WHITEMAN

TONY D'SOUZA was born in Chicago to Indian-American parents. At 18 he rode a bicycle across Alaska, at 19 crossed India, at 20 planted grapefruit orchards in Israel, then attended college in Wisconsin and Virginia, spent a year working on fishing trawlers out of Oban and on construction sites in Fort William in Scotland, before serving three years in the Peace Corps in West Africa. He is now 30 and this is his first book. His writing has been published in the *New Yorker*, the *Literary Review*, *Playboy* and other journals.

From the US reviews of *Whiteman*

'One significant virtue of D'Souza's storytelling rests in his ability to present [his] experiences of African life with a vividness that reveals the continent's allure without sentimentalizing its romanticism... It's this quality of vision that makes [*Whiteman*] notable and, for a first book, unusual. Where many a fledgling novelist would aim a protagonist's awakening solipsistically inward, D'Souza directs it generously outward. He resists the temptation to use Africa as a colorful backdrop, to mill a *bildungsro* American goes to Africa to change t has changed. Instead, in original, un with force and restraint, why a you however haplessly, might not relish the prospect of having to return home.' *New York Times*

'Peace Corps veteran Tony D'Souza manages... to neither over- nor under-romanticize the culture or the way his presence [in rural West Africa] affected him and his hosts. *Whiteman,* an intimate and unabashed account of how a young American man would live when dropped into a completely foreign environment, reads with a startling honesty... Authentic and intriguing.' *Minneapolis Star Tribune*

'An exceptional account of West African village life, written with enormous affection and you-are-there immediacy... Africa may be ultimately unknowable for the author, but this non-fiction novel, his debut, represents a thrilling partial discovery.' *Kirkus,* Starred Review

'A compassionate and compelling look at a people and a way of life that you can't help feel are doomed.' *BookPage*

'Ultimately, what makes *Whiteman* so affecting is D'Souza's understanding of what it's like to fall in love with people who will never be like you, with a place that will never be home and with a troubled continent that – despite your best intentions – you can do nothing to save.' *People,* Critic's Choice, four stars

'A powerful debut, full of insight and sly humor, about a man who desperately wants to belong to a place that has little need of him. This is a visit to Africa you will not soon forget.' *St. Louis Post-Dispatch*

WHITEMAN

TONY D'SOUZA

Portobello
BOOKS

Published by Portobello Books Ltd 2006

Portobello Books Ltd
Eardley House
4 Uxbridge St
Notting Hill Gate
London W8 7SY, UK

First published in the United States by Harcourt, Inc., in 2006

A CIP catalogue record is available from the British Library

9 8 7 6 5 4 3 2 1

ISBN 1 84627 049 9

www.portobellobooks.com

Designed by Linda Lockowitz

Typeset in Dante MT

Printed and bound in Great Britain by William Clowes Ltd, Beccles, Suffolk

For Hélène,
In regret

AFRICA UNCHAINED

At nine A.M., the doorbell rang. I couldn't see who it was because of the high wall surrounding the house, but after a moment's debate whether I shouldn't just ignore it, I picked up the crowbar we'd been keeping handy and started across the courtyard to the security door. I'd talked with the girls about getting a gun in the black market, but we hadn't gone that far yet. "Jack's a man. He'll protect us," Samantha had winked and said, and I'd shaken my head and told them, "Then consider yourselves dead already." Because while I didn't like to think of myself as a coward, my first impulse on hearing gunfire was to hit the floor and crawl under something. At the door, I raised the crowbar like a baseball bat. I'd never swung a weapon at anyone, didn't know if I could now, but I held it like that anyway. *"C'est qui?"* I shouted, trying to sound larger and more menacing than I really was.

"Adama, restes tranquille," a woman's voice called to me. *"C'est Méité Fanta, ta voisine."*

I quickly turned the lock and pushed open the door onto Ama Méité, a weathered old woman with a steel tub on her head, the heads of the fish in it peeking down at us like children eavesdropping on adults. She also had a stick poking out of the corner of her mouth, an extra-large toothpick. Ama Méité was grandmother to the rabble of naked children who played dust-raising ragball on our street in Séguéla, hollering all day like they owned the place, which they did, and who had brought us water, bucket-by-paid-for-bucket, from their well during the last coup when the water and electricity had been cut in the city. Méité's face did not change when she saw the crowbar in my hand. She went on chewing her stick, the local version of a toothbrush, as though it were a carrot, or a tasty piece of licorice. But I knew from experience that it wasn't tasty at all, that it was infused with a bitter oil as succulent as varnish. People were like that here.

We quickly went through the morning salutations in Worodougou, a cultural requirement you couldn't ignore in the biggest of rushes, even if, say, you felt like the world was ending.

"Manisogoma," I said, lowering my eyes in respect. 'Good morning, respected mother.'

"Say va! Ah see la," Ama Méité said like shouting, which was how it was done. 'Thank you, respected sir. Did the night pass well?'

"Em'ba, Ama," I said. 'Thank you, respected mother, yes.'

"Allah bis sonya!" 'God bless your morning.'

"Amina, Ma." 'Amen, Mother.'

"Allah kenna ahdi." 'God grant you beautiful health.'

"Amina, Ma," I said, touching my hand to my forehead as if bowing in thanks and deference to her benedictions.

"Allah ee balo," she said. 'God grant you a wonderful youth.'

"Amina, Ma."

"Allah bato luma." 'God nourish your home and family.'

"Amina, Ma."

"Allah bo numa." 'God bless all that you do.'

"Amina, Ma," I said louder than before, indicating in their way that I'd received all the benedictions I could bear. *"Iniché, iniché. Allah ee braghee."* 'Amen, Mother. Thank you, thank you. God bless you in thanks for your benedictions over me.'

"Amina, Va!" 'Amen, sir.'

"Allah den balo, Ma." 'God bless and protect your children, Mother.'

"Amina, Va!"

"Allah kenna ahdi." 'God grant you beautiful health.'

"Amina, Va!"

"Allah sosay djanna." 'God grant you long life.'

"Amina, Va!"

"Allah bis sonya." 'God bless your morning.'

"Amina, Va! Iniché. Adama Diomandé." 'Amen and thank you, respected Adama Diomandé.'

Then we were done with that and Ama Méité said to me, *"Bon,"* flatly in French because we could now get on with our lives. I could already feel the sweat starting to stand out on my forehead, and the fish in the tub on Méité's head seemed to me to be wilting in the sun now, hanging over the rim like the melting watches in the Dalí painting. She rolled her eyes from the weight of the load and planted her hands on her hips, which were wrapped in a wildly colored bolt of cloth depicting cellular phones. The cloth was a *pagne* celebrating the arrival of Nokia to our stretch of West Africa two weeks ago, and many women in Séguéla were wearing them, were tying their infants snugly onto their backs with them. Coups and guinea worm and female circumcision and HIV and mass graves in Abidjan full of the Muslim north's political youth and the women had turned traditional dances all night around bonfires to celebrate the arrival of the cell phone. This was what West Africa was about: priorities. "So you already know about the coup," Ama Méité chewed on her bitter stick and said.

"Know about the coup?" I said. "All I know is that I got up this morning and turned on the radio and there wasn't any radio."

"Oui," she said, "so you know about the coup. But what are you going to do with that stick? When the bandits come, they will have guns. Therefore, you should buy a gun. A rich man like you, Adama, with so many wives—"

"They're not my wives!" I started, like a thousand times before. "They're my colleagues. I work with them. Nothing else."

"If they're not your wives, oh, then why won't you marry my daughter Nochia, oh?" she sang in French to embarrass me. "She knows how to cook and likes to work in the fields. If you know how to do anything, she'll give you many healthy children, maybe even twins. And even if you don't know how to do those things, she will teach you. Like that you will be rich in America and make your mother proud. Then you will bring us health and happiness and, of course, many gifts, oh, when you come and visit. Anyway," she said, spitting wads of mulled wood on the ground between us like hay, "you should buy a gun. My son knows a man who can sell you a strong gun washed with good magic."

"We are a humanitarian organization, Ama," I said lamely. "We don't believe in guns."

And she said, "In all the films from America, all is guns. So don't tell me! What I've come to say is this: Don't open the door today, Adama Diomandé. There are many looters and bandits. They will come and rob you. Everybody knows whites live in this house. And who knows what riches you have in there, anyway? So do not open the door. Now I have to go to market and sell these fish. They don't care if there's a coup or not. All they care is that they want to stink soon."

"Thank you, Ama," I said as she turned to walk back to her compound, where the children were kicking a soccer ball that was really half of a coconut shell, were playing hopscotch in the dirt and clapping and singing like it was the best day ever, like always. She waved her hand back at me and said, "You whites are bizarre, oh! Going to chase away bandits with a stick, Allah!"

I could not remember if this was the third coup or the fourth in the two months since I'd arrived up north, and anyway, talk of coups was a very complex thing because you had bloody coups and bloodless coups and attempted coups and aborted coups and averted coups and rumored coups and the coups that happen that nobody knows about except you go to the post office one day to mail a letter to your retired mother in Florida to say everything's getting all blown out of proportion in the Western media and there's a new general-president smiling at you from the stamp like somebody who's gotten away with something big, and also there were the *couvre-feus,* which is pronounced somewhat like "coup" but means you can't go out at night or you'll be shot, which should not be confused with *coups de grâce,* which is how chickens were killed for dinner. All of this is to say that every three weeks the country was erupting into general mayhem from the capital to Korhogo, producing very little change except for a mounting body count and the ulcers growing in my stomach. Oh yes, there was also the matter of a few towns in the far north like Kong and Tengréla that had declared themselves independent states and were being deprived of all services by Abidjan in an apparent attempt to siege them into submission. There was also the small matter of the new guns the traditional hunters and witch doctors were showing off in the villages, shiny AKs that they said came from Mecca, and other small matters such as the Christian military kicking in people's doors like storm troopers and beating old women, and the list could go on for a very long time, but after I locked the door behind Ama Méité, I went inside to call the Potable Water International office in Abidjan—my organization—for an update and found that the line had been cut, which wasn't reassuring. Then I sat on the couch and fiddled with the shortwave's antenna. Just as I was able—with many strange maneuvers of my arms like a semaphore—to draw in the BBC, where the female announcer was calmly saying in her lovely British voice, ". . . rebel forces in the Ivory Coast . . . ," all the power was cut and then I was suddenly very alone in a dark and quiet house in what the U.S. embassy security officer had referred to just weeks before as "the most unstable city in the country." I switched the shortwave over to its batteries. Of course nothing happened. I turned the radio over. The cover to the battery compartment was missing, and so were the batteries. One of the girls knew where they were no doubt, as one of them was out in the bush right now, humming softly as she dug a new latrine, working to the music playing from her battery-powered Walkman.

To make a long story shorter, I had to go out. For one, I was hungry, and for two, I wanted to know what was going on. I got on the bicycle we kept at the house and pedaled out into the city, chased by the vast throng of my neighbors' kids hurrying barefooted and bare-bodied over the piled trash and foamy sewage rivulets of our street, shouting after me, "Everybody! Everybody! *Regards! Regards!* It's the whiteman! *Toubabou! Toubabou! Le blanc! Coutoubou!* Crazy!"

The best thing about the coups was the opportunity the lawlessness afforded an otherwise-subdued people to have some real fun. I turned onto one of the three paved roads in town and started down to the city center scattering sheep and goats and chickens and beat-up and mangy dogs and children and women carrying huge loads of firewood on their heads as I went. A long chorus of *"Regards le blanc! Coutoubou!* Crazy!" shouted by even the adults for a change kept me company and then I came onto a large gathering of young men watching a house burn down. They seemed very excited and happy to see me, so much so that they decided to block my way, their chests glistening with the sweat brought out by the heat of the fire. A leader stepped out from the crowd, set apart from the others, typically, by his massive size, and also by the rainbow-colored clown wig he wore like some kind of insignia of rank—who knows where he got it. I wondered then what this minor general would decide to say to me.

"Whiteman!" he decided to say.

"Oui, je suis blanc. Ya rien je peux faire. Papa blanc, mama blanche. Donc, je suis blanc."

"C'est ça! C'est ça! C'est toujours comme ça! You are white and I am black. There is nothing we can do," he said with enthusiasm, and we shook hands to seal the agreement.

"The fire is pretty, is it not?" he asked me, and I had to agree because after all it was: a two-story pillar of flame rising up from the gutted shell of a one-story house. It lifted its roaring face into the cloudless and suddenly beautiful sky.

"Whose house was that?" I asked him as we appraised this work.

"A swine-fucking policeman's," the young man told me.

"And who lit it?"

"We did," he said, and thumped his chest.

"Yes, it's very beautiful," I said.

The young man turned to me. He glowered under the wig, a completely different person now: the person who had lit the fire. He said, "You are French."

"No, I'm American," I assured him, glad for a change to actually be one.

"Not French?"

"No."

"Certain?" he said, and cocked his head.

"Yes. Very certain."

"Well . . . ," he said, and looked me up and down as if unsure about what to do. "Well, that's really great," he said, and smiled broadly. As easily as that, we were friends again. In English, he said, "Are you fine?"

"Yes, I'm fine."

"Eh? You say what?" he said, tapping his ear and making a hard-of-hearing face. "Speak more slowly."

I said very slowly, "I-said-I-am-fine."

"Yes, okay. Mama fine? Daddy fine?"

"Yes-every-body-is-fine."

"Yes, okay. Sister fine, brother fine?"

"Yes-every-body. Every-body-is-fine."

"I speaking English."

"You-speaking-good-English."

Then he puffed up his thick chest and looked around the mob to make sure they had seen and heard his linguistic display, and why not? None of them could do it. Then he was back in French again. "You know Michael Jordan?"

"Yes," I said.

"You know Jean-Claude Van Damme?"

"Yes. Him, too."

"Me, I want to go to America," he pronounced. "You will take me when you go?"

"Yes."

Then he said, "Your bicycle is very pretty. Here in Africa, we don't have bicycles such as this. I admire your bicycle very much. Give me your bicycle. A gift."

"Unfortunately," I said at the prospect of having to travel at the same speed as everyone else on a day like this, "I have to go and see my friend. The older brother of my great, great friend in fact. I have to pay him many respects. Also, his mother, who is very old. Also, their quarter's imam. The house is very far away, so I need the bicycle. Please forgive me for being so rude. Tomorrow, I will see you and I will definitely give you the bicycle."

"Tomorrow, hey? So, whiteman, you know our ways, is it? Well," the young man the size of a bull and wearing a clown wig and surrounded by a crowd of other young men standing before a house they had destroyed said to me with a smile, "no problem then. Tomorrow we'll meet and you will give me the bicycle. A gift."

"Tomorrow," I assured him. "Don't worry. I won't forget!" I pushed past him, and the crowd of them parted and let me go.

"Hey, whiteman!"

"Yeah?"

"Have a good time!"

At first, I pedaled away at a regular speed because we were friends and everything was normal, wasn't it? Then, away from them, I pedaled as fast as I could. Down by the big intersection where the meat vendors in their shacks lined the roadside among their hanging sheep carcasses and pools of blood, a troop carrier full of grim soldiers holding rifles upright between their knees came barreling along, and I tumbled out of the way and into a gang of goats. Not bothering to brush myself off, I kicked the goats away, hopped back on the bike, and rocketed down the opposite alleyway. When those soldiers met that mob, I guessed it would probably turn out bad. I thought it best to leave them all to it.

First, I went to the bank, the reason I had come in to Séguéla from my village in the bush. The heavy metal doors were shuttered and the long iron bar with the padlock as big as my chest was drawn down across them as though the bank would never open again. It wasn't really a very big building. Now it looked like the most secure shoe box in the world.

A very old man in rags was lying on the steps with his eyes open. He looked like a scrap of trash, like someone had tossed him there. First I thought he was dead, but then he turned his head, hacked, and spit, something I understood he'd been doing for a while because of the running gob of spit dripping down the steps beside him like raw egg whites. When he noticed me looking, his bearded face brightened as though something funny had just happened. He said loudly in excitement, "Hey! A whiteman!"

"Allah noya kay," I said to him, 'God soothe your illness,' and he said back to me, *"Amina, Toubabou-ché,"* 'Thank you, whiteman.' I knew from the filthy rags he wore that he was wildly insane. Though the insane were mostly left to fend for themselves in this part of the world, they were also treated with courtesy. If you ever bothered to ask them a question, sometimes you'd even get a useful answer. "Papa," I said, "what's going on with the bank?"

"The bank? This bank? This bank behind me? Ha ha! It's closed!"

"When is it going to open again?"

"Open again? Ha! Don't ask me crazy questions," he said, and laughed. "You whites. You walk on the moon before you walk on the ground."

"Hasn't anyone come by and said anything about the bank opening?"

"Everyone came by and asked about the bank opening. Look at the bank, whiteman. Ha ha! It's closed!"

"I need money," I said, mostly to myself, and the old man said, "Money! You need money! Ha ha! Why don't you go find money on the moon! Don't you know what time it is? It is time for the bank to be open and the bank is closed. So you tell me what time it is now! *Les blancs!* Don't you make the time, too? Ah, *les blancs!* Bank and time! Money and the moon! Oh, whiteman! Hahahahaha . . ."

Next, I decided to go see an acquaintance, Diomandé Kané, at his compound. He had recently gone from being my preferred Séguéla cigarette vendor to a Muslim insurgent. I'd had beers with him at the Club des Amis Christian bar on my odd weekends in the city, but in the past week I'd heard he'd bought a *boubous* and started praying. So it was serious with him, and I knew he'd have news. His narrow compound was set in the vast camp of impoverished Dioula south of the main market square, beyond the towering and yellow-painted Grand Mosque of Séguéla, its minarets capped in brown onion domes, its latticed windows intricate and mysterious and dominating everything.

As I rode toward the market—a sprawling shantytown of corrugated tin shacks in whose passageways one instantly became lost like in a North African souk—a mixed mass of women and children came spilling out from it like a school of baitfish chased by sharks. They were darting and changing course together suddenly just like fish, coughing and shouting, *"Lacrymogène!"* which meant 'tear gas,' and nobody stopped to call me 'whiteman,' so I knew they weren't exaggerating. The crowd swept me down the hill past the mosque to Timité Quarter, the poorest section of town, until I pulled myself out of it at a compound I knew there, and where I'd taken refuge before, when I'd newly arrived in Séguéla, just as I'd been waiting for a logging truck to take me into the bush to my village posting for the very first time.

Back then, a throng of young men had come running down the road, stopping only to pick up and hurl stones at another crowd of young men who were chasing them, who were stopping in turn to snatch up the bouncing stones and throw them back again. I'd been carried away by the crowd of onlookers who'd gathered themselves up to run away from that, carried down to hardscrabble Timité as though in a wave. In my fright, I'd found shelter in the first compound after the omelet kiosk with the big mango tree rising up beside it like a giant in a coat of green feathers by banging on the gate as hard as I could and yelling, *"M'aidez! M'aidez!"* and passed an afternoon in silence, stared at by four assembled generations of a Fulani family freshly arrived from Mali to try their luck in relatively prosperous Ivory Coast as many from the neighboring countries did. They'd never seen a whiteman up close before, and the smallest children pulled my toes to see if I was real, while the women simply stared. Now I was at their gate and banging on it again.

"C'est qui?" someone shouted, trying to sound larger and more menacing than he really was.

"Sidibé, restes-toi tranquille. C'est Adama, ton blanc."

The gate was pulled back to reveal the old patriarch of the family in his flowing blue *boubous* and wide-brimmed hat with the circular Peul designs tooled into the leather. His face was thin and bright beneath the hat, his beard stringy and white. He said in stumbling French as he tugged me in quickly by my shirt, "Oh, Adama. How nice of you to come and pay us a visit again! Please come and sit with us like before. Tell us all of your news."

I passed some hours in Sidibé's dirt-floor parlor listening to the ticking of his wall clock—a round-faced Seiko, his only real possession—after we'd run out of things to say. One of his grandsons made periodic forays into the city to assess the situation, and came back again and again so breathless and worried that the old man folded his hands on his lap and said, "Oh, Adama, it has been so long, isn't it? Let us drink another tea."

The one time I left the parlor to cross the courtyard to squat over the flyblown latrine hole seething with fat maggots, I saw the smoke from the fires rising up into the sky in columns from the different quarters of the city like trailings, vultures circling lazily around them, high up, as if there was all the time in the world for what they had to do. Then there was gunfire, automatic and small-arms, staccato, right here, far away, patterned layers of jarring sound, just like the Fourth of July in Chicago, where I was from. It was the smoke from the fires that did it, the way it curled into the sky like the black smoke of sacrifices of people invoking the ancestors for help. It filled me with a stunned dumbness, a weight, a dread, a fatigue that spread through my body like exhaustion. Was this really happening? I mean to say, I did not know how to feel. Fear, exhilaration, nerves, adrenaline: These were all the same species of creature, and ever since I'd arrived in Ivory Coast, life had been this way. Did they really want this fight, this North-South, Muslim-Christian, colonization's hangover civil war, or did they not? Did I? I don't believe anyone could truthfully tell then. Yes, of course people would die, but didn't everyone think, 'Not I! Not I!'? And didn't everything taste sweeter since the violence: that cold, cold Coca-Cola, the last Marlboro of the day, sex with your girl, the joy of breathing because the day had ended and you were still alive! Everything had become heightened, everything myopic and refined. How much fun to be had by all!

And of course I couldn't help but pick a side. Forty years of abuse and neglect by the Christians since they'd inherited power from the French at independence, forty years of watching roads and electricity and schools and development traverse the south, while here in the Muslim north it was all hunger and *harmattan,* military harassment, the men gone to labor in the cocoa fields, coming home once a year with AIDS, no money, no medicine, no schoolbooks for the kids, and even the northerners' nationality stripped away because of the new interpretation of the Constitution. There were good guys and bad guys and I could see them, and over all of this stood the basilica in Yamoussoukro, the largest church in the world, air-conditioned seats, miles of stained glass and Italian marble for a congregation of three hundred on good days, none on most, to spell out the way things were as clearly as its gold dome and crucifix standing up against the horizon. How many hospitals could have been built with that money? How many deep-bore water pumps? And Boigny, the first president, had himself placed at the feet of Jesus Christ in the glass, unleashing this mess! Where was the mosque to stand beside that church? What about this half of the country?

Lastly, there was reality. I was a whiteman. No matter how well I spoke Worodougou or *gnushi* French or Dioula or that I obeyed my village's customs and let them take my old name, Jack Diaz, from me, and baptize me with a new name, Diomandé Adama; no matter that I lived with them as they did and was ready some days to take up arms with my friends, to stand with them as though their families and grievances were my own, this was a place I did not belong and, more than that, a place where they would not let me belong.

We were the last foreign-aid group still in the field. The last round of rioting had seen even the missionaries driven out. It was only three weeks ago that that Dutch woman, Laurie's friend, was sitting in our living room, where we'd gathered for safety, gabbing, fingering the wooden cross on its rope around her neck, laughing nervously, saying, "Well, now that those funny Japanese people have packed up and left, you know, it looks like it's you water people and us Bible people."

Then it was only us because the churches were burned all over the north and they went to the Dutch woman's house in Séguéla in a mob where she lived behind where they welded bicycle frames beyond the military post, thought she wasn't home, and proceeded to loot everything. It was only while they were dousing the walls with kerosene that someone—maybe my friend with his rainbow wig—noticed the bed that they had forgotten to take in the back room, and lifted up the mattress, and there she was like a dusty treasure found in the back of a closet, an old dress your grandmother wore seventy years ago to the prom: a middle-aged Dutch woman who had come to Africa to bring Jesus to Muslims, her skirt damp from her own urine, crying with her hands hiding her face like she wanted to be a child again, and did she curse them as black devils finally is what I want to know? But the crying and her age and the piss struck a chord in someone, because they helped her up, helped her to gather herself together—to brush her hair from her eyes, to wipe the tears away—helped her find her keys, helped her pick them up when she dropped them from her trembling hands as certainly she did, helped her stagger out of that house on their shoulders, shook her out of her dream of her childhood in Amsterdam—the clouds reflected in the canals, the yellow hay fields of the countryside of Gouda—ducked her head down with their hand so she wouldn't bang it as she got into her car, let her drive away. Then they torched her house, anyway.

On the road south, she was joined by a convoy of them, whites with their Bibles piled around them in their Land Rovers like sandbags, their churches and missions burned, for some of them their life's work burned, and nothing left to do now but sift the remains from the ashes of their memories and turn the other cheek. In Sidibé's house then we could hear the singing of the muezzin, a long and mournful wail, like an air--raid siren in the shock and length of it. Sidibé winked at me and tapped the side of his long nose. "If God says that it is all right to go out now, Adama," he said, smiling, "then certainly it must be all right."

And I did go out into the city again, and I did see many other things to make me feel very quiet inside myself in the memory of them, but here now in the telling of this story, I've lost my direction. What I'd like to tell about now is a monkey.

Across from our house in Séguéla, where I would go on to spend the night under the bed with gunfire and the shouts of angry men around me in the city like the madness in a crazy man's head, there lived a monkey on a chain. This was in the courtyard of our neighbor Méité Fanta, the same woman from the morning, the grandmother of many, many happy children, a kind enough woman who sold us water once on a hot day when we didn't have any. Anyway, they kept a young monkey on a chain attached to a pole in the courtyard and the monkey was really a baboon, but if you were to ask anyone what sort of animal it was, they would simply say, "A monkey."

This monkey's name was Rita—I asked—and I grew fond of her. The children spent many long hours teasing her with leafy tree branches, with bananas she could not reach, and there was also a famous game in that neighborhood called Touch the Monkey, in which each child brave enough would venture forth when they felt Rita was not looking, cross into her sandy area—the radius of her chain, the chain being as long as two or three paces, enough space for a monkey in a poor compound in West Africa, if that can be accepted as a unit of measure—touch her like slapping, scream and flee, and often I was pleased to see her leap onto a child's back and sink her short-yet incisors into a neck. I harbored untold sympathy for that tormented creature who somehow managed to keep her spirits up. I got it into my head that she could recognize me, that she could pick me out of the crowd as the one person who did not want to amuse myself at her expense, and she would break into a funny little half-step dance on seeing me, banging her fists against the sand and then leaping and turning as she howled. Of course, this was because I brought her bananas and papayas and other things monkeys like to eat every time I came to town.

"Oh, thank you, Adama Diomandé," Méité Fanta came to me and said one day with the sun beating down on our necks, the gritty *harmattan* wind caking our pores with dust, chapping our lips and the insides of our nostrils. "Thank you for feeding the monkey. When she is grown and fat we will call you and you must come and share the meat of her with us."

There is little sentiment to be wasted in a place where hunger is a real thing, where meat is scarce and a small and personable baboon like Rita would help the children grow. Still, I chased the children away from her when I could, bribed them with cheap candies to leave her alone, trying to make her short life more endurable, chained as she was around the hips to an immovable pole in a dusty courtyard where chickens scratched for ticks. I honestly believe that she came to recognize me, that she would say to herself on seeing me, 'That is the good one among them.'

Then one day when I was caught in Séguéla while Séguéla burned around me, I opened my door in the late afternoon to a small gang of bandits. They showed me knives, and then they hid them in their sleeves again. I could not get past them or close the door on them and still I did not let them in. In my hand was a crowbar, which in the end I was not able to swing. "You will give us money," the leader of the trio said, and I tried to see his face behind his mirrored sunglasses but could only see my own reflection. It startled me, how white I seemed, and then, how odd. What was this white person doing in this place? I opened my wallet and gave them the money that I had. It was a few U.S. dollars in their currency, perhaps ten, not much by any standards, not much by theirs.

"This isn't enough," he said, holding the money on the flat of his hand as if offering it back, giving me a second chance. "This is nothing. You must give us more money."

"Please," I said. "The bank is closed today. This is all I have. Please." Some long moments passed. I do not know how many. In the silence I heard myself say to them from a faraway place, "Please. Please."

They went away. I cannot remember what direction they took as they left, or what they looked like as they walked away. I could not now pick them out of a crowd. I cannot know how much time passed as I hung there in my doorway, but then, as if waking from a deep, deep sleep, I was in the world again. And what a raucous world it was! In the distance, gunfire, and here, the explosion of goats and dogs and chickens and sheep and dust and feathers and the many and bare-bodied grandchildren of my neighbor screaming as they were chased through the street by Rita—a baboon mistaken for a monkey—her chain broken and free, pursuing wildly now these children who for so long had tortured her. For an instant, I felt a wave of pleasure course through me like love at the sight of the mayhem of her freedom, and for that one instant I can say this: I was happy, I was happy to my core. Then the monkey spotted me, and my happiness turned to white-knuckled fear as barreling toward my doorway was an openmouthed creature with fangs and shrieking and I don't know what she planned on doing, on seeking asylum behind my legs, or on sinking her teeth into them, for suddenly I was face-to-face with what I wanted to know but couldn't, Africa, Africa unchained, and there was no other recourse at that moment but to guard hearth and home, and slam shut the door.

THE LAHOU BIRDS

Mazatou was all bust and butt. One morning a few months after I arrived, I got up and opened the door of my hut, and there she was, framed in the doorway like a painting, standing and pounding rice in a wide mortar on the edge of my courtyard. When she saw me looking, she unhitched and opened her wrap so I caught a brief flash of her full and bare thighs. Then she shut the wrap, refastened it, smoothed its folds over her ample rump, and began to sing and pound that rice in a way that tossed every curve she had at me.

I was in Tégéso, a Muslim village in the bush near Séguéla, where I had been sent to help the people find a way to have clean drinking water. Life was more basic there, harder in many ways, tied to the natural world. Many were the mornings that I did not want to leave my hut, had trouble working the heart up to it. People called me Sergio at first, the name of the lead character on the Mexican soap opera the whole village watched on a black-and-white set they ran off a car battery. Nothing about me resembled him but my white skin and dark hair, but to some of them, Sergio and I were one and the same. No matter that I'd begun to live among them as humbly as they did, I was a creature set among them from the magical world of television. Even after a year, children would sit in a group on the dirt of my courtyard to watch me do the simplest of things as though watching television still: sweeping out my hut, coughing from the dust, spitting, mending my sandals, sharpening my machete, taking a sip of water from my gourd. "What is the whiteman doing now?" I'd hear a small one whisper in Worodougou, and another would whisper back, "Don't know. But it looks like he's drinking water." "Do whitemen drink water, too?" "Don't know. But that's what it looks like he's doing."

Other mornings, in a burst of assertion, I'd get up and chase them away with a stick. Adults, for the most part, did not treat me like such an overt novelty; to some who had seen whites in the city, I wasn't, and others acted as if I was a normal thing among them because they wanted to seem more sophisticated than they really were. Still, even the old chief, who should have known better because he'd fought in Europe in World War II as a forced conscript, called me Sergio from time to time with a wink and laugh, and I understood that at the core of each of them in that Iron Age village was a child who looked at me and wondered, 'Do whitemen drink water, too?' I'd been eager to get in the field for PWI, but since 9/11, project money had dried up. I kept my notes, urged people to boil, dreamed about all that clean water—silent and vast and dark as time—waiting to be tapped in the aquifers below us, but without money for new deep-bore pumps, I spent most of my days in Tégéso waiting for the world to right itself and the aid valves to flow again. I didn't have much to do but live among them, and I didn't want to go home. Many were the nights I went to sleep praying I'd wake in the morning with my skin turned black.

Sometimes, when the stares and giggles of the children reached through the hard veneer I'd learned to cover myself with, I'd hike into the forest for a respite. The children were afraid of the forest—even the adults were—and I'd sit in the long roots of a towering ebony tree as if in a hammock and listen to the clacking of the long-billed lahou birds in its canopy, their calls like the sound of people laughing at a party. In conversations with the *dosso*—the witch doctor—I'd learned that lahous were one of the birds a hunter must never kill, or the ancestors would kill him with an illness in turn. Lahous watched the world of men for the ancestors from the tops of the tallest trees, remembered what they saw, wove the incidents into funny stories that they would tell to each other again and again. For this reason, every storyteller mask had a carved lahou bird perched on its crown, the long toucan bill seeming to curve down all the way to where the mask could hear what it had to say. The lahous clacking in the tree above me were the birds telling funny stories of men to each other, and listening to their raucous laughter awhile, I'd feel I had joined them in it. Then, in the forest twilight with the night spirits beginning to dart about in the gloom in the corners of my eyes, I'd go back to the village and give it another try.

Mazatou was my neighbor's granddaughter come from a village in the near west. My neighbor, an old woman, had injured herself badly while chopping palm nuts out of a tree in the nearby swamp. This otherwise ancient old woman had climbed the trunk of a palm tree to get at the bundles of nuts in its crown, and in chopping them loose with an ax in one hand and hugging the tree with her other as she'd been doing all her life, something happened and she'd fallen out, impaled her hand clean through on a stick on the way down.

"How did you fall, Old Mother?" everybody in the village wanted to know.

"A genie pulled me out," she had explained, and cried, sitting on a stool outside her hut with that stick through her hand like a pencil. "That tree belonged to my sister who died. She doesn't want me stealing her palm nuts even though she can't use them anymore. She was always jealous of me. So she sent a genie to pull me out."

"Maybe you are too old to be climbing trees, Old Mother."

"Too old? It was a genie! I saw him. He was white all over, and he had a terrible white face. He pulled me down and laughed and then ran off into the swamp. Everybody has seen genies there. What do you mean saying I am too old to climb trees!"

One of her sons came, chastised her for going to the swamp by herself, gave her a piece of goat hide to bite with her gums, and while she looked away, he yanked the stick free. Her hand bled freely until there was a pool of blood in the dirt, and he put leaves on both sides of the wound, and wrapped it tightly with an old rag. The old woman made dinner for herself that night, and of course, before the week was out, she was feverish on her mat in the dark of her hut, her hand swollen up like a latex glove filled with water.

"Adama," she called to me weakly from her mat when I poked my head in to give her the morning greeting, "the healer wants to cut my hand off. Don't you have whiteman medicine for me in that box of yours? Can't you make it heal?

If they take my hand from me, I'll be no good to anyone. Then I know I will die."

"I can probably heal it," I told her. "But if you let me treat it with whiteman medicine, you have to follow what I say. You can't put mud on it again after I've cleaned it."

"I promise, Adama."

I boiled water, washed her hand in her hut as she cried, squeezed the pus out so it dripped in gobs to the mat, and washed it again with soap. Then I smeared both sides of the wound with triple-antibiotic cream and covered it loosely with sterile gauze. I had no penicillin to give her, but knew she'd get better if only she'd keep it clean and dry. Her fever broke in the night, and after three days of my cleaning and dressing her wound for her, she was chopping wood again. Healing the woman's hand was one of the small ways I justified my presence among them as a rural relief worker, when really, I spent most of that first year simply trying to make it through each day. She pounded sweet *foutou* for me from plantains she'd gotten somewhere, and in our morning greetings, she would bow deeply to me as she invoked Allah's name to bless me. Then Mazatou arrived in the village, and I wondered if she wasn't a part of the old woman's thanks as well.

Every morning, Mazatou would shake her curves as she pounded the hulls off the day's rice, and I would blush, pretend as I washed my face that I didn't notice her. It was the height of the dry season, and there wasn't work to do in the fields. Men repaired their thatched huts and lounged about; women spun cotton and cracked palm-nut pits with rocks under the mango trees for the seeds inside that they'd turn into soap. I played soccer with the men my age, listened to them tease each other about women, learned new and important words. Families spent hours together under their compound acacias, and young men and women went for walks around the village in the dark at night, trying to find a secluded corner to start families of their own. The way Mazatou flirted with me brought the blood up all under my skin, made my body feel as hot around me as the intense heat of the noontime sun. It began to make me crazy. It began to make me consider doing crazy things, like waving her to come into my hut when no one was looking, and closing the door on us. But I didn't want to offend the village's hospitality or trust, and so she shook her hips and licked her lips, and I became as frustrated as a tethered goat.

"Have you seen this girl Mazatou?" I said to my friend Mamadou as we sat on our haunches outside his hut, brewing Arab tea, the night sky a vast and spangled drape around our shoulders.

"Who hasn't seen her? She's as ripe as a late-season mango."

"Anyone get to her yet?"

"People from this village are afraid of people from her village. Haven't you noticed that nobody talks to her? Besides, they say she has a fiancé in Abidjan. He's trying to make a little money, and then he's going to come back to claim her."

"Why would people from here be afraid of people from there?"

Mamadou poured some of the tea into a small and dirty glass on the tray between us. He blew on it, tasted it, poured it back in the pot, shrugged. "They live by a great rock where there's a python that eats men's souls."

"Oh," I said.

"Yes. Nobody from this village has the magic to go there. Anyway, her people are crazy."

Mamadou was the companion the village had given me when I'd first arrived. They'd chosen him because we were roughly the same age and he spoke French. It was his duty to teach me how to behave politely, to know what was taboo and what wasn't. Mostly what he did was watch me make horrific mistakes, and then, after weeks of letting me make them, he'd say to me in a small voice, "Are you sure you really want to sweep your hut out at night, Adama? The ancestors take it as a great insult. It means you are sweeping away their welcome as they look for a place to sleep."

"Really?" I had said to him that time as I'd stood up with my broom.

"Oh yes. It's a really terrible thing to do. All your neighbors are complaining."

"Why didn't you tell me that weeks ago?"

"Why remind a blind man that he is blind?"

Or, walking around the village with me one morning as I saluted old men as they came out of their huts, just as I did most days, he said to me in that small voice of his, "Are you sure you want to salute people before they've washed their faces?"

"Since you put it that way, Mamadou, I know that I don't. Now that you've let me do it for months, please tell me why I shouldn't."

"Talking to people before you've washed your face in the morning is like talking to them with shit on it. It's very humiliating. People have been complaining for a long time that you make them humiliate themselves each and every morning."

"Wonderful," I'd said to him, because I'd learned there was no use in arguing. The secrets of the village would reveal themselves to me in their own time, if they ever would.

But four months in, much had happened, and I felt that I knew my way around their taboos, even if I didn't. At that fire where the tea was brewing, I said to Mamadou, "I think that girl looks at me in a way she shouldn't if she's got a fiancé."

"Are you sure, Adama?" he said, and lifted his eyebrow. "Maybe she's only got something in her eye. As the ancestors say, 'A hungry goat will eat even his brother's wool.'"

"I'm sure, Mamadou. As the ancestors also say, 'If a cripple tells you he will win a race, know that he knows the other runners have no legs.' Isn't that right?"

"Okay, Adama," he said, and laughed. "Take her. Call her into your hut. If she looks at you that way, then she's yours."

"But what about her fiancé?"

"One can never say with these things. She isn't married until the bull is slaughtered. And even if she was, you could still call her into your hut."

"And no one would care?"

"Oho," he said, and laughed in the dark, rocked on his heels. "No, Adama. If she was married, people would care."

"What would they do?"

"They would whip you and chase you into the forest. If you came back, they would kill you. Then they would drag her to her husband's family, and her husband's family would whip her. Then they would stuff her vagina full of chili peppers."

"God."

"Yes."

"But if she's not married?"

"Nobody cares."

"Are you sure?"

"I'm sure, Adama."

Mamadou leaned back against the trunk of the mango tree we were under, looked at me with hooded eyes. "You're hot all of a sudden, aren't you? That's good to know. People here have been wondering if it's just African women you don't like, or if it's women in general. That's a very dangerous thing, Adama, to be a man here and not like women. But don't worry. I've defended your honor. I tell them that you have a wife in America and that whiteman ways are not like ours. An African could not wait for his wife for two years, or even one. I'm glad to see this new vigor you have for Mazatou. But remember, when you pray for rest, you also pray for work."

The next morning, I washed my face, and when Mazatou tossed her hip at me, I spoke the first words I'd ever said to her in the few weeks that she'd been there: "Mazatou, where is your fiancé?"

"My fiancé, Sergio?" she said, leaned that long pestle on her shoulder, unhitched her colorful wrap and gave me a glimpse of her waist and thighs, arranged it again. "Who said I have a fiancé?"

"Everybody says it."

"Why are you asking everybody about me behind my back? I've been here for how many weeks now, Adama? Why haven't you asked *me* that, or even said hello? It's almost as though you are shy. Like a boy. A shy whiteman boy," she said, and curled her lips around her teeth in a dangerous smile.

"Mazatou?"

"Yes, Sergio?"

"Come here. Come inside my hut and let me show you how shy I am."

She set that pestle like a long and heavy spear against the mango tree, looked around through the morning half-light at the village, which was only beginning to wake, then sauntered across my courtyard until I felt charged and dizzy. From a few feet away, she ducked down her head to peer beneath the thatch and into the gloom of my hut. "I've been wondering what the inside of a whiteman's hut would look like. But it's too dark in there, Adama. I can't see anything."

"Come closer," I said to her. "Come inside and I'll show you everything there is to see."

She inched one sandaled step closer, waved her hips behind her with her hands on her thighs and said, "Hmm, Adama. I still can't see. Is there gold in there? Silver? Everyone thinks that's what you have. What do you want to show me?"

"It's better than silver and gold, Mazatou. I promise you. Come inside and find out."

"Better than silver and gold, Adama? What could be better than silver and gold?"

"A red stick, Mazatou."

"A red stick, Adama? Bring it out here. Let me see it."

"Come inside. You'll see it. I'll even let you touch it."

"Is it very big, Adama? Is it a big red stick?"

"It's long. Like a pestle. A long pestle you hold in your hand for crushing shea nuts into butter."

"Adama!" she said like blushing. She stood up then so she seemed even taller than she really was, rubbed her belly with her hand so her breasts lifted and fell under her blouse, grinned down at me when I was crouching inside my hut's low doorway, and said, "I don't know, Adama. Maybe I'll look at your red stick tomorrow. You can show me how you crush shea into butter with it then. But I'm hungry right now. 'Morning opens the mouth.' I have to finish my work if I want to eat rice."

I cast a hand out to catch her wrist, missed, and she stepped back and turned up her nose. She said, "If that's how you whitemen act, maybe you should keep that red stick thing of yours to yourself." She stomped across the courtyard in a great show, picked up the pestle, leaned it in the rice in the mortar, and winking at me, opened her wrap to give me a glimpse of those dark thighs, shutting them away again as she cinched it around her waist. By the next morning, this torturous ritual was established between us, and often were the times after making a snatch for her hand that I'd fall back on my mat in the pulsing rage of lust and frustration she stoked in me with every wink and tease, my red stick a painful thing, angry with me, too, for not having been able to put it to the use for which it was made.

When I had first come to the village, the chief had tried to give me a girl. It was the custom in much of West Africa, I'd heard in training, as much as offering a visitor water, a girl to help around the household, a gift the village could afford to give to an honored visitor for his time among them. The girl they offered me was in her midteens, and she followed me to my hut that first evening with a broom as though to simply clean it out for me. When she was done getting out all the cobwebs, I thanked her in French because even despite my three months of training, I hadn't been able to speak passable

Worodougou yet, and my first sense of disquiet occurred when she didn't go home, but sat on the root of the mango tree growing by my doorway. I tried to shoo her away, but with all my neighbors looking on with blank faces and the girl not moving, I had stopped that. I went to Mamadou's hut with my hurricane lamp in the evening and passed a quiet meal with him, fumbling to eat rice with my hands from the pot we shared. When I went back to my hut, I was relieved to see that the girl had gone home. I opened the door to go to bed, and there she was, stark naked in the lamplight, her body flat as a board on the mat, her arms at her sides, her eyes looking at me and trembling. It took me a moment to understand it, then I picked up her wraps from the floor and covered her with them. Somehow, I remembered one of the Worodougou words banging around in my head: *Taga*: 'Go!' She wrapped herself covered, then grasped my leg as I tried to push her to the door. She shouted scared things at me, and I at her, and my neighbor, whose hand I would heal six months later, came and dragged the girl by the wrist from my hut.

Mamadou was at my hut door at first light. He pushed open my door, came and crouched above me. He said, "What did that stupid girl do?"

"She didn't do anything," I said, sitting up.

"Her mother will whip her, don't worry, Adama. We're very sorry. We'll find you an even better one."

"Mamadou," I said, and grabbed his hand, one of the only times I had touched him in any way but greeting. "Don't send me another girl. In my country, a man always finds his women for himself. I won't stay here if you send me another."

"The chief is upset, Adama: with the girl, with her family.

If you didn't want her, why did you take her? Girls are offered as is custom, but nobody ever accepts one. You did."

"I thought she was going to sweep."

"She *did* sweep. I saw her."

"And the other part?"

"You didn't like her? You don't think our village daughter is pretty?"

"No, she's very pretty. Look, this is all getting very confused. Let me thank the chief and tell him the girl didn't do anything wrong. Then we'll start things over, and I'll take care of my hut with no girl."

"But it's good to have a girl, Adama. Good for you, and good for the village. If you don't have sex, you'll get sick. And also, the other men won't have to worry about their wives and daughters."

"They don't have to worry about their wives and daughters now, Mamadou. Not from me."

"Ah," he said, and nodded. "I understand. Crickets sing with crickets, ants march with ants. You don't like African women."

"For God's sake, Mamadou, I like all women. All colors."

"Of course you do, Adama," he said, and winked. "You are like the Lebanese merchant in Séguéla. He doesn't sleep with black women, either."

"Mamadou, don't go around telling people that I don't like black people. That girl was too young. In my country, it's a shame to sleep with any girl who is not very close to your age."

"Really?" he said, lifting an eyebrow.

"Yes."

"Let's go see the chief."

Because I was new there, everybody was still interested in

absolutely everything I did, large or small. So this thing with the girl was a large thing, and everyone who was on hand came out to watch. It was my punishment, I felt, for having so easily accepted having someone else do work for me that I could have done on my own. The chief sat in his chair in his courtyard wearing his long green *boubous* like a robe, his white Muslim's prayer cap on his head like a crown. He was ancient and thin, his left eye clouded with a thick blue cataract. Flanking him on either side were the assorted old men and sages of the village on stools in their many-colored *boubous,* holding their chins in their hands. Mamadou helped me work through the salutations for a chief, shaking hands with each of those men, greeting them in the name of Allah. Then we sat on stools across from the chief with the bodies of the village a thick ring around us. I wasn't supposed to look the chief in the eyes, and I didn't.

The chief said something. Mamadou said, "The chief asks if you slept well."

"I slept well, tell him."

The chief said something and the whole crowd laughed. Mamadou said, "The chief asks if you like girls."

I looked at the chief and laughed, and he smiled at me. I said, "Tell him I like girls."

The chief said something and everyone was somber. Mamadou said, "The chief says, 'Your ways are as confusing to us as ours must be to you. Don't ask for food again, Adama, if you are not hungry.'"

I sent a kilo of sugar to the girl's mother later in apology, and almost two years to the day after that, the girl, Fatoumata, much taller now and a woman, came and rapped on my door with a smile and her eyes lined with ceremonial kohl. She said in her husky woman's voice, "Where's my gift, whiteman? Haven't you heard that I'm getting married?"

Living in the village was much like living on a farm, though I'd never done that either. All about us in that maze of huts with the mango and acacia trees standing up between like light poles were animals: goats and sheep and dogs and chickens, some cows, even a few donkeys. Everywhere if you looked, sex was happening, anytime, anyplace. Just sitting on a stool in front of my hut of a brief morning, I could watch a rooster strut about, chase and mount and rape a half dozen chickens, shake out his legs after each act, dizzy and disoriented from it, and in a few minutes, he'd be chasing and raping another one. Stuck-together dogs were always great fun to watch; to watch the children toss rocks at them, the dogs trying to run away on eight legs, other dogs trying to mount what was already mounted, their penises erect like skinned sausages, humping the ribs of the couple in question. Male goats worked together to pin a bleating female against a tree, taking turns mounting her roughly against her wishes. Even the ducks made love, the drake on top of the hen's back and pressing her to the ground with her neck in his bill, his tail wagging in quick jerks like waddling as he did what he had to do. It was easy enough to ignore, but if you were in that sort of mood, it was all that you seemed able to see.

Mazatou came one morning as I sat on my stool and asked me for some of the peanuts I was eating. There were people around; boys shooting marbles, an old man sleeping in a hammock, an old woman chewing tobacco under her mango tree and looking off at nothing, and I couldn't have grabbed her if I wanted to. She held out her rough hand and I spilled nuts into it. She looked around, opened her wrap so her bare hips and thighs were only an arm's length away, then closed the wrap up as nonchalantly as though she herself hadn't noticed what she'd done.

"Keep that up, Mazatou, and you're going to get in trouble," I promised her. "Don't the ancestors say, 'The fly who plays near the spider's web risks feeding the spider'?"

"What are you taking about, Adama? Adama, what are they doing?"

I looked where she was looking, and a yellow dog was mounting a black one, his tongue hanging out happily and he looked around and seemed to smile, his haunches thrusting into her. Then Mazatou pointed in another direction, and it was a rooster, pinning a squawking hen to the ground with his body, shaking his hips an instant, hopping off her again in a dizzy way as he tried to find his footing. Then she pointed straight ahead out to two donkeys in the distant field, the male with a long black pole erect between his hind legs. He reared up, and the whole of that pole's grand length slid into the female. "What are they doing, Adama?" Mazatou asked me, and winked. "Do you know what that is?" I could only grit my teeth. And then, like a joke on both of us, the old man roused himself from the hammock, coughed and spit, waved to the old woman chewing tobacco who was one of his wives, and she followed him into his hut and shut the door.

The idylls of the dry season ended with the first sprinkling showers of April. Like all the men of the village, I went out into the forest to clear the tract of land the chief had given me for my farm. Because I was a whiteman and considered much weaker at field work than they were, I was given two hectares that had lain fallow only one year. Therefore, the brush I had to clear from it was only twice my height.

Helping Mamadou with his father's farm from my very first days there, I'd learned to swing a machete efficiently, and more than that, how to build a field hut. It was an easy thing, once you knew what to do. You buried two main supports, each a forked pole as tall as you were, a half dozen paces apart, then laid a pole in their forks. On each side, you did the same again, with short poles, low to the ground. Then you built a lattice of stripped palm branches for the framework of the roof, and cut and bundled grass for thatching. It took two days to build. But it could last the whole rainy season, giving one shelter from the afternoon monsoons. Children could do it; I did it. Then I sharpened my machete under its shelter with my file, went out into the bush surrounding it, and began clearing my farm.

At this time, all the hundred men of the village were occupied clearing their own farms as I was. My days were spent like this: I ate rice and oil at Mamadou's mother's hut in the morning, then walked the three kilometers on the trail through the forest to my farm. I'd cut and cut that brush, leaving it behind me in piles. Blisters on my hand opened and bled. I wrapped my hand with cloth strips and went on. All the men there did. This was what growing your own food meant. At night, I'd trudge back to the village, my whole body aching, my bones in pain, and I'd smoke a cigarette in the village center near the chief's hearth with other tired young men and listen to the smallest children drumming on old coffee cans, the virgin girls singing. It was a time of fatigue and not really talking to your friends. My arms would be so worn and tired from the work that I could not bend them completely down as I lay on my mat.

The only thing different about the work I did on my farm was that I did it alone. The other men had their women and children to help them, and besides, nobody liked being in the forest by himself. The forest was rife with haunts and genies. Among the most important parts of having a woman was that she prepared lunch in the field. This was always the simplest of dishes, often nothing more than rice sprinkled with salt. Not having a woman, I didn't even have that. I ate green mangoes that were just starting on the wild trees, and green papayas that grew in my field from the last farm that had been there. It gave me diarrhea, but I wanted to build a great farm and be a man. Mazatou tried to continue our flirting morning ritual, but I was too tired for it for now.

After weeks of slashing and cutting, the weeds fell and dried behind me like kindling, and with four acres cleared for the first planting, I lit a match and watched that bracken roar up in flame. When the ash settled, the area was open and clear. I had my farm.

The way to sow corn and beans there was to take a short-handled hoe and walk in lines. Each half pace you stepped, you chopped the earth open with the hoe, tossed in some seeds, patted the wound closed again, and stepped another half pace. Like this I planted my first four acres by hand, cleared ever more.

The heavy rains fell just as the ancestors promised. And then one morning I went out to my farm, and it was green with shoots, each one in its appropriate place. Now was the time for weeding, because the weeds rose up between the plants as quickly as they did.

How many weeks passed when I didn't even notice the setting of the sun, the rising of the moon, the cycle repeated again in the morning, the passing of days? All was work. And I did it until my arm felt made of cement, did it almost as well as any man there. When my beans were ankle high, my corn as high as my knee, my fields long and clean of weeds between the rows, I set down my hoe, went and lay under my field hut on its soft and dry earth, closed my eyes, and thanked the ancestors. I fell asleep. What did I dream? Plants growing to fruit, the earth fertile and alive.

Someone shook me awake. I blinked my eyes open to Mazatou.

"Adama! You've worked very hard out here. I wondered what you were doing in the forest all by yourself, why you don't play with me anymore like you used to. The village is empty. It's very boring there."

"What are you doing here, Mazatou?"

"I know you have no woman," she said, kneeling before me where I lay, setting down a calabash of rice. "I thought you must be hungry, so I came to give you food."

I was hungry, always was then. I reached for the calabash, and she pulled it away, smiled. I reached for it again, and she let me have it. I ate greedily, ate every last grain of that rice, the fish bones mixed in it. Then I lay back and began to feel alive again, food in me, the major work done and my fields green and growing. In a minute, I opened my eyes and looked at her face above me, the thatch of the hut I'd built beyond. She said, "Whiteman?"

"Yes, Mazatou?"

"You look like Sergio. You're Sergio, aren't you, from the television?" The Mexican soap opera was called *Marimar;* Marimar was Sergio's girlfriend. Sergio and Marimar had all the same problems of any couple in a Western soap opera. One night they were kissing, the next night fighting, the next night they'd have split up completely and taken new lovers. Mazatou approached me in that hut on her hands and knees. She said, "Kiss me the way Sergio kisses Marimar."

My body awakened. I said, "You know that they aren't real people, Mazatou, that it's a story made up for fun?"

"Kiss me like he kisses her," she said with her eyes closed.

I held her face in my hand, and I kissed her. Our tongues met and danced briefly against each other. The red stick came to life in my pants as she'd made it do so often before. I grabbed her shoulders and pulled her close down onto me, wrestled her a minute trying to kiss her more, and she shook me off and ran away. Like this, she'd managed to tease me yet again. "Take your calabash with you," I shouted from my knees, watching her run off through the corn, throwing it in a long arc after her.

At Mamadou's in the evening, I told him what had happened. We smoked cigarettes after the rice his mother had prepared for us and were tired. "Are you sure it was her?" Mamadou asked me, leaning against the mango trunk, seeming too tired to care.

"What do you mean?"

"If she didn't go to the fields with you, how can you know for certain that it was her? Genies like to take the shape of people we think we know, and they like to take the shape of women. It causes men problems. The next thing you know, you think you are sleeping with your neighbor's wife. If she didn't go to the fields with you, she could be a genie. You have to be careful. Genies like to torment and embarrass us. That is what they do."

"That was a real girl I kissed out there. That was the real Mazatou."

"What I am saying, Adama," Mamadou said, and released a slow plume of smoke, "is that it could be Mazatou, or it could be a genie. Unless we watched his birth, how can we know that a man does not have a twin?"

"Can a man sleep with a genie?"

"Genies like to trick men into sleeping with them. It gives them pleasure. Then, sooner or later, you reveal your heart to them and they eat your soul."

"If she comes back again, genie or not, I'm not going to let her get away."

"'Genie or not'? Adama, I see now that you're too lost for advice. But maybe it won't cause problems for you. Who knows what kind of power genies have over whites."

She did come again, the very next day. She came at noon, with food. She bowed and presented it to me. "Eat, whiteman. Eat until you are full." I looked at her carefully. Every pore of her seemed to be the same Mazatou who tormented me in the village, so why wouldn't it also be her here now, doing the same? I ate until the rice was gone, then lay on my back and smoked a cigarette. Mazatou kneeled close by, as she had done the day before. She said, "You work too hard. All by yourself." All around us were my growing corn and beans.

"Work with me," I told her.

"Whiteman, Adama, I can't work with you. What would my grandmother say?" She shuffled forward on her knees. Her face close to mine, she said, "You're Sergio."

"You're Marimar."

"Kiss me, Sergio."

I stubbed the cigarette out in the dirt, exhaled the last of the smoke to the side, then reached and touched her face, and she leaned down with her eyes closed to kiss me. There was still a little rice in my mouth, but she didn't mind. We kissed longer than the day before, and I reached and touched her breast through her blouse. She let me long enough that I felt her hard nipple beneath the thin material. Then I moved to snatch her around the waist, and before I could, she was off again through the rows of corn, her sandals slapping up against the soles of her feet.

Every day went like this until I became as frustrated and flustered as I had been when I'd woken up to her those many mornings pounding rice and shaking her hips at me. She came to my field hut and brought me food, called me Sergio, and we'd kiss like on *Marimar.* Even my scalp itched from it. Evenings I'd tell Mamadou, and he'd shake his head and look away, warn me about genies. "Maybe it's a genie that likes a fight, Adama. Next time, don't let it go, and make love to it, and it should leave you alone."

"And if it isn't a genie? If it really is Mazatou?"

"Make love to her, anyway. The rabbit that plays with the leopard is waiting to be eaten."

When I'd see Mazatou in the village and other people were around, she'd act as though we hadn't ever exchanged words; as soon as we were alone, she'd show me her hips and thighs, come close and whisper, "Kiss me like Sergio."

My every thought was of Mazatou, of sating myself in her body, and in doing so, becoming a real man of that place. What else was there to think about in the quiet of night in my hut before sleep? Everyone and everything was satisfying themselves around me just as they wanted. Mazatou had brought me to the point that I would do anything to find satisfaction as well.

"Kiss me like Sergio, Adama whiteman," she said, and bumped my shoulder with her hip as she passed me sharpening my machete that final evening before my hut. I rasped that blade to a razor's edge and decided that next time I would kiss her for good.

That last morning—the last morning I ever woke up to her—Mazatou didn't flirt with me. She pounded her rice with the monotony of a robot, and I could see that something was wrong. "What the matter, Mazatou?" I called to her from my stool.

"My grandmother is sending me back to my village today, Adama. My fiancé hasn't come from Abidjan for me. So now I must go and all our playing will end."

"I'm sorry that he didn't come," I told her, and took up my machete and calabash of water to head out to my farm.

"Adama, it's all right. We stop crying for rice when we've filled ourselves with yams. Playing with you has been fun."

"Maybe for you," I told her.

"I'll carry food to you today. Bring your red stick. Maybe today is the day I'll finally see it," she said, and winked.

I tried to work out there, but with Mazatou on my mind, I couldn't. I went and lay under the cool shade of my field hut. I hadn't had contact with a woman since coming to the village, just this girl who had frustrated me endlessly for months. The corn was waist-high now, my fields were very healthy. It rained a bit in the late morning, and then the sun came out and burned the rain to steam. Mazatou came through that clearing mist in her colorful wraps and set a calabash of rice beside me. I ate a few mouthfuls and pushed it aside. She crawled to me on her knees. "Kiss me like on *Marimar,*" she said. We kissed awhile, and then she broke away. "You can show me that red stick now."

"Are you sure you want to see it?"

"Yes, Adama, of course."

"And you're not going to run away?"

"Why would I run away?"

"You have every time before!"

"Well, this time I won't."

I didn't trust her, but what choice did I have? I unbuttoned my pants, slid them down, and there was the red stick. She looked at it as if it were a strange creature; it was as red as I had promised. She wrapped her hand around it like a pestle and began to pound it up and down. I drew deep breaths, enjoying: her hand thrummed like a piston; at first I wanted her to slow down; then I didn't; then I stopped breathing altogether. Suddenly, I was at the cusp of release. I grabbed her, pulled her to the ground, rolled and pressed the weight of my body on hers, stripped her wrap free from her thighs, and my stick touched her where it was supposed to go in. Could it have been inside her an instant? With the strength of a girl who pounded rice day after day, she pushed me off, scampered out from under the hut on her hands and knees; I was close on her heels, a goat, a dog, a rooster, a man, everything about me fire, hunger, lust, desire. I grasped for her wraps which flew about her like ribbons, and for a moment, had them in my fingertips. We ran deep into the corn, she just inches away from my outstretched hands, my pants falling around my ankles. Then, as had to be, my pants tripped me. A girl ran through the corn as I shouted her name from the dirt. The force of my pleading raised the lahou birds from the great trees, laughing already as they turned circles through the air, remembering forever this new story I had given them.

L'ÉTUDIANT

A boy in a school uniform came and sat in the dust outside my hut one evening. Six months had gone by, and I felt settled in the village. I was in my field clothes, a rough T-shirt and jeans, which had dried around me like cardboard. The day had been long and I'd worked hard putting up corn to dry on racks I'd built. Despite my fatigue, the boy didn't bother me. I'd gotten used to people staring at me, understood why they did. I didn't mind someone like this who simply watched, was otherwise respectful.

The boy's name was Abou, one of the witch doctor's many sons, the one he had sent to school. Most families chose to educate at least one son—sometimes even a daughter—to help them make certain they weren't getting cheated when time came to sell the cotton harvest, and the government men would arrive in the village with their badges and thick ledgers to buy it. No one expected these children to go on to be doctors or lawyers. It was enough if they could add and subtract, and follow the buyers' quick French.

"Adama," Abou said, his thin wrists lank over his knees, "you've labored well in your fields today. You cleared many weeds with your machete, isn't it? You've cleared back brush and told the forest that you are a man."

I didn't like his tone, guessed he was mocking me as the children often did. Beyond us in the witch doctor's courtyard, women were pounding dried cassava to powder in their wide mortars for the evening *toh*. I said, "How do you know what sort of work I did today, or if I did it well? Did you skip school again, Abou? Were you in the bushes watching me like a genie?"

"A genie, Adama? No. You are sharpening your machete. Why would you sharpen your machete if it wasn't dull? Adama, why do you work so often in the fields? What is it that you've come here to do?"

It was a question they'd all begun to ask. No matter how often I'd explain 9/11, that money wasn't available to do my job the way it had been in years past, this never seemed to get through to them. "I'm here to help the village have clean drinking water," I told him, my patent response. Lately, it had begun to sound lame even to me.

"Ah, Adama, that is good. So you are growing clean water in your fields. That is why you go to them every day."

"Of course I'm not growing water in my fields, Abou."

"Eh? So why do you work in the fields if it is not to grow clean water? Clean water is a thing we need very badly. The water my mother brings from the swamp has bugs in it."

"Times are tough, tough all over the world," I said, and looked down at my hands, humbled again at my inability to accomplish there what I'd promised when I'd arrived. "Once there was money to do many things. But now my country is at war, and there isn't. Without money, I can't do anything. Now I wait."

"You mean you don't have a money machine in your hut?"

"A money machine, Abou?"

"A money machine, Adama. All Africans know that whites have machines to make money. That is why whites are rich while blacks are poor. You have machines to fly in the air, machines to fly to the moon, machines to grow food. Therefore, you must also have machines to make money."

I smiled to myself, raked the file quickly over the blade pinned upright between my bare feet. "We have machines to do almost everything. But we don't have machines to make money. Believe me, if I had a machine to make money, that's what I'd spend my days doing. I'd work that machine so hard, we'd all be rich."

"Also, white babies are born with gold teeth. When the teeth fall out, you collect and sell them, and that is also why you whites are rich."

"Who told you that?"

Abou shrugged, looked at me with a serious face. "White babies can walk just after they are born."

"Anything else?"

"White eyes can see into a black man's soul."

I shook my head, looked across the village as the drape of evening settled onto it. Women and girls stood upright, lifting and dropping their long pestles like derricks, men and boys in their field rags sat at the fires and looked at nothing. Why argue? I'd once tried to explain what a microwave oven was to Mamadou, came away from that discussion wondering myself if the guiding science behind microwaves wasn't magic. "It's a box. You put the food into it. You press a button, it makes a sound, and then the food comes out hot."

"No fire, Adama?"

"No fire, Mamadou."

"Then how? Like magic?"

"Not like magic. Like science."

"Like science how, Adama? How can a simple box make food hot without some magic involved?"

"It's not just a simple box," I'd said, shook my head. I didn't for the life of me know how microwaves worked. A satellite had arced above us in the heavens that time, a steady red dot in the stars. I'd decided against pointing it out to him as well.

Here now, Abou appraised my work on the machete with the same sort of cocked eyebrow that Mamadou had lifted at my mumbled excuses about the microwave, shook his head. They all did that. Nothing I did seemed to conform to the proper way. I handed the machete over to Abou, tossed him the file, and he braced the long blade between his knees and went to work on it. In his hands, the file rasped thin curls of metal from the blade like ribbons. "See, Adama? Anyone can sharpen a machete. Anyone can grow a field. But it is schoolwork that is hard. Why don't you come to the school? There are already plenty of people who can do these things you do. Come and teach us about America. Teach us how a money machine is made so that we can make our own."

Abou's mother called him to dinner from their hearth, and I tested the blade on a corner of the callus on my thumb. The blade ran through it as if it were a cheese rind. Yes, the machete was sharp, much sharper than I had a knack for making it yet. I lit a cigarette as the last of the stars came out, and Abou and his brothers sat on their haunches and ate with their hands from the bowl of *toh* their mother had set down for them. The youngest waved to me when he saw me looking. Above them hung the tilt of the Southern Cross and as I settled into my cigarette, I asked myself again, 'What are you here to do?'

I'd been to the school before, had an open invitation from the director to visit anytime I wanted. The school was a three-mile walk through the forest on the logging road to Séguéla, and was a world of its own. It had been built in the '70s, when cocoa was still an income-producing commodity for Ivory Coast, and though the then-president, Boigny, had robbed the nation's coffers shamelessly to build the world's largest Catholic church on the site of his mother's village, there had still been enough money to construct schools. Along with the schools' two long buildings were six cinder-block houses for the teachers. There were flowering acacia trees and periwinkle shrubs, a dirt soccer pitch, and one of the only working deep-bore pumps in the region. Every day during the school year, children left the surrounding villages at daybreak to walk to it.

When our school had first opened thirty years before, the plastered and painted walls, the shining metal roofs, must have been a marvel for those mud-hut villagers to see. But the crash of the commodities market in the '80s, along with the humid wear of the surrounding forest and the political trouble of the past years, had taken their toll. The paint had long since peeled off, the roofs had rusted, the mortar between the cinder blocks had crumbled, and the school complex looked as though it had been ravaged in a war. The teachers' homes were squalid; the water from their pump was red. These days, they rarely received their salaries on time, and they hadn't had a raise in fifteen years. The teachers, Baoulés of the ruling Christian tribe, were angry and overworked, and the students packed the six classrooms so thickly that long rows of them sat on the floor between the crammed benches. No one had any supplies to speak of, whole villages of students shared a handful of textbooks; the soccer terrain was covered in cattle dung, the classrooms had to be swept out each morning for the pellet droppings of the goats that bedded down in them at night, the bush around the school was a minefield of students' shit because the school had no latrines. To visit the school was to glimpse the decay of Ivorian society.

The teachers were seated around a low table under a mango tree outside the director's house when I arrived that morning. They were drinking *bangi,* palm wine, a slow buzz that could be prolonged all day, and eating lush plates of rice and sardines with spoons. Behind me, the school buildings were alive with the sound of children sweeping, laughing, preparing the classrooms for the coming day. It had been months since I'd come to salute the teachers, and even though the village was far away in terms of distances in the bush, that I hadn't come to salute them was an insult they couldn't immediately forgive.

They were all big men in colorful *pagne* shirts, well fed compared to the Worodougou; they were heavier and blacker, proud because of their positions. The director, the oldest and largest among them, shouted back into his house as I approached, and his wife in her wrap came out quickly with a chair for me. When I was seated, the director swallowed from his drinking gourd, wiped his mouth on the back of his hand, rubbed his face like waking up, glanced at the others, and then at the lightening sky. My presence seemed to burden him like a chore. He sighed and said, "Tell me the news, Jacques."

"No news, Director. I have only come to salute you."

He grunted, glanced about. "That is good. That is the proper way. But what is not the proper way is that it is now two months since we've seen you. You don't like us, is it not? If you liked us, you would have come and honored us more often. Too much with the Worodougou. Perhaps you have taken a wife and pray at the mosque with them as well. They call you Adama, isn't it? A Muslim name."

They were looking at me, their eyes red, their faces blank. A breeze rustled the mango's leaves, but that didn't matter. The director had one lazy eyelid that made him look perpetually sleepy, more imposing because of it, and his head was frosted with gray. The teachers' shirts were neat and professional, and sitting before them was like suffering an interview.

I lowered my eyes. "I must ask forgiveness. My mission is to live among the Worodougou as they do, to learn their language. I have grown a field so that they can see that I understand their work. It has taken much labor, and I've been in the forest every day. Today I have come to salute you. I ask forgiveness on my knees. Every day I have wanted to come. But every day has become a new day when there is work."

Everyone burst into laughter. Even the wife doubled over. Then the director chuckled and said, "Get up off your knees, white Worodougou. This thing about the knees; only Muslims say this. Can you believe this, my brothers? Here is a whiteman, Muslim words spilling out of his mouth like the morning prayer."

The teachers swallowed their last bowls of wine, muttered to the director in Baoulé, sauntered off to their classrooms to begin the day. Though I waved it off with my hand, the director passed a gourd of *bangi* to me. I liked to drink, but didn't in the village because I didn't want to offend my neighbors. The constant pressure to drink was one of the reasons I'd stopped visiting the school. But Mamadou had recently taught me how to get out of this one. I took the gourd, poured a long sip of it into the dirt beside my chair and said, "So that the ancestors may drink."

The director shook his head. He said, "Too long with the Muslims. I am a Baoulé. Baoulés drink *bangi;* therefore I drink *bangi* no matter where I am sent to live. Why have you come today, Jacques? What do you want?"

"I'd like to help at the school, Director."

He looked at me a long time with his one eyelid half closed, swallowed the last of the liquid in the gourd, stood, and considered the morning. In the yard, the teachers were arranging the students into regimented lines before the flagpole to sing the anthem while two older boys raised the Ivorian tricolor. The flag was faded and tattered; another boy hit a scrap of metal with a pipe to call everyone to attention, and when the flag reached the top of the pole, the children followed the teachers' cue and began to sing. Despite everything, it was a pretty sound.

"Two more months until vacation," the director said as we listened to the children's singing. Just before he started off for his classroom, he said to me, "Don't think that we need your help, white Worodougou. We are trained and have certificates. But come tomorrow nonetheless. We will find something for you to do. Now, stay and eat. Perhaps it's the diet in the village that has made you lose your sense of respect."

I sat and ate the sardines and rice that his wife placed before me. We had nothing like sardines in the village, and the time of yam had long passed into the time of horrid *toh:* cassava gruel. It was a good and decadent meal, and I ate until I was full. The thought of that food made me look forward to the coming days.

Under the stars that night, I told Mamadou my plan to help at the school. After months of dejected ineffectualness, I was excited about something, but as I spoke, he chewed his *toh* like a steer mulling a cud; he didn't seem happy for me at all. He said in an even voice, "It is good that you've got something to do finally, Adama. But take care of that director. He is not popular here. Everything may not be as it seems. Perhaps he can't open his one eyelid because he has many secrets to hide behind it."

Abou was waiting for me at my hut. He met me as I entered the courtyard, took my hand, and led me to my door. He said, "I saw you at the school today, *Tonton* Adama. How pleased I was. Soon we will learn about the money machine of the whites. Sleep well tonight, so that in the morning you will be ready to teach us."

In the morning, the director was waiting for me under his tree. The teachers were there, too, drinking *bangi,* eating sardines, listening to the morning news from Abidjan on a transistor radio. The radio seemed oddly incongruent—a lost artifact of technology in the bush—but there it was. The past months of uprisings by northern Muslims against the government soldiers who controlled their cities had the teachers scared. Deep in enemy territory, they knew their lives depended now on things they couldn't control, on interpreting the news.

"Drink, Jacques," the director told me, with his sleepy eye. I emptied the gourd he passed me to the ground and said, "For the ancestors." The teachers muttered at this. "Like a Muslim," one said under his breath.

"*Bon,* Jacques. This is what we have decided. You know that we are overworked, don't have time to travel and attend to the needs of our relatives. They demand much from us because we are salaried professionals, and grow angry when we do not visit them. Therefore," the director said, and handed me a box of chalk from his breast pocket, "we will take turns visiting our villages, and as we do, you will supervise our classes. Today Isidore will travel, and you will teach second grade. None of us are happy that someone without a certificate will be in charge of students. But the times being what they are, we have decided to make do."

The students were lining up in the yard, the boys already raising the flag. I began to protest, I said, "Director, I've never taught anything—"

The newscaster on the radio said, "The RDR has called a general labor strike today in Abidjan."

"Muslims," Isidore, the second-grade teacher, muttered under his breath.

As the children began to sing, the morning drinking session broke up. Isidore hugged the others good-bye. He was the youngest of them, and the tallest, his first time in the bush after his years at the teachers' school in the city. He patted me on the shoulder, handed me a long rubber strap cut from the inner tube of a car tire. He said, "I'll bring you a fresh baguette from the city when I come back, little Worodougou. Don't worry. But use this. Don't spare them. The children in the second grade, they are the worst of all. If it breaks, the director will give you another. This is the only thing these children understand." Then he ran across the soccer terrain to hop on the approaching logging truck.

What was there to do but walk with the teachers to my class, to the seventy students in a motley of uniforms that their parents had pieced together for them smiling at me already from the benches and the floor? They stood like recruits as I entered the dim room. "*Bonjour,* monsieur!" they shouted. Had anything in my life prepared me for this? For all these children? For teaching in a language I didn't even speak well? The strap was a repugnant thing in my hand, and the students stood smiling. They were tiny versions of human beings, some covering their mouths with their hands to stifle their laughter. Already, I could hear the straps flying in the other classrooms, the children in them crying out. Corporal punishment was meted out for wrong answers, for daydreaming, for any sort of offense at all. "Sit down, children," I told them in French, and they sat like falling. Then I said, "Can someone please tell me what your last lesson was?" They blinked at me as though they hadn't understood.

I saw Abou in the back. I said to him, "Abou, what was your last lesson with Monsieur Isidore?" He looked stricken, scared. "What page are you on in your textbooks?" He shook his head, looked down. "Anybody? Please. What have you been studying?" Those in the front row looked like they might cry now. I shook my head. Flies already worried my eyelashes. "Don't any of you understand French?"

A small girl, one of the few girls there, raised her hand. I nodded at her. She stood and said slowly, "*Bonjour,* Monsieur Adama."

"Yes, good morning, Salimata. What was your last lesson?"

"*Bonjour,* Monsieur Adama," she said again. Someone in the back giggled.

I said, "None of you understand French, do you?" They all blinked at me. I said, "I could say anything and you wouldn't understand." They stared blankly. In Worodougou, I said, "Can anyone speak French?"

"We can sing the anthem!" a dozen of them called.

"*Akain. An be touba kan fô?*" 'Good. But can you speak French?'

Abou raised his hand. He said sagely, "Adama, why are you speaking Worodougou in school? Everyone knows that if we speak Worodougou in school, then we must be whipped."

"I give you permission, Abou. Can you speak any French?" Abou nodded his head solemnly. "Speak," I said.

"*Bonjour,* monsieur," he said.

I set the box of chalk on the table, went out and across the yellow yard to the director's class. The students were drawing on their slates with nubs of stone. The director was at his table, reading a newspaper from a stack of them beside him on the floor. The table was old and flimsy, and I noticed that he'd slipped off his shoes beneath it. He blinked at me with his sleepy eye as the students stood. "*Bonjour,* monsieur!" they said. I waved for them to sit down. The director folded his paper, seemed concerned. He said, "Are they giving you trouble, Jacques? Come, I will show you how to whip them."

"They can't speak French, Director. Not a word. How am I supposed to teach them if they can't speak French?"

"If they don't answer your questions, you must whip them. Then they will answer. Let's go. I will show you."

"I don't want to whip them. I'll teach them in Worodougou until Isidore comes back."

"Impossible. Tribal languages are not allowed in school. French is the national language. The students must study in French."

"I'll try again," I said.

"Use the strap. That is what the children know."

Back in my classroom, the students had helped themselves to the chalk, had drawn crude gazelles and elephants on the board, were playing soccer with a rag, many were stretched out and asleep, others had painted their faces completely white with the chalk. They stood when I came in, the sleeping ones jerked to their feet by others. They said in unison, "*Bonjour,* monsieur."

"Sit down, children," I said in Worodougou. "What did you do yesterday?"

Abou raised his hand. He stood and said, "Monsieur Isidore taught us one to ten."

"To write it or to count it?"

"Both, Adama," Abou said, and smiled.

"All right. Let's count to ten."

They counted to ten perfectly in French, like singing a song. I felt a ray of hope. "Now, someone come and take this chalk and write one to ten on the board." No one raised a hand. There was much embarrassed giggling. Finally, Salimata raised her hand timidly. She was one of those who had painted her face white with chalk. She looked like a mime. I waved her forward and she took the chalk I offered. She was only as tall as my hip, her hair in neat plaits. I urged her to the chalkboard. After a long deliberation, she glanced at me a last time and wrote a perfect capital *L*. Then she looked at me nervously. I glanced at the crowded class. They were nervous, too, as though all of their fates depended on Salimata's answer.

"Sali," I said in a soft voice, "what number is that?"

She looked at me a long time, then at the *L*. She said, "It is this number?" and pointed at the *L*.

I felt hopeless. I said, "And that is what number, Sali?"

"This number," she said again, and pointed to it with her finger.

"Which is what number?"

"This one. This number, *Tonton* Adama."

"Don't call me *Tonton*. I'm not 'Uncle' at school. I'm 'Monsieur.' What is the name of that number, Sali?"

"*Tonton,* I don't know," she said, and tears fell out of her eyes.

Abou raised his hand. I pointed at him and he stood. He said, "Now you must whip Salimata, *Tonton* Adama."

"I don't whip children," I said. A murmur went through the class. The murmur rose, and they began to have loud conversations. Abou stood again. He said, "Adama, you must whip her. She drew this crazy number that is not a number. So you must whip her. That is the rule."

Salimata was trembling and crying. The students offered their consent in loud voices: seventy ten-year-olds urging me to use the whip. I lifted the rubber strap off the table. "Salimata, come here." She shuffled forward, tears leaking freely. She raised her palms to me like an offering, turned her face away in anticipation of the blow. I lifted the strap high above my head, felt the class draw in its breath. Then I let the strap fall over her palms like a wet noodle. The whole class laughed, and she laughed. For an instant, I felt happy, drowned in the ridiculous situation. Then everyone shut up as the director came in.

He took the strap from my hand, whipped Salimata three times in the face. He erased the *L* with a wipe of his hand, wrote a perfect *1*. Everything had happened in the blink of an eye.

"What is this laughing, hey? Imbeciles. Jacques, it will be a long day if you let these children have the best of you. The school is not the village. And an *L* is not the number *1*." He took a quick tour of the classroom, whipping children indiscriminately. Then he handed me the strap, and Salimata lay on the floor, weeping. I wanted to comfort her but didn't. We spent the rest of the morning taking turns writing the number *1* on the board, and more than half of them wrote the letter *L* anyway. I understood then this was the first time most of them had written anything.

Isidore didn't come back that day, or any other. I asked the director about it constantly as he and the other teachers drank under the mango tree in the mornings, and he placated me with plates of rice and sardines. There were reports on the radio about an uprising in nearby Mankono, and the teachers were concerned with that. For two weeks, I did my best to teach second grade. Though the textbook was well into addition and subtraction, we worked on counting to twenty. Even I began to use the strap, though I could see in the students' eyes that they did not fear me. Wednesdays were supposed to be set aside for extracurricular activities: sport, or song and dance, but what Wednesdays really meant was that the teachers took their classes to work for them in their personal fields. The girls chopped firewood while the boys weeded between yam rows. Beatings were general and often. First grade was spent mostly on memorizing the national anthem; after that, it was learn what you could.

During training, we'd been taken to visit a "typical" Ivorian elementary school. That had been in the well-funded Christian south. The teachers had been kind, and the students well dressed and polite. Everyone had his own textbook, and not once had I seen a strap. But that had been during training, a three-month-long illusion designed to keep the reality of Ivory Coast at bay and us from quitting and going home.

Being at the Tégéso school depressed me in a profound way. The deep sense of hopelessness that had pervaded the whole country since General Guei's coup settled into me as well. I longed to return to my fields, where at least the plants still grew. I did what I could mornings and afternoons. At lunch, I ate with the director, the rich food the only good part of any of it.

Under the director's mango tree at noon, the teachers

gathered to drink and eat, while the children formed long lines for the meager bowls of plain rice that the teachers' wives sold to them for twenty-five CFA each—about four cents. Those whose parents could not afford this sat in the shade and didn't eat. They stared blankly at nothing while flies settled on their faces; starving people. At the director's, in the meantime, we feasted on rice drenched with palm oil, on tins of Moroccan sardines. I'd tease Mamadou in the evenings about the good food I'd had to eat at the school, and he'd look away at the stars. I wished I'd never gone to the director to offer my help, envied my friend's life in the fields. Teasing him about the good food I'd had to eat was my only way of making my present life seem bearable.

I wrote to my friend Ryan about the awful strappings, about the illiteracy of the children. He wrote back from his village, "Sounds like the same problems here, Jack. The teachers are underpaid and overworked, trying to foist an unrealistic curriculum on children whose people they are at odds with. It lets them justify stealing the children's food. The rice, oil, and sardines are provided for free by the World Food Program."

I asked Mamadou that night if it was true, and he waved his hand like warding away dust. He said, "A Christian from Abidjan came here in a big car. He said they would give food to the children. For a while it was so. Then the director came and said the program had ended. Now the children pay. Who knows what is really true?"

In the morning, I asked the director bluntly where the sardines came from. He and the teachers laughed uncomfortably for a moment as they drank, and his wife went into the house.

Then the director looked at me with even his lazy eyelid lifted. He said, "You've eaten with us as we have, Jacques, have you not? Hasn't it filled your belly? Hasn't it given you the energy you need to make it through the difficult day?"

"I've enjoyed it, yes. But where does it come from?"

They drank their palm wine and looked at nothing. The radio reported another massacre. Then they went off to teach their classes.

It was the strappings, the hatred toward the Worodougou, Isidore's extended jaunt, the difficulty of teaching second grade when I wanted to be in my fields. After a few days of pointedly refusing to eat lunch with the teachers, of getting no explanation from them about it, I went to the chief. He was lying in his hammock, looking at the stars in his old-man way. I sat on a stool before him. After a time, his cataract-clouded eyes rolled onto mine. "Adama," he said and grinned, "you've come to tell me that you've finally secured a tractor for us, is it not?"

"The director of the school is stealing food from the village."

Mamadou was with me in his *boubous,* as always. He looked at his toes while the chief rocked back in his hammock and gazed at the stars. Some long moments passed as he swung with his hands folded over his chest. It was as though the chief had heard something he didn't want to know. Then he looked at me again and said, "Is this true, Adama? Think cautiously. Is this something I need to know?"

Mamadou didn't offer me any support. I inhaled deeply, almost sadly. I said, "It's true, Father. The food at the school has been given to the children for free. The director takes the best things for himself, makes the children pay for the rice that remains. He shouldn't have any of it. It all belongs to the children."

"Mamadou, Koné's son, is this something that I need to know?" the chief asked.

"Adama has discovered it. It is a very important thing, as he says."

The chief shook his head. He said, "Adama, I have welcomed you here as my son. You have come to tell me something, and now I know it. Every gift is held by two hands: the one that gives, and the one that takes away."

It was still early evening. Mamadou and I followed the chief on the logging road to the school. The director and the teachers were drinking at the table like apparitions by lamplight, bowls of rice and sardines before them. They didn't rise as we approached. Then we were standing before them, Mamadou holding the chief's arm to support him. The director nodded to the chief without looking him in the eyes. Then he asked, "The news?" in French, and for the first time, I heard French words leave the chief's mouth. He said in a soft village patois, "Adama has been teaching at the school, is it not?"

"It is," the director said, and nodded into his gourd of palm wine.

The chief said, "If one allows the *agouti* to thrive in one's fields, then one must expect corn to fall. You will send the foreign gift to the village in the morning. So you have enjoyed awhile. Now it is finished."

The director nodded and the chief called us away. As we left the school under the stars, I understood that the chief had known about the theft, that I had caused the collapse of some delicate system they had devised among themselves.

"You should have told me," I said to Mamadou as we smoked on stools outside my hut in the night. He exhaled a long plume of smoke at the stars, scratched his foot, and said, "You are the whiteman. It is your place to tell us. We didn't ask for that gift, or this trouble it has brought us. Why are you upset, Adama? The monkey eats guava, the francolin eats rice. Don't be upset to have done what was right in your heart."

In the morning, boys brought the sacks of rice and crates of oil and sardines to the chief's compound on their heads, and the teachers used the pretext of a Muslim uprising in distant Boundiali to leave for the city. "How long will you be gone?" I asked the director on the roadside, but he only shook my hand good-bye as he stepped up onto the bush transport, which was already crowded with his family and bags. He winked his lazy eye. He said, "Thank you for these past weeks, for your help. Adama! What a great help you have been! Maybe the old chief will guard the food better than we have. *Inshallah,* isn't it? For the food and for our return. *Inshallah*. It all depends on God." As the truck lifted dust in the breaking morning, I went to the school and dismissed the classrooms. The students would not leave. Sitting in the classrooms was better than laboring in the fields, as their parents would make them do if they went home.

For some long days, I thought about quitting, about leaving the village and going home. When Abou would come and sit outside my hut in the evening, he'd look at me with a pained face. "White babies can't walk when they are born, can they, Adama?"

"No, they can't."

"And there isn't any money machine."

"No."

Abou didn't offer to help me with my machete any longer.

Soon enough an old man died. I didn't know him, but Mamadou told me he had been important. Everyone in the village put on their best *boubous* and went to the chief's compound to mourn. I did, too. Soon, long trains of mourners began to arrive from surrounding villages. We all sat on mats, the women on one side, the men on the other, the colors of our robes a vivid pageant against the dirty village. An old and toothless griot told stories of the ancestors and the seasons, the old women wailed, the young women cooked over great pots. Then the funeral feast was served. It was all the rice and sardines from the school, gone in a day.

A calabash of food was placed in front of me, the chief's eldest wife brought me a spoon so I wouldn't embarrass myself in front of all these strangers. The day was long and yellow, a faint wind in the mango leaves above my head. I set the spoon aside, dipped my fingers into the calabash to eat like everyone else. Beside me, Mamadou watched as I fumbled with the food. "Like this," he said, tucking his long fingers into the rice, drawing a dollop of it to his mouth with grace and ease. I took a breath, focused myself on that one simple act. Everyone seemed to watch as I tried again.

THE FRANCOLIN HUNTER

I'd undergone three months of training in a modern, Christian village, near the capital, Abidjan, before being sent to Tégéso. During training, I and the seventeen other volunteers of my group had daily classes in West African French and the individual tribal languages we'd need in our villages; we also learned other things, such as how to build wells, and how to treat those wells for cholera, which broke out every rainy season all over Ivory Coast. We were energetic young Americans during training; we studied frenetically, shook hands with everyone we met, made messes of ourselves eating *foutou* and peanut sauce with our fingers, talked politics. We diagrammed extensive theories of rural development on the blackboards of the schoolrooms the organization rented for us. We went to church on Sundays with our cocoa-growing host families; we made sweaty love to each other late at night under the blossoming mango trees on the sandy bank of the dark Comoé River. Some of us made plans of marriage, of the children we'd have once we'd finished our service, how we'd tell those children as they grew, "Mommy and Daddy met in Africa." But first, we were going to change the world.

A year in, nine of us had gone home, one to a mental asylum, and two more were laid up in the Western hospital in Abidjan with malaria. I managed to stay, and when I'd get sick, I'd sweat it out on my mat in my hut. Part of it was I liked it there. Another part was that I was afraid to fail. Even those days that I wanted to spend alone in my hut, I would rise, wash my body from a bucket in the tall grass, take a few deep breaths as I searched the pale sky for answers to the new questions forming inside me, and I'd wind my way to the chief's compound at the village's center. At each hearth, I would offer my morning salutations. It was difficult to give of myself that openly, it was work, and I knew the Worodougou found my white presence in their village ridiculous. For a long time, I spoke their language and fumbled with their customs like a child. Then one day, I didn't anymore.

This was nearly one year to the day that I had arrived with my small backpack off a logging truck whose Burkinabé driver, as I signaled him to stop, looked at me with a nervous face and said, "What? Here? What is it? You got to pee?"

"No, man. This is it. Tégéso. This is where I'm going to live."

He didn't even come to a complete stop, as though he thought that if he did, he'd have to live there with me. Hopping off the truck, I felt I was stepping down onto the unknown surface of an unexplored planet. The truck rolled away, the red dust settled, and as I turned to face what would be my home for the next three years, the villagers set down their implements and gathered: the women their pestles, the men their machetes and short-handled hoes, the children their rag balls, hoops, and sticks. The village was a collection of thatched huts surrounded by the tall walls of the forest. We stared some long moments across the short road at each other. The primitiveness of the village fell on me like a sudden weight, and as I looked at all those people looking back at me, I'd never felt so white. For the first time I allowed myself this thought: What am I doing here?

Of course the organization had sent an envoy to prepare Tégéso for my arrival, but that had been months before, and though every day during training we had been reminded that soon we would each have to step down from a vehicle and into our lives in Africa, the reality of that had seemed as theoretical as our optimistic plans for starting pump-building cooperatives and fish farms. I understood two things immediately: that I was white and would be no matter what I did, and that not one thing I'd learned in training would have a practical application in this place. I set down my pack, crumpled inside myself. The crowd rushed to me, and my bag was hoisted onto a small boy's head, and another child led me by the hand to the compound of the chief.

I would never see the village assembled in its entirety as I would that first day. It was hot; I felt like crying. I was afraid to even look at my hands; I knew they would be shaking. I sat on a stool across from the chief in his chair, and many words were said, but I don't know what, and by many voices, but I don't know whose. Flies landed on my forearms and I let them. One pair made love. I had never been so closely examined by so many people. I had never been so acutely aware of my own existence, or wanted something so desperately to end. As the great flux of those first moments ebbed, words came through the heat to me. The thin old chief spoke in his rasping and weathered voice. He said, "Know that you are welcome here, Adama. Adama Diomandé," and he tapped his staff down on the earth with finality. In this way I lost my American identity, was given my Worodougou name: Adama, the Muslim version of Adam, the first man, and Diomandé, Dio—'of the,' Mandé—Mandé, or Malinké, people. No one there ever really learned my Western name, or cared. With time, even this wouldn't matter to me.

How can I say when trust was built between myself and them? The most important thing was simple time, and a close second was language. Each evening in the early days, I sat in the chief's courtyard by the fire among his young sons, and I'd point to my nose, my ears. They would laugh and tell me the Worodougou words: *"Nu-ay-o,* Adama, *now-o,"* and I'd write them in my notebook. In the mornings, I'd walk through the village, teasing the children that followed me, "These are my eyes, this is my nose."

"What's this, Adama whiteman?" a naked seven-year-old would say and lift up her leg.

"Bau-o," I'd say, and they'd all laugh.

"What's this?" another would say, and point to his penis, and I'd blush and say, *"Mogo-o."* Then they'd all cover their mouths and run away.

I enjoyed the forest, found it mystical, overwhelming, secret, beautiful. Perhaps I didn't fear the forest because I didn't know enough about it. When the jibes of my neighbors about my white skin and hairy legs would get to be too much to bear, I'd often follow a path between the trees, find a tall mahogany to sit against, and listen to the birds and monkeys chattering in the canopy. It was hot there, and I sweat even sitting down. I'd sweat like that for three years.

Because I didn't have a wife or children, I wasn't a real man to the Worodougou, and I took up hunting to compensate for that. After a year of hearing the reports sound from deep in the forest as I'd sit in the village cleaning my toenails with a matchstick, I went to Séguéla, the regional capital, and spent some of the only real money I ever would there, $100, for a handmade twelve-gauge shotgun. This was a traditional weapon, the sort that Samory Touré's men fought the French with before they lost the Malinké homelands to the colonizer: an imitation of the real thing, a handcrafted copy of what the Africans had seen, and wanted for themselves.

For three days, I stayed at the blacksmith's compound in Séguéla, watching him make my gun for me. He was an old man, nearsighted, a pure and devout Dioula from Odienné, his prayer cap on his bald head dirtied from the grime of his work. Guns were outlawed by the ruling Christian government, and the blacksmith's compound was situated in a secluded thicket of grass along the marsh at the edge of town. His small boys played marbles and kept watch along the road; his wives were polite and modest, as was in keeping with the household of a respected man. I conducted business with him in Worodougou. Getting my gun felt racy and exciting. I knew I was breaking important rules, and I didn't care. To make the gun, the blacksmith sawed a three-foot length from a long water pipe, heated the end, and tapped into it a round length of metal to widen the bore to take a shell. The action he made from metal scraps, hammering the hot pieces into shape on his anvil, a discarded engine block. It was delicate work, stunning to watch done so efficiently. The lush voice of Oumou Sangaré from the old man's tape player relaxed us as she sang songs from the desert, and beside him, his blind son carved the stock from a marbled piece of ebony. We drank tea and smoked cigarettes. The blacksmith asked me, "Do you miss your mother, Adama whiteman?"

"Very much so, Father."

"So why is it that you have left her?"

"I want to know your people. I want to go home and tell her about you and how you made this gun."

"Ah, that is good. A cub must make a long journey before he returns home as a lion."

When the gun was finished and assembled, a lesser imam was called, and after he'd chanted over and blessed my weapon, I gave him coins and kola nuts from my pocket. The blacksmith appraised the barrel's line a final time with his one eye. Then, with a smile, he handed it to me. I shouldered the gun, pointed it at the sky, pulled the trigger, and the action clicked. It felt good.

"Adama?"

"Yes, Father?"

"When you kill the animal, thank his spirit like you would a brother."

"I will."

"Adama?"

"Yes, Father?"

"Bring meat to the people you love."

To bring the gun back to the village, I had to negotiate three government checkpoints. This was a very scary trip. Violence had been flaring up again between the Muslim and Christian tribes the past months, and everyone was on edge. Whole villages of Muslims had been hacked to pieces by drunken Christian youth, and as foreigners, we should have been pulled out by the organization. But the U.S. government supported the Christian tribes, just as the French had all through the colonial days, and to pull us out would have meant admitting that things weren't as stable for their puppet government as the western companies, trading in Ivory Coast for cocoa, rubber, and timber, and selling Coke and cigarettes, wanted to hear. Not one of the northern Muslims I lived with had a positive memory of a white person to speak of. Some of the old men in my village had been forcibly conscripted by the French to fight in World War II, and many others remembered when their grandfathers had been taken away in chains to work the French cocoa fields, and build their mansions at Grand Bassam. Still, they gave me a hut, and a bowl of rice or *toh* three times a day.

Living among the Worodougou, I saw firsthand how the Christian southerners kept the Muslims in a state of poverty so that they'd have no other option but to work as laborers on the commercial plantations. The soldiers at the checkpoints knew I knew this. I didn't go to Séguéla often anymore because every time I did, I was subjected to humiliations. One soldier in particular, a sergeant, an older man with buck teeth and a paunch at the Kavena checkpoint, liked to press the barrel of his sidearm to my temple and make me sing the U.S. national anthem. Another time, he made me do push-ups. And once, when he was very drunk, he reached in the window of the bush truck I was seated in and slapped me across the face.

"Do you pray to Allah yet, white Worodougou?" he shouted at me. "How is it that you've lived here all this time and you haven't once come to the barracks to salute me in front of my officers?" The villagers traveling with me, mostly old women taking yams to market, kept quiet out of fear, and even after the soldiers had drawn the nail-studded plank from the roadway to let us pass, no one said a word. I know this was because they didn't want to call attention to my shaming. I also know that they told their families about it, and in this way I became known in Worodougou villages where I'd never even set foot.

I put the pieces of my gun in a rice sack under my seat, and for how awful trips like that usually were, the ancestors were on my side this time and the soldiers simply waved us through. If they'd found it, they would have had the right to shoot me. But they didn't find it. In my hut, I assembled my gun, wiped its length with a cloth like praying, filled my pockets with shells the blacksmith had acquired for me from a Peul contrabander, and went into the forest to kill something. Everyone was occupied with chores and nobody saw me go.

All through the forest were paths, and now and again through the gloom, sunlight would glimmer ahead like at the end of a tunnel. This would be someone or other's fields, and in this way, the forest around Tégéso became for me a sort of labyrinth of adventures. Some of the paths led to golden fields of rice, others to symmetrical quilts of yam mounds. Even better were the silent rows of cashew trees. These were spaced widely enough that I could walk easily through them on the clean and weedless earth. I knew that these fields and orchards were full of animals that troubled the crops. There were long-toothed *agouti,* a kind of giant rodent that was prized for its succulent flesh and could fell a quarter acre of corn in the short expanse of a night. There were short-haired bush pigs that liked to uproot cassava. There were troops of red monkeys that would take a single bite out of every papaya in a tree. And above and beyond all were the double-spurred francolins, a grouselike wild chicken that ravaged rice and scratched sweet potatoes and yams loose from the soil.

The francolins were what called me. Now and again as I'd work in the fields, a pair of them would flush from under my feet in great and heart-stopping explosions of wing, and before I'd even had time to understand what had happened, I'd see the heavy-bodied birds coasting on their outstretched wings to drop in the distant crops again. I felt that this was a greater challenge than even the larger game offered: to stalk a waving field of rice, gun at the ready; to stop when my senses flared; to hold my breath; to concentrate even the hairs on my arms to the when and where of the flush; and just when I'd give up the moment to a false trick of light and desire and wind, the francolins would leap up like firecrackers. I shot at a dozen and missed them all.

Chauffeur, my neighbor, came to my hut in the dark depth of the new night. All through the village, the night fires burned like markers of humanity, and above, the stars were talc tossed across black paper. I sat on the dirt and the older man took my stool. He lit a cigarette and released a plume of smoke to the night.

"Adama?" he said in his measured and graveled voice.

"Yes, Father?"

"You're not afraid of the forest, are you?"

"No."

"I've never known a whiteman before."

"I never knew Africans until I came to this village."

He sighed, smoked, scratched his knee through his worn field trousers. Even though a year had passed, I had spoken to him rarely, was surprised and flattered that he had come to me in this way. He was old enough to be an elder, but he seemed to participate in nothing. Even on Fridays, I had never once seen him in a bright-colored *boubous,* heading to the village mosque.

"Do you have a wife in your country, Adama?"

"No, Father."

"Is your father living?"

"No. He joined the ancestors seven years ago, just when I became a man."

Chauffeur grunted, as though a truth had been told. His difference from the other men, even from the chief, was pointed. While they asked me for cigarettes or coins now and again when no one was looking, asked me questions like, "Adama, did you whitemen really travel to the moon?" Chauffeur seemed to take my presence in stride. He was a thin man given to field labor; he had four hardworking wives who never seemed to quarrel amongst themselves as the other men's wives always did. What I knew about Chauffeur was that he brought strange herbs, roots, and vines with him in bundles from the forest in the evenings, and that he was a great hunter. Mamadou had also told me that Chauffeur had driven a cab in Abidjan as a young man; hence his name.

"Adama, do you understand that the people here fear the forest?"

"I've seen that they are nervous in the fields as the sun begins to set, Father."

"Adama, this village, we as people, we are only visitors here. The village is carved from the forest, and it is our true place. It is only in the village that things are as they appear. When we leave the village on a path, we leave the world of men and enter the world of the spirits and ancestors. Here, we stand on real ground and the sky above us is as it should be; the village is a small scrap of floating bark that we cling to like ants in water. When we enter the forest, all is as though upside down."

"Yes, Father," I said.

"Adama? Why have you brought a gun to the village?"

Something embarrassed rose in me, and I made it settle again. I said to him, "The men have guns here. I wanted one for my own. I want to hunt. I want to contribute in some way."

"You are not a man here."

"I know," I said, and looked at my hands in the dark.

"You have fired twelve shots in the three days since you've brought the gun. You are shooting in the air, so it's green money, or francolin, or bat that you are hunting."

"It's francolin, Father. I'm hunting the francolin."

"Do you know his name, Adama?"

"No."

"U-a-o."

"U-a-o."

"Would you like to be a hunter of the *u-a-o,* Adama?"

"Very much."

He drew on his cigarette a last time, inhaled the smoke like swallowing it, crushed the butt out under his bare heel.

He said, "I'll wake you in the morning. Don't wash your face."

Islam came late to the Worodougou. Of the varied Malinké peoples, the Worodougou are unique because they live in the southern forest. Because of their relative isolation—Tégéso, for example, means "The Cut-Off Village"—they were able to retain their belief in the power of the ancestors. Samory Touré, the Malinkés' greatest hero, was in some ways the Worodougous' worst enemy. He fought the French colonizers late into the nineteenth century, and as first Bondoukou, then Kong, Korhogo, and Odienné fell to the white armies, Touré fought a last-ditch scorched-earth campaign. He arrived with his cavalry in Séguéla in the early 1890s, the French close on his heels, and as with any desperate cause, he needed a focal point around which to rally the people. Touré chose Islam, and when he arrived among the ancestor-worshipping Worodougou, he gave the villagers an ultimatum: Convert to true Islam, or his men would force the village mothers to crush their infants in their millet mortars. Most villages acceded. But in a few, like Gbena, five miles to the east of Tégéso, so great was the peoples' trust in their beliefs that a whole generation of Worodougou were pounded to pulp in their forming bones. In the end, the French cornered Touré in a dark forest near the Cavally River in Liberia. He had nowhere left to run and legend says that they cut him to pieces.

Now, all Worodougou villages have two things in common: a baobab tree, thick and mighty, planted when the village was founded, and a small cinder-block building with a cupola, often painted yellow, which is the village mosque. Genies and witchcraft are still vibrant among them, and while they turn to the imam to settle simple disputes of marriage and land, when there's a real problem, they turn to the witch doctor, the man charged with guarding the spiritual health of the village. Chauffeur was the witch doctor of Tégéso. I lived next door to him.

I followed Chauffeur into the forest that morning. It was a great honor that he would spend time with me. Even in the dark, he knew his way with ease, and my gun slung over my shoulder, I followed the whisper of his feet on the hard dirt of the path, and the acrid smoke of his cigarette. The forest was silent and black, seething, seeming in that silence even more stupendous than it really was. Beside the trunk of a great teak, Chauffeur stopped us. The sky was indigo now between the moving leaves of the canopy, and America and my life there felt as far away as they really were. I could feel the beating of my heart. I can say this: In the forest, I felt alive.

"First," Chauffeur said to me in the dark, "take off your sandals."

I did what he said even though I worried that my whiteman's soles were too soft to not be cut by some stray twig or stone.

"Now eat this," he told me, and passed a small handful of dry powder into my hand. I tossed it into my mouth, mulled it with my tongue until it formed a ball, and then I swallowed it. It tasty woody and rotten. It tasted like dirt mixed with gunpowder.

"We'll sit among the grass at the edge of this field. Imagine that you are the grass, Adama. That is all I want you to do as we wait for the *u-a-o*. The *u-a-o* is afraid of men for all that we have done to him, as with all the animals but the ones who live with us. Grass to the *u-a-o* is as the village is to us, and if we are grass, he will not be afraid. Give me your gun."

I handed Chauffeur my gun and he set it against the tree. Then we moved into a cashew orchard, sat in the thick elephant grass that grew at its edge.

I tried to think of nothing, to become one with the growing plants and the soil. The first light fell between the cashew trees, and in it, all sorts of animals came forth from the forest. First came the striped ground squirrels that sniffed and reached out their paws as they went, as though testing the ground for solidity. Then a troop of red monkeys came through on all fours, the males looking about like soldiers, the group stopping a minute to sit and groom each other like a family on the move. At one point, the monkeys were close enough to speak to, and I wondered if Chauffeur would shoot this easy meat. I looked where I knew he had been sitting, a few arms' lengths from me, and was surprised to find that I could not pick him out at all. Yes, the light was still faint, but I knew he was there and I made myself see him; he could have been stone, he sat so still. As he rested on his haunches, even his eyes no longer seemed to move. Three bush pigs jogged through with their tails erect, and then the animals cleared the field. The light gathered its first hints of yellow. I held my breath. It was then that I heard them. On the dry leaves of the forest floor, their footsteps sounded like those of cautious men. They seemed to be all around us, the world noisy with them. I looked at Chauffeur and saw his eyes turn at mine; a smile when he could not offer one.

There they were: in the open expanse under the trees, the francolins, a dozen of them, already close and closing, stepping and scratching, bobbing their heads as they fed, raising them up to scent the air like deer. They seemed beautiful in their speckled breasts; arrogant and sure; everything a chicken would have been if it could be what it once was. Some were close enough now to kill with a slingshot, and I noticed the dark stripes by their sharp eyes, the brown and white plumage of their dun breasts. For an hour we watched them. I saw how the chicks, almost grown, waited for the hen to gurgle "all clear" before they followed, how the males strutted and kept guard. Sunlight fell all over the orchard, and the francolins filled their crops with the black ants that had converged on the fallen cashew apples.

Just as suddenly as they'd appeared, they hurried to the cover of the forest. I looked at Chauffeur and he set his fingers against his lips. Along the way, on the path, two young boys in shorts came laughing into the field with calabash bowls under their arms. They pried the nuts from the fallen fruit, filled their bowls, and went away again. I understood then that we could have killed them, too.

Still we sat, and when I looked to Chauffeur for guidance, he gave me none. When all had quieted, the francolins came into the field as they had before. Chauffeur passed his gun to me stock first, and when the dominant male of the flock leaped to a termite mound to cry his health and position to the morning, I sighted him in at his bulging breast, exhaled, drew back the trigger, and killed him.

"U-a-o fa," Chauffeur said to me, touched my back as we walked through the orchard to collect the bird's body, 'Francolin hunter.'

Over the next two years, I killed a hundred francolins, discovered my own methods of taking them on the wing. The most important thing I learned was this: If your senses told you they were there, then they were; and if you waited long enough matching your will to theirs, they would flush from even the thickest of rice. I learned many things about the francolins those years. I learned that if you shot an old male and didn't reveal your position, in time his sons would come to mourn his body, and then you could shoot them, too. I learned the call of a lost chick to draw the hen from the forest, and the call she made to attract a mate. Most important, I learned the dominance call of a fully fledged male. When I'd make this from a thicket of grass, soon enough a young male would rush into the clearing, his wings spread and ready to fight with his spurs. Many were the evenings I'd return to the village with three francolins tied to my belt. I shared the meat among my neighbors and wove the francolins' tail feathers into the braiding of my gun's sling. Even in neighboring villages on days when I'd go to their markets for news and shells, young boys would touch my elbow as though trying to absorb something from me and whisper, *"U-a-o fa."* No one but the smallest children ridiculed me anymore.

What I wish to tell here is about my neighbor Chauffeur, who taught me to hunt the francolin, and how once he did, I began to understand who we both were.

My proximity to Chauffeur gave me a new standing in the village, and the young men at the chief's compound who had once been happy to tell me that my nose was my nose and my eyes were my eyes now addressed me as *Va,* 'Father.' Mamadou began to call me *Dosso,* 'Mystical Hunter,' and all about me I felt a certain space that in English we call respect. People stopped asking me for gifts, and sometimes among them, in a line and harvesting the season's rice, I'd forget that I wasn't black.

Until Chauffeur had paid attention to me, I'd worn blinders against the goings-on of his compound. Now, he was all that I noticed. My hunter training didn't end with that first day, but continued in increments. One night, he made me sit in the frightening forest by myself until dawn, and another time he told me to bring him a stone from the top of a granite hill twelve miles to the west before dusk fell. Everything he asked of me, I did. Always, I was eager for more. The bundles of foliage he brought from the forest in the evenings made me wish I'd studied botany. But it's enough to say that under the eaves of his hut dried all manners of leaf and flower and vine, and of mushroom. Why had I thought that the people who came to his hearth each evening were simply villagers paying him his due respect as an accomplished man? Now I saw that they weren't. They were women with their shawls drawn over their heads and obviously sick. Chauffeur would listen to them patiently, talk with them a bit as he smoked, then pass a bundle of herbs to them, which they'd accept with profuse thanks. He knew the plants of the forest and how to heal with them, and his wives didn't quarrel amongst themselves because they understood the importance of what he knew.

Chauffeur was the keeper of magic inherited from the reservoir of his people's culture.

There are two stories I must tell to end this one. This first is about Bébé, and the second is about something else.

The first is this: Bébé was the strongest young man of the village, built like an ox; he could clear a line of thick brush in half the time it took Yacou, the next-strongest man. But for all his bone and muscle, Bébé was also simple, and he fell in love with a clear-faced girl from Sualla, the neighboring village. Khadija was beautiful in every sense of the word; her long arms were like calf's legs, her rump was like a hen's, but there was something wrong with her as well. Some said she loved a Senoufo brush-cutter who worked as a slave in her father's cotton fields. Some said genies counseled her in her dreams. Whatever it was, Bébé wanted her, and brought a red steer to her father's hut. Who could say no to Bébé when he was the best one of a strong village like Tégéso? But even Mamadou would shake his head in the night as we'd eat rice from a bowl with our fingers under the mango tree of his mother's compound, the stars on our shoulders. "If the viper lifted its head at you, Adama," he'd say to me, "would you offer your hand to it?"

Bébé brought his bride to his hut, and three times she ran away. Each time, Bébé's brothers and brothers-in-law brought Khadija back kicking and screaming. But Bébé was strong, and after the final time, he closed the door of his hut with a slam, and in many respects, that was that. This was at the end of my first year there, and it seemed a sort of joke to me. Soon enough, Khadija was seated on the dirt under the mango tree of Bébé's compound, and as the months went by, her pregnancy grew. Bébé was ecstatic, and he labored in the fields even harder than usual. I suppose many assumed that with the birth of the child, Khadija's will against her husband would break.

I was a francolin hunter only a short time when it happened. Khadija was due, and Bébé was talking openly in the fields about the son he knew he would soon have. Then his bride was so pregnant, it seemed she was inflated with water. We came back from the fields one day, and Bébé's mother and sisters rushed to him, touching his arms. Khadija had gone.

Khadija disappeared for three days, and even in her home village, no one knew where she was. On the morning of the fourth day, she came back to Tégéso, haggard and worn, her maternity *pagne* torn to ribbons about her. She wasn't pregnant anymore.

The chief called a council, and all the men went. Khadija sat on a stool with her head in her hands, and Bébé sat beside the chief in his finest blue *boubous.* "Where is the baby?" the chief asked Khadija, and she rolled her head in her hands and moaned out her story again:

"The pains came on me and I fell into a dream. The ancestors called to me and told me to walk to my village. While I was in the forest, white genies came on me. They took the child from me and I could only hold on to a tree as they did."

She led us all to the place in the forest where she said the white genies had taken the child. Bébé's brothers hacked about with their machetes, but there was no blood, no sign of the child.

"Is this the place?" my old chief asked Khadija, condescending to talk directly to a woman because of the importance of the situation.

"Here, Father," she whispered, and gathered her shawl about her. "This is where they took it. Please, Father, believe me. I have told you everything. Let me go home to my mother."

There was nothing to do, and we all went back to the village. For some days, a terrible cloud hung over the village, and Khadija sat under the mango tree looking at nothing. Mamadou wondered at night to me if the chief would release Khadija to return to her people. I didn't speculate at all because I knew now that it wasn't my place.

Soon, one night, Bébé came to Chauffeur's compound; they went together into Chauffeur's hut. For a long time, they sat in the darkness, and all of us, Chauffeur's wives and sons and I, didn't speak to each other, but let the weight of the stars lay on our chests. Then Bébé came forth with a bundle in his hands, and Chauffeur stayed inside. "Medicine," Chauffeur's first wife said under her breath as we watched Bébé go.

For three days, Khadija vomited blood, and then she was dead. Bébé's brothers buried her at the edge of the village, and not even her mother came. The cloud that had hung over everything lifted, and for a few weeks I noticed that the village was calmer than usual; that everyone's wives seemed to get along, that the pubescent girls ready for the dry-season excision weren't moaning about what they were about to undergo.

The last part of the story is this: The more secrets I learned from him, the more Chauffeur took an interest in me. One night when the moon was new, he came to me smoking a cigarette and said, "Could you live among us forever, whiteman?"

"I could, Father."

"Do you respect our ways?"

"I do."

He told me to lift myself up, and I followed him barefoot into the forest. For a long time, we walked in that black ink. He led me far into it, to a place I'd never been. Then he said to me, "Adama, whiteman, tell your people about what you are about to see." I followed him to the edge of a small clearing where a fire was burning. My eyes adjusted to the light, and we did not enter the clearing, but stood at its edge. In it, I saw young men, the quiet and respected young men of the village. All were naked and glistening with sweat, as though oiled. None knew we were there. Half of them, a half dozen, were writhing on the dirt that someone had swept clean, moaning, some screaming, and the other half seemed to be in trances, seated and fanning their writhing brothers with fistfuls of broad leaves. On the post before the fire was a mask. The light of the fire shone through its eyes. The writhing young men seemed to be in the throes of a vicious death, and while I knew that I could never understand the visions they were experiencing, I also knew that it was what I wanted.

"Give me the medicine, too, Father," I said to Chauffeur.

He took my shoulder in his hand and turned me. He said, "I know that you are strong, Adama. But there are things we must keep for ourselves if we are to go on in this world as a people."

I followed him to the village through the forest. All the way back I felt as lost as on the day my father had died. I was the francolin hunter. But what was that? All the things I had been doing suddenly seemed as ridiculous as they really were. The forest, the people, they would never reveal themselves to me.

I lay in my hut a long time that night. I thought about the witch doctor, about Bébé, about the village and what it had done to Khadija. When I finally slept, I dreamed of those writhing men. Who did they invoke to tell them what was right? Where did they go in their dreams, what answers did they bring back with them?

I dreamed of stars, of moving through them like swimming underwater. I saw a field of grass: calm, quiet as the land itself, the first sunlight falling on it, wind rippling through it like fingers, beautiful: the world free of men. Then I was in it: breathing, hidden, my mind clear, as African as I would ever become, not African at all. A francolin stood on a mound to sing, his breast filling with air to rend the quiet morning with his life. I dreamed my gun lifting, the sudden crack of the shot; the tumble of the bird; its death: The proclamation of my life to this world.

DJAMILLA

Shortly after Khadija's death, Mamadou brought me a sack of mandarins from his father's orchard. I wasn't much in a mood to be with the Worodougou after what had happened, and each morning when the families would set out for their fields, a wife or husband would salute me as I sat on my stool. "Not going to the fields with us today, Adama?" they'd ask. I'd wave them off with my hand, hold my side and say, *"Djekwadjo."* 'Malaria.'

I was often down with malaria, everyone in the village was now and again, but this time it was something more serious, a sickness of the heart. In my early months there, I had romanticized the Worodougou, made them out to myself to be better than they were. But I now understood that they were as flawed as anyone.

It was nice to be alone in the village those days, everyone gone to the fields but a few scattered old women tending to their families' hearths. I ate mandarins and watched the clouds scud across the sky.

One morning, the village empty and quiet, a Peul girl came in her fancy wraps and silver anklets, a wide calabash of milk on her head, trading ladles of it for yams from hut to hut. The Peul were nomadic cattle herders from Mali, and a family of them lived on the village's far western edge, near where they corralled their herd at night. Aside from trading milk, they did not bother with the Worodougou, nor the Worodougou with them. The Peul considered themselves a superior race because they did not work the soil, and the Worodougou thought them contemptible for the same reason. Despite this, Peul girls had the reputation of being the most desirable in the region. Perhaps it had to do with their mystical desert roots, the pride of their tall carriage, their shyness, their exotic language and culture. But perhaps, too, it was because of their beauty.

The girl stopped in her tracks, surprised to see me. I had never before been alone in the village in this way: in the daytime, the time when the village belonged to women. She was tall and slender, old colonial coins hammered into a necklace that hung over her collarbone, strings of amber beads hanging from her long earlobes. Her lips were tattooed around with black ink, and her hair was woven into tight plaits, coins arranged in them, too. Of course I knew who she was: Djamilla, the Peul patriarch's unmarried daughter. She would have been beautiful anywhere.

Djamilla looked at me defiantly, set her hands on her hips. Maybe she didn't like being surprised; maybe again it was because she was used to the village men calling lewdly at her for everyone to hear. She was far enough away that if I wanted to say something, I'd have to shout. Instead, as though propelled by a force other than myself, I rolled a mandarin to her. It crawled over the dust as though time itself had slowed, came to rest between her bare feet. Her eyes lined with kohl made her seem dangerous. The heavy calabash on her head made her seem taller than she was. I wondered what she would do, why I had rolled the fruit to her in the first place, why I cared. Then, like a wading bird, she ducked and picked the mandarin up.

"I know your name," I called to her.

"I don't speak Worodougou, whiteman," she said back at me fluently in that language.

"Dja-mil-la," I called, the syllables rolling off my tongue like a song.

"Who are you to say my name, you dirty Worodougou farmer? Aren't your fingernails covered in soil and filth? Don't you know I'm a Peul?"

"I'm not a Worodougou," I told her, and grinned. "And your name is in the village for all to know, as pretty as the moon and stars."

"I'll tell my father!"

"I'll tell him myself."

"Then tell him. See what I care."

"I'll come tonight."

"I'll hide in my hut."

"You'll hear my voice."

"I'll plug my ears with cotton."

"You'll know in your heart that I've come."

"I'll cut my heart out, feed it to the dogs."

"Then I'll pet those dogs because they've eaten your heart."

"Then those dogs will bite you because they have my heart inside of them."

"Djamilla, put down your milk. Come inside my hut. I want to show you pictures from my country. I want to show you a picture of my mother."

"You have pictures to show to me? Show them to my father. You will see what he says. Then you won't roll mandarins at me like a Worodougou monkey."

"And then you won't pick them up."

Djamilla looked at the fruit in her hand as if understanding what it meant. For an instant, I thought she would throw it at me, but instead she folded it into her wrap. She said as she turned and left, "My father likes to eat them, so what?"

The funk I had been feeling dissipated into the air. I stood in my morning wrap as she receded, my chest bare, struck a pose as vivid as I suddenly felt. Then a stooped old woman came by—the witch doctor's mother—chasing a duck away from her compound with a scrap of blue cloth tied to a stick—which is what old women used to chase away ducks—and she saw me, the parting Djamilla, understood something, and straightened. "Adama! Get in your hut," she said, and poked me in the ribs with the stick. "That you are white is bad enough. But you are also hairy! Cover up! If you let Djamilla see how ugly you are, then she may not marry you."

Usually after dinner, I'd sit with Mamadou under his mother's mango tree where we ate, and talk late into the night about life. As a third son, Mamadou didn't have any other options but staying in the village and helping his father work in the fields. But his dreams were vast: He wanted to go to Abidjan to look for work like his older brothers had. He wanted to own an Aiax soccer jersey and leather shoes and a cell phone, and one day, a car. I'd try to extol the pleasures of a traditional and honest life in the village to him, but he wouldn't hear it. The lights of Abidjan called to him, France and America after that.

"I'll work in a cloth factory like my brother, I'll tend a big field for a rich man. I will send some money here to my father, save the rest, and then I will open a kiosk and sell omelets and Nescafé. I'll buy a stereo so my customers can have music. You will visit me, I will visit you in Chicago, America. We'll be big men together. I will drive you in my car, a Citroën—"

There wasn't much else to do at night but talk. People were talking at the hundred hearths of the village. Voices droned on in this way, simple worn laments for rain, for love, for money. I stood, brushed off the seat of my *boubous,* and Mamadou was startled out of his reverie. He said, "Hey? Where are you going so late?"

"For a walk. To salute some people," I said vaguely, and waved at the dark.

"I'll come with you—"

"Stay here. Spend some time with your *go.* Isn't it time you had another child anyway?"

"Adama, where are you going? Where is there to go? Adama, are you feeling unwell?"

"Unwell?"

"You are behaving strangely. When you behave strangely, it means you are getting sick. If you get sick, I will have trouble with the chief. Tell me where you are going so late. If you don't, I will follow you."

"I'm going to salute Bukari."

"Bukari? The Peul?" he said, and shook his head. "The only time we salute the Peul is when there is a business of milk or meat. Do you want to eat meat, Adama? I will tell my father to send some yams to them and we will eat meat tomorrow."

"I want both milk and meat, Mamadou," I said in a low voice.

"We will send for them."

"You can't buy this milk and meat with yams."

"Milk and meat that you can't buy with yams? Adama, why are you talking in riddles? The moon is not full. Why are you behaving mysteriously?"

"Every night I listen to you, little brother. Has it ever occurred to you that I might have a few dreams of my own?"

"Dreams, Adama?"

"Desires. I'm going to see Djamilla."

Mamadou lifted his eyebrows, then grinned and rubbed his knees. "I thought you were sick, whiteman. But you are not sick. You are a goat. Many men turn into goats when they see Djamilla. Go and try your luck. Soon enough, you will be my friend again."

Bukari wasn't in his hammock as I expected an old man such as he was to be, but cross-legged on his mat, sipping mint tea under the stars. He had a long Arabic beard streaked through with gray, and his flowing blue robe made him seem as foreign as he was. The fire burned low in the circle of stones beyond him, and nobody else was around. He had a second glass waiting on the small steel tray as though he'd known I was coming. "Oh, Adama, come and sit," he said in his Fulani lilt, patting the mat beside him. "Too long it has been that you have not saluted me. Let us drink tea. I want to know all about life in America."

I sat with Bukari a long time as the crescent moon carved its way across the sky. I talked about Chicago, about snow; he wanted to know how cattle were raised there. From the dark hut behind us, I heard giggles now and again. Once I heard a slap, and a child's voice cried out in protest. Then it was quiet again.

"What is this 'cowboy'?" Bukari asked me. I explained as best I could. Bukari reclined back on his elbow, said, "But what does one need with a horse? To know cattle, one must walk with them. Your Peul do not seem very strong to me, Adama. We drive our cattle by foot from Bamako to San Pedro. We sleep in the grass, move them slowly so they do not thin. It takes many months, and we are alone in the bush with our herds and Allah. This is how we are Peul."

"I'd like to know cattle as I know planting," I told him. "If you invite me, I'll come and visit your herds."

"Oh, Adama, this is good. But what about your Worodougou people? Will they not be jealous to see their whiteman drinking tea with a Peul?"

"I've had enough of the Worodougou. Too many genies. Too much digging in the soil like moles."

"Ah, Adama, this is good. Tomorrow, come before the sun and we will take the cattle to graze."

Bukari offered me his hand good night, and I shook it and bowed low in their way. I felt distant Mali calling me—the land of cattle and true Islam, of the Sahel and stars as embodied in that calm old man—and for a last thing as I stepped off into the dark, loud peals of girls' laughter emptied from the hut where they'd been gathering all through my visit.

It began first thing in the morning. As I walked across the village through the morning mist that would soon burn off, women set their long pestles on their shoulders, hitched their wraps higher on their hips, and called to me in laughter, *"Anisogoma Fla ché, oh! I be i muso chulla?"* 'Good morning, Mr. Peul! Are you off to salute your wife?'

At Bukari's compound, Djamilla pounded corn for flour while her younger sisters tended the fire. She blushed when she saw me, dropped her pestle to the dirt, hurried into the hut, and shut the door. Her sisters sat on their stools and hid their faces in their hands. Their shoulders trembled as they fought their laughter, they snorted and choked, the coins in their hair rang like chimes. Bukari was on his mat, praying. The Peul were real Muslims, while the Worodougou guessed at it. The language of Bukari's prayer was Arabic.

When he finished, he sat a moment looking at the morning sky as if meditating, then rose, smiled, and took my hands in his. He had a clear and open face beyond his beard, was as tall as I was, though thinner. He said, "Adama, so early you have come. Like a son. This is how sons come to their fathers in Mali."

At the corral, Bukari leaped over the barring pole in his robe, and then I did. The long-horned and humped Brahmins stamped and lowed like prehistoric creatures, larger in the mist than they really were. It was warm among them; there were flies and dung piles everywhere. I waved flies from my face while Bukari separated calves from their dams with his staff. The calves cried and the cows lowed, but none of the beasts made a move at him. He tied the dozen calves to the piled brush that made the fence, and while they strained at the ropes like dogs on leashes, Bukari milked the cows into a great calabash one by one. He nickered at them to calm them in an ancient language of man and kine, and though they could have easily thrown a hoof or horn, he petted their shanks and they didn't. It was a fine art, gentle. Bukari lifted the gourd over the gate pole to the head of one of his young girls who had come, and she bowed beneath its weight, found her legs, straightened, and set off into the mist for the village. Then Bukari raised the pole, and the cattle filed out in a long and dusty train toward the brush, their hips shifting like women's.

We followed the cattle for miles to where the forest opened into thick savanna, sitting and chatting now and again in the grass as the herd grazed, sometimes sleeping, only to awaken with the hundred head lowing calmly in the distance like wild buffalo at ease in the world. Bukari talked to me about Allah, about how every blessing of his life—his cattle, his daughters—came to him from God, and I asked him to tell me Peul words, which I recorded phonetically in Roman letters in the notebook I'd brought. For lunch, I climbed a wild guava and he made a basket with his robe to catch the fruit I tossed down to him, and then Bukari bent water-lily leaves from a pond into wide cups, milked the cows into them, and we drank the hot liquid, thick as cream, like princes. When the cattle crossed a stream, we waded across with them.

When they came to a Worodougou rice field, Bukari ran ahead, warding them away from the golden crop with whistles and clicks. Not once did he hit or curse them in any way. They were his children and he knew each one's name. It was a long and tiring day, pleasant in the walking, and when the sun began to sink, the cattle turned around as though on instinct. By the settling of evening, the forest was a dark wall before us again on the plain, and I was whistling and clicking at them, too, patting their high haunches like old friends. My notebook was full of Peul words: sun and moon and grass and water and stars. The cattle entered the corral, lowing as though glad to be home, and when Bukari untied the calves, they rushed to their mothers, found their teats, and began to suckle vigorously.

"Now we pray to Allah, Adama," Bukari said, and cleared a patch in the corral with his staff as if wiping a trowel across wet cement. He took my hand and led me down to my knees. "Like this, Adama. Follow," he said, and genuflected his face toward the earth, touched his forehead to it. He said the Arabic words, and I knew them, too, from hearing the Worodougou say them every day. But with the Worodougou, the words were rounded, slurred. Bukari knew the words as they were meant to be pronounced.

"Now you, Adama," Bukari said, and he sat on his heels and smiled at me. I lowered my forehead to the dirt, and the coolness, the softness of it calmed me. Arabic was like singing. I felt happy when I rose again.

Bukari held my hand on the way back to his compound, and I felt close to him. The women had dinner waiting—corn *toh* and peanut sauce—and Djamilla sat on a nearby stool and smiled off into the night. Something was happening now. Bukari squeezed my hand and said, "All day together. Like a son."

Mamadou came and found me outside my hut that night. We sat on stools and smoked cigarettes and enjoyed the stars, the last sliver of the moon. He said, "Eh, Adama? How was your day with the Peul?"

"My day was fine."

"Ah, that is good. And did you make progress with Djamilla?"

"Maybe," I said, and shrugged.

He was quiet awhile, considering. It was a cool evening, and at the witch doctor's hearth, his sons huddled over the fire against the chill, the fire standing up between their shapes. Then, as if giving up, Mamadou said, "So you are a *Fla ché* now. That is as it will be. It is as the ancestors say, 'When food is plentiful, the dog will wander. When he feels the pinch of hunger, he will crawl to the fire with his tail low.'"

"You're jealous of the Peul."

"Jealous? No, Adama. It is only a proverb. It is good to tell proverbs. It is good to talk and make our hearts known. Adama, what has been troubling you these past days?"

I wanted to say nothing, to go on as we had all been, as though nothing had happened. But something had, and I was tired of carrying it around. "I don't like what happened to Bébé's wife."

"No one liked that here."

"Why couldn't the village just let her go home to her mother?"

Mamadou looked at his hands. He said, "Khadija killed her child. What precious thing do we have if not children? Her life ended when the baby disappeared. Even her own mother would have poisoned her. Adama, can I tell a story? Two stories."

Mamadou had told me a hundred stories over the past year, proverbs by the dozen.

"One dry season when my father's father was a young man, three boys went into the forest and found a beehive in a stump. For a moment, they thought to come back to the village and tell the honey collector, but instead they decided to poke sticks down into the hive. The first two boys ran forward, put their sticks into the stump, then dashed back onto the path. Then it was the third boy's turn. The sound of the bees caused him to lose his courage, but the other two teased him. So he ran forth with his stick, put it into the hive, and the bees rose out in a black and angry swarm.

"They ran through the forest. If they'd been wearing sandals, they lost them. They ran so fast that perhaps even their clothes fell off. Behind them came the bees, the sound of them angry. When they reached the clearing before the village, the boys began to shout, 'Bees are coming! Angry bees are coming behind us!'

"Everything ran for shelter; the goats and ducks for the tall grass, the old women for their huts. The boys dashed into their mothers' huts, shut the doors. All through the village, the angry bees circled like smoke. At one hearth, a mother had stayed home from field work to rest, her small children with her. Back and forth she ran, picking up her children, taking as many as she could inside the hut. Then the bees arrived.

There was nothing she could do but shut the door. She watched through a crack as the bees descended and stung her infant daughter to death. Do you see, Adama?"

Then Mamadou told me this story: His uncle, Mustafa, had a bitch dog that was a good tracker. She was such a fine dog that Mamadou's uncle fed her meat from time to time. The dog loved the uncle, and if anyone would approach the old man, the dog would lift up off her haunches and growl.

"'Why don't you kill that mean bitch before she bites someone?' the people would come to his hut and argue.

"But the old man would say, 'She is a fine hunter. The best in the village. I'll tend to her odd ways.'

"The old man fell sick and was bedridden. His dog began to wander in his absence, became pregnant. All around, people watched the old man's hut for signs of recovery. He had been a hard worker in his life; with his cotton profits he had managed to purchase things people desired: a portable radio, a Dutch wax *boubous,* a number of well-formed calabashes that could be used for many purposes. When he died, the dog guarded the door to his hut with such a fury that no one could get past her to claim his possessions in the night. Then his son came from a neighboring village, Somina, gathered up what was his, and buried his father.

"The hut was empty and no one bothered to feed the dog. If anyone dared approach the hut, she would rise up and growl. A wave of rage swept through the village dogs, and she caught it, too. When the witch doctor went through the village killing the dogs with his machete, he found that the old man's bitch had given birth to a litter of six. Somehow, she had managed to wean them. Many people of the village, out of curiosity, followed the witch doctor about as he chopped the sick dogs to pieces. They followed him to the old man's hut, and the bitch dog came out from her place in the bushes, growling, foaming at the mouth. With a quick blow to her neck, the witch doctor killed her. The puppies hid themselves in the bushes and he went home.

"After a few days, the puppies came out again. They growled and barked like grown dogs, their fur bristling. They also had the rage. The witch doctor went to kill them, but all the people said, 'No. What can they do? They are small.'

"For a week, people would go to the old man's hut and the rabid puppies would come out of the bushes on their short legs, growling and foaming at the mouth like angry, full-grown dogs. Imagine, such small creatures acting as though they were greater than they were? No one had seen such small angry dogs. Everyone laughed about it. Then the puppies thinned and died on their own.

"Do you see, Adama?" Mamadou asked me as he finished his story. He stood and brushed off his *boubous* as though the storytelling had taken something out of him. "I am not jealous of the Peul. I know that your life here is difficult. But know that ours is difficult as well. Wander now. But do not circle about like bees if you don't intend to sting. Do not foam at the mouth if you don't have the teeth to bite. Good night, Adama. Sleep and dream of Djamilla. Make progress. I will be pleased when you come back."

The Worodougou did not make it easy on me. Everywhere I went over the coming days, it was, "Good morning, Mr. Peul," and, "How is your lovely Peul wife?" I went to Bukari's and we grazed the cattle. Djamilla seemed to inch her stool closer to us every night.

I can't say that Djamilla entered my dreams the way true love should, but she was beautiful and I enjoyed the tension. I also enjoyed being with the Peul. The food they ate, the soft lilt of their language, even praying to Allah with Bukari in the corral was like escaping the Worodougou world I lived in.

Every night as she sat closer to us, Djamilla seemed more at ease. Would I really marry her, stay in Africa with her as my wife? Would I take her home to America, return to the village in a long car with her and our children, bearing gifts for everyone? Wrestling the calves and following the herd was hard work, as demanding as any. I begged off one morning, told Bukari that I needed a rest loudly enough for Djamilla to hear where she stood pounding corn. I hoped that she hadn't closed her ears to me as she had once promised she would.

I sat on my stool outside my hut in the empty village, waiting for Djamilla. Soon, she came. If I had thought she would rush into my arms behind her father's back, I was wrong. She stood across the courtyard the way she had before, the wide calabash on her head, her hands on her hips. I rolled a mandarin to her and she picked it up. She peeled it, ate it, spit out the seeds. Then she said, "Why are you always at my hut, whiteman?"

"The moon and stars," I said in Peul. She blushed despite herself. For an instant, her kohl-lined eyes looked less like a raptor's than a doe's.

"My mother lives in Mankono, you know. We are only here while there is grass for the cattle."

"Are there moon and stars where your mother lives?"

"Adama, enough. Don't you understand? With us, it is the mother one must speak to after one has spoken to the father."

"Mankono is far. I don't even know where Mankono is."

"Eh? Then why have you done all of this? Forget it, white-man. I must sell my milk."

I let her start to walk away, and then I called after her, "Moon and stars, I will even go to Bamako, if that is where your mother lives." I rolled another mandarin to her feet. She looked at it, at me, narrowed her eyes.

"Why do you tease me?"

"Dja-mil-la," I said.

"Why do you say my name like that?"

"Dja-mil-la."

"Stop! It makes my ears itch."

"Djamilla, come here. I want to show you something. A picture of my mother. If I must go to see yours, then you must come and look at mine." I went into the dark of my hut, waited, and my heart began to pound. Soon again, she came, the mandarin in her hand. She lowered the calabash from her head to the ground, and I could see flies sucking moisture from the cheesecloth covering the milk like black jewels. She peered under the thatch of my doorway, said, "Show me here."

"Not there," I said from the shadows of my hut, "here. These are only for you to see. I want to show you here."

She glanced about the deserted courtyard, bit her lip, ducked her head under the thatch, came in. I offered her a stool, and she sat on it. Her feet were powdered with dust, and she seemed smaller somehow now close to me. She glanced all about without turning her face, and I saw my hut through her eyes: a worn raffia mat, a mosquito net hanging over it from the thatching, my trunk where I kept my few Western things: T-shirts and jeans, vials of malaria pills, notebooks; then my machete and short-handled hoe, my field clothes, my ceramic cistern of water, my shotgun and shells, my bathing bucket. If she had hoped to see something in there to reveal my soul to her, she was disappointed. I had less than most of the Worodougou did. I rummaged through the metal trunk, came to her with a short stack of photos. She looked at me warily, and I kneeled and offered her the photos.

She took the first one up carefully, as though she was afraid of damaging it. It was my mother and sister in Hawaii, where they'd gone together after my father had died. They were trying to smile, though the sun was in their eyes. They were on a deck somewhere, piña coladas in their hands, pink cocktail umbrellas in the drinks. My mother had a yellow flower behind her ear. My sister looked pale and tired.

"Your mother is fat!"

"Not that fat."

"Is this your wife, Adama?"

"My sister."

"Is this your village?"

"More or less."

"What is all this water?"

"That's the ocean."

"Your mother's hair is the color of ripe rice."

"She put the color in it."

"But henna makes things dark, Adama."

"It's another kind of henna."

Djamilla accepted the pictures one by one, studied them closely as though trying to enter America through them: the house I grew up in covered with snow, my sister beside some boyfriend or other in his new Camaro, my mother at her retirement party, me in my black coat on Michigan Avenue, snowflakes on my shoulders.

"What does snow feel like?"

"Cold like the moon."

"Where is the grass?"

"Far from where we live."

"Who do these pigeons belong to?"

"To no one. They live like that. Nobody eats them. Old women whose children have left like to feed them peanuts and talk to them."

"Is it a good place to live?"

"Sometimes."

"You must be very rich, to have pigeons you do not eat, to let old women throw away the harvest to them."

Without realizing it, we were sitting close together on the floor. Our fingers touched again and again as I passed pictures to her, as she pointed things in them out to me: a girl in a background's red boots, a woman wearing green mittens. Djamilla smelled faintly of cream and butter, the amber beads of her earrings familiar to me now, the tattoos around her lips as though all women had them.

"What is this? A dog in a bed? Is America so rich that even the dogs sleep in beds?"

It was my sister's rottweiler, Daisy, up on her bed when she'd been a puppy. I held the picture and smiled. "Sometimes they do," I said.

"How could I live in such a filthy country? Where dogs sleep in beds?" Djamilla said, leaned against me as she laughed. Her body was warm, almost heavy. All around us on the floor now were pictures of a faraway place, the people in them looking back up at us from gray landscapes of concrete and snow. Djamilla touched a picture of my mother with the back of her hand, like trying to feel the curve of my mother's cheek. I held Djamilla close to me as she did.

"Your mother won't accept me because I am black."

"My mother will accept anyone I choose."

"I will pound corn *toh* and peanut sauce for her."

"She might like that."

"I will make it so your mother will never touch a pot the rest of her life."

"I don't think my mother has done that for a long time."

"And how can I honor your sister?"

"You can plait her hair."

A shadow darkened the doorway. It was the old woman, her stick in her hand for chasing away ducks. She peered in, let her eyes adjust. "*Fla muso,* come out of Adama's hut. Take up your milk before it curdles. Go to your father's house," she said in a low voice, stern but not angry. Djamilla went out, and the old woman helped her lift the calabash to her head. Then I went out, too, to watch Djamilla walk away.

"Adama," the old woman said to me, "don't you have women where you come from?"

"We do, Mother."

"Then why do you trouble this girl?"

"I'm not troubling her, Mother."

"Adama," she said, and poked me with her stick, "is this all that you are? A man? Another man to trouble a girl? Go to the fields and work, you lazy goat. 'The whiteman this, the whiteman that.' Since I was small, people have said it. Ah, Adama, if your mother was here, she would scold you. Go to the fields now before I beat you with this stick. *Toog gbenna aug gbenna, konani fo la whella.*" 'In the forest or fields, the duiker is the duiker.' "What a disappointment!"

Did I love Djamilla? I loved Africa, loved being in the fields with Bukari and his cattle, the tender hands he laid on their haunches. I loved the sound of the children singing at night, the long drape of the stars. I loved the forest and being in it. I loved it when it rained and the air was so clean it wasn't like there was any air at all.

After a long day with Bukari, the herd corralled and lowing, I'd say good night to him, salute a few hearths here and there, and then Djamilla would find me in the dark. We'd walk the paths in the tall grass along the edge of the village like lovers from an older time, the moon waxing above us. She'd worry that she'd be cold in America, and I promised her that I'd buy her a coat to keep her warm. I'd tease her that she could sell milk in those steel labyrinths she'd seen in the pictures, that she could trap those pigeons that belonged to nobody and sell them, too. She'd laugh and slap my hands, this tattooed girl from Mali.

As we reclined and sipped tea one night, the moon finally full, Bukari said to me, "You are truly like my son, Adama. Anything you desire, ask and it shall be yours."

I went to Mamadou's. I'd neglected him a long time, but

he still brushed off a stool for me. He smiled and said, "Ah, Mr. *Fla ché*! Long time. Are the cattle well?"

"I think I want to marry Djamilla."

Mamadou's smile faded. He looked at me in earnest. The night was dark, the hearth fires glowing in it. He said, "Djamilla is very beautiful. She is calm and works hard. Any man would desire her for a wife."

"I need you to talk to Bukari for me."

"Does it mean that you would always be near me?"

"Perhaps."

"And are you certain that this would make you happy?"

I nodded.

After a day alone hunting francolin in the forest, I felt sure of my love for Djamilla, and I came home to the village and told Mamadou to visit the old man. I looked at the stars from under his mother's mango tree and smoked cigarettes as I waited. Here it was, my life. When Mamadou came back, he sat down beside me and sighed as though spent. He said, "Adama, Bukari accepted almost as soon as I stepped into his courtyard."

"What happens now?"

"We wait. He will send word to Mankono, and the mother will decide. That is their way."

The days became long. I avoided Djamilla's compound as was the custom, and she avoided me. A hush ran through the village. I could tell from the long looks people cast at me that they knew. What they thought of it, I couldn't tell. But they didn't call me Mr. Peul any longer, as it wasn't any longer a joke. Many nights and lying awake in the dark of my hut, I felt that I'd made a terrible mistake that I couldn't now undo. Then I'd see Djamilla in her beads and wraps and coins across the village, bent at the waist and drawing water from a well, and I'd think to myself, 'That is my woman.'

I went to work in the fields with my neighbors to pass the time. For some reason, I was glad now to be with the Worodougou again, singing the hoeing songs and back in that familiar rhythm. I looked at pictures of my mother and sister now and again in my hut. They felt like people I had never known. A young and somber Peul came from Mankono on foot. Word had finally arrived. A buzz ran through the village. I waited under the stars with Mamadou for the messenger to present himself at my hut, to tell me which way my life would turn.

He was tall and lean. His *boubous* was green satin with gold filigree embroidered about the neck. He stood before us like a desert prince. Mamadou offered him a stool, but he refused. He said, "If the whiteman wants Bukari's daughter, then Bukari's daughter is his. That is the word of her mother. It is finished."

The young man asked leave, and I heard Mamadou give it to him. Then Mamadou shook my shoulder. He said, "Rejoice, Adama! What you have desired is delivered. *Allahu akbar!* You are to be married!"

I wasn't married to Djamilla that time, or any other. In the morning, I jumped on a logging truck to Séguéla, stayed in the city a week, two. When I went back to the village, Djamilla had gone. I didn't explain myself to Bukari; I was too embarrassed. Also, he was a Peul, and I didn't have to.

For weeks, no one said anything to me about it. Then one night as we lit cigarettes and leaned back against the mango tree after dinner, Mamadou said to me, "Milk or meat, Adama. Those are the only times we deal with the Peul."

I nodded, smoked my cigarette, considered the stars.

A wandering bead trader came through some days later with a story. I was in the fields and didn't see him. A beautiful Peul girl in Mankono had fallen in love with a whiteman, and had been scorned. For some days, she had been very ill, and then she was well again. Now she was becoming famous for giving alms of milk to the albino beggars in the Mankono market. When people asked her why she did, she told them it was because the albinos reminded her of the man she loved. The villagers found the story hilarious. They would stop me now and again over the coming years to recount it, laughing hard to remind me that it wasn't a funny story at all.

SABINA

The job allowed me to travel down to Abidjan every few months, and as a respite from the rigors of the Iron Age, I began to. I dated an Abidjan hooker during my second year: Sabina. Even then, I knew those girls standing on the Rue des Jardins corners were brave: Linda, Sandra, Jan, Fatou, Celeste, Bintou, Margarite, Awa, Judith, Luce; tall in their lithe bones, long in their fleshed limbs. Their braids, synthetic fibers grafted onto their slender heads, reached down to their waists like the manes of ponies. They were riddled with AIDS, though they didn't know it yet. They were Liberians and Nigerians and poor Dioula girls from Kankan and Odienné. They'd all been raped a dozen times. They were what was left in a place where all that was left were whores. It cost $2 for an hour, $5 for the whole night. And if you paid them for it, they would tell you any lie you needed to hear:

"Your penis is so huge."

"You are a magnificent lover."

"You are handsome, baby, so good-looking."

"I love you, man."

Sometimes soldiers would round them up for kicks, fuck

them, beat them, drop them off in some faraway quarter. They were always back the next evening.

Sabina wasn't the prettiest on the street, but she didn't gather her things together and leave as soon as the transaction was over. Maybe she had nothing better to do in the early mornings. Maybe that dull hotel room I took her to was better than where she actually lived: the grim Abobo quarter, perhaps? In a plywood shack with six other girls, sickness all around, open sewers, a brutal pimp, rats? The hotel was nasty, all I could afford on my relief-worker's salary: hot cinder-block rooms with no fans, televisions in wire cages playing loops of white porno that the owner must have thought the whiteman liked. Now and again it was a white woman getting fucked by a dog; other times it was a white woman getting fucked in both holes by two men at once. The bed was a foam mattress on a plank frame. The night attendant, a sleepy old man who seemed to keep his eyes shut through everything, tossed sheets as thin as tissue over the lovemaking platform. No matter how much I tipped him in advance, there were always dark stains on those sheets. There were roaches stilled on the walls, gathered together in shiny armies up by the crease of the ceiling. And bolted on the wall, a long and filmy mirror let me watch my white body humping hers if I'd chance to glance over. That scene always startled me. Even when I wasn't drunk, I couldn't imagine that those people were also us. The toilet was a hole in the floor in the only other room, logs of shit floating in it, the flies, torpid with the cool night, clinging to the shit like black men on lifeboats.

In the silver glimmer of the television after sex, I'd become human again. We'd sit up and smoke cigarettes together in bed, drink the remainder of the beer I'd brought with us. As we sat there one of the first times I was with her, I asked Sabina, "Why are your breasts flat like that?"

"Why the fuck not, man?" she said, the sweat drying on her upper lip in the hot night.

"You have children, don't you?"

"Two. So what? The girl is dead. The boy lives with his father in Monrovia."

I said, "Why do you do this, Sabina?"

Sabina said, "Don't you know that it's for money?"

I said, "Are you free tomorrow? I'd like to buy you lunch somewhere. I'd like to take you shopping for a nice dress."

She said, "Where will you take me? To Sococé? To some rich man's place like that? There will be people there who will look at me. I don't want them to look at me the way they will if I am with you."

I held Sabina to me, stroked her hair, and after time, she slept. Every few months after that when I'd come down, I'd cruise Rue des Jardins, ask around for her until she appeared. "It's my boyfriend," she began to say, snapping gum as she materialized from the shadows. I gave her too much money every time, imagined strolling down Michigan Avenue back home in Chicago with her on my arm. Why not? We'd look at the Christmas displays together in the windows of Macy's; I'd dress Sabina in long furs so she would never be troubled by the cold. We'd have hot chocolates in some warm bar in Lincoln Park, and my mother and friends would drop in to greet her and say hello. In Western clothes, she'd fit right in. Who knows where the money would come from?

One night, I trolled for her, couldn't find her. There were a dozen to take her place. "Where is Sabina?" I said to a slender Sierra Leonean in an electric blue vinyl miniskirt.

"Sabina? Who's that?"

"Sabina. Liberian. Little nose. Long legs. She talks about me. She's tall."

"You go with me if I tell you where she at?" the girl said, cocking her head, snapping gum.

"You won't tell me otherwise?"

"Man, this is business. Out here is business only."

"Then yeah. Just tell me where she is."

"Sabina, she go there. Other side. Her daughter, you know. She got to do something about that daughter."

The first time I knew it was possible, that sleeping with those girls standing on the corners was a thing that men really did, was after the second serious outbreak of violence.

Fighting between tribes had flared up again all over Ivory Coast at the beginning of my second year, and the organization had pulled everyone down from the villages to Abidjan for safety. Though there were still a hundred of us in-country at that time, half would soon be going home, and the organization put us up, four to a room, in the small luxury hotels scattered all over the Rue des Jardins foreign quarter in Deux Plateaux.

All day during the consolidation, there were meetings at the U.S. embassy where the clean-cut CIA men asked us for information about what was going on up-country. Though they were responsible for our security, they couldn't even pronounce the names of the most important tribal leaders correctly. The

CIA men's shaking us down for information irritated me; the man from Washington charged with running the consolidation in his three-piece suit did, too. Even in the air conditioning, his face was red, and the time gunshots rang loudly outside the embassy, he ducked the way I had when I'd been new.

It was good, at least, to see the others: those hopeful friends who'd suffered through training with me, three months in a comfortable southern cocoa village, Africa all around, and still, in the draconian regulations of training, at arm's length. Everyone now had their tribe, their African name, their hut. They had changed physically. Gone were the closely shorn haircuts, the makeup and Western clothes, the softness. Now the men were lean, the women in African wraps. People seemed older, darker. We told stories fueled by alcohol on those hotels' pool decks: a cobra killed on a doorstep, the first dance of the village masks, the dark trails through the jungle, the pubescent girls marching out in a line with the old women for their excision rites. We talked about births we'd witnessed, deaths. "Do you still believe in AIDS?" we asked one another. Some said, "Oh, hell, yes." Others shrugged and said, "People die of everything here."

And there was violence to talk about. The young men of one girl's village sharpened their machetes, smoked ganja, wove crowns of mango leaves around their scalps: the war dress. Another girl had hidden behind the counter of the Elf gas station in Korhogo while mobs burned the city, lit piles of tires on fire on the street corners as though claiming territory.

Everyone dealt with what was happening in their own ways. Yes, many did decide to go home, and a bus was charted to take them to the airport in an exodus. "Good-bye," we said to them on the steps of the embassy—no real good in it—their Embassy Marine escorts stone-faced in the flanking jeeps. Of those who stayed, some ate too much pizza from the Lebanese shops, some danced all night in the clubs, some went shopping in Cocodi for sandals and trinkets, some smoked Grand Bassam beach pot, many, many got drunk, and a few took Valium and went to bed.

Ryan and I went out into the Abidjan night to drink tall and sweating bottles of 66 among the Africans in the open-air bars, where the Cameroonian music, *makassi,* Sam Fan Thomas, blasted from the tape decks so loudly, we couldn't even say who it was we were any longer. What was the plan those few hours before the shoot-to-kill curfew fell over the city like a drape? To talk about our lives in our villages, to be friends in this shared experience, to be drunk, in an easier, jocund place.

On the dimmest corner of that street, the most bustling, too, for all its lack of light, was the Hacienda. Maybe the owner had dreams of traveling to Spain, maybe he'd actually made it there. Who knows why it had that name? It was another open-air place with a woman frying fish on the smoking grill in the corner, a sleepy boy on a stool peddling loose cigarettes from a cup. The beer was cheap, tall and sweating bottles of Bock Solibra, and at a table in the corner behind a potted palm sat a veteran volunteer named Charles. He was with a girl, an African. Ryan and I approached him. I said, "Can we join you? Say the word if not. We're cool. We don't want to bother you." I'd already learned that the one thing that could really bother a whiteman in Africa was another whiteman who still thought that everyone white in Africa shared something in common.

The stars were wide in the sky about the bustling street, and Charles lifted his sweating beer bottle, shrugged as though he didn't care. "You want to sit down with me? Really? Be my guests. It's still a free country after all, isn't it?"

This was Chuck: Two years in, he'd made it out from his village, Berebi, on the coast, where the worst massacres of this killing season had happened. He'd been there for it; he'd seen the bodies, had known some of them. And even before that, we'd heard of him: His best friend, another PWI worker, had died the year before in a motorcycle accident outside Odienné. Still, he stayed. Maybe he stayed to see his service through for them both. He spoke his dialect with a liquid fluency; he seemed aloof. Whenever the Americans in-country gathered for a holiday—Thanksgiving, the Fourth of July—as with Ryan and me, he didn't go. He was tall and lanky, good-looking in a tired way; I understood that behind his glasses, he knew more about life than I did. Beside him as we sat down, the girl, black and thin, looked away.

"Surprised to see you out," Chuck said after a minute, and put on an uncomfortable smile. "Africa suiting you well?"

The girl didn't understand English. She glanced at him, at what he was saying, like looking at strange and dangerous wasps: the English words.

We drank, didn't talk much. What was there to say really? I began to look at the girl, to inspect her, to take in her presence and attempt to decipher it. Chuck said something to her softly in her language, which he knew, and she blushed deeply, hugged her beer bottle close to her heart. In her eyeteeth were fillets of gold. She was dramatically beautiful, her hair close cropped, her long limbs perfect, her tribal scars feathered around her eyes making her seem even more beautiful than she was. I said to him, "How long have you known her?"

"Twenty minutes," he said, and shrugged.

Far below the music, Chuck whispered more things in the girl's ear that made her draw her knees up so she set her sandals on the table. What was he saying to her, I wanted to know. She sipped her beer awkwardly, as though the bottle was too big for her, as though it wasn't a thing she did. The alcohol animated Ryan, and Chuck answered his questions about where he thought the violence was going, about the bleak future of Ivory Coast. But really, it was as though we were at two tables now: one where three young American men discussed Ivorian politics, and another where a man and a woman were finding intimacy. Chuck rested his hand on the girl's thigh as though she belonged to him, and the girl smiled. If she was lying about that smile, I could not tell. He rose, tossed bills onto the table, took the girl about her waist. "Well," he said, "welcome to Africa. I've got no advice for you. It's not a place for everybody."

The barmaid brought more beers. I said to Ryan, "I could do it."

Ryan looked away at the night, exhaled a plume of cigarette smoke, said as though to himself, "Not me."

Then they were there, born from the black night itself, two tall girls in tight pants, glass bangles rattling, perfume as thick as flowers, sitting down across from us as though they'd been invited. Had they? The near one leaned across the table, her face a delicate palette, said, "You Frenchmen? Soldiers?"

"Americans," I told her, "relief workers."

"Oh, so you're poor, don't got any money," she said, moved to get up.

I reached across the table and grasped her wrist. I said simply, "We're not that poor."

"I'm not going to do it," Ryan said in English.

"We'll just talk to them."

"Talk to them about what?"

"I don't care what. Keep me company."

The girl was black as oil. Her nose was a petite thing on her face, neat and pretty. Her braids hung over her shoulders like cords. Her tight white outfit made her look as if she was about to participate in some sort of sport. She said, "English? That what you speaking? You Englishmen?"

"Americans, I said."

"Not the same thing?"

"No."

"Do Americans like to fuck?"

"Sometimes they do." I nodded.

She snapped gum. I couldn't tell if she was bored. She whispered to her friend in a language I'd never heard. The friend nodded, snapped gum, and looked bored, too.

I bought them drinks, tried to make conversation about the war. They wouldn't. "What's your name?" I said to the girl across from me.

"Sabina."

"You're beautiful."

"I thank you, man."

She looked at me like she was trying to decide if mine

was a face she could manage. Something electric ran all through my body. I said to Ryan, "I'm bringing her back to the room."

"She's got AIDS, Jack."

"I know that."

"Wear two condoms—"

"I only want to hold her."

Sabina shifted her chair beside mine. She set her hand on my knee in the casual way an old girlfriend would. I looked at her hand, noticed the fingernails bitten down to the quick. Instantly, she tucked her fingers down under her palm. The African functionaries drinking at the other tables in their fine *pagne* shirts glanced at us, looked away as though they'd seen nothing. I said to Sabina, "Do you do this much?"

"Do what much?"

"This."

"This? What is this? No, man, I don't ever do this. Never. Only you. I see you, you are handsome to me, I come and I sit. Okay?"

"Okay."

The barmaid came and warned about the curfew, and we took a taxi back to the hotel. Ryan sat in front beside the driver, and I sat in back between the girls. The other girl set her hand on my knee, and Sabina barked something sharply at her in their language. The other girl took back her hand and looked out the window.

"Your brother don't like my sister? She not beautiful for him?"

"She's beautiful."

"My sister, she come with me even if she not beautiful for your brother. I watch for her."

"She can come. She's already here."

"Your brother don't love?"

"No, not tonight."

Sabina rested her head on my shoulder, snapped gum slowly as if she'd fallen into a dream. The streetlights played over us in the dark as the cab carried us through the silent quarter.

At the hotel, the uniformed guard let us in as though nothing was out of the ordinary. I understood then that nothing was. In the hallway, I heard a party raging in another room; the others achieving their release. Our own room was empty. I put on MTV, cracked beers for everyone from the fridge. Sabina came from her armchair to sit beside me on the couch, glanced at MTV an instant as if absorbing the images of the black women dancing there, turned to me, kissed me. Ryan and the other girl sat in armchairs across the coffee table from each other, their legs crossed, uncomfortable, as though at a formal function.

Sabina smelled like soap, like sweat, tasted like the sugar of her gum. Her lips were soft. Her tongue roamed in my mouth. Somewhere far away, Ryan was talking awkwardly to the other girl about the chicken farm cooperative he'd started in his village while waiting for funding to build a deep-bore pump. I heard the other girl say, "You really living in a village, man? In a dirty backward village where they living like worse than animals?"

"Yeah," I heard him say.

"In a house?"

"A hut."

"Got to be so difficult, man!"

"It is."

I was touching Sabina's breasts now; she was moaning in my ear. I lifted my body over her, felt her body softening beneath me under her clothes. Behind me, I heard Ryan say to the other girl, "Well, shit. What are you doing sitting over there?"

In a minute, Sabina touched the side of my face, whispered in my ear, "Look, man. Look at your no-love brother." I looked, and Ryan had the other girl on his lap, was kissing her with his eyes closed. Sabina and I laughed together. I carried her into the bedroom, turned out the light. "How much you give me, baby?"

"How much you want?"

"Ten thousand."

"Five."

"Give it now."

"Use condom, man," she whispered in my ear. Though AIDS was everywhere, inside Sabina it didn't seem such a frightening thing; I ignored it, found it worth the risk. Life was about living, about doing this. I thought about taking the condom off. She let me hold her body tight to mine all through the night. Then I slept soundly, and in the morning, she was gone.

We had a picture taken together once, a Polaroid at the amusement park in Zone 4.

Sabina had been in a mood. She hadn't liked going out in public with me, but I had this desire to do other things with her besides fucking. The amusement park was a rusted Ferris wheel on a desperate asphalt slab, and a few frayed bumper cars that boys pushed in their bare feet for coins when the power was cut, as it regularly was. The Ferris wheel had frightened Sabina, the long looks the Lebanese families threw our way in the night hurt her pride. She wouldn't hold my hand no matter how many times I tried, wouldn't attempt to have fun of any sort at all. After an hour of it building in me, I grabbed her arm and said in a low voice, "What am I paying you for, Sabina? To act like a bitch?"

I tossed rings over bottles again and again, wasting money, until I got it right and won her a yellow teddy bear whose foot was already leaking stuffing. I'd regretted what I'd said instantly, needed this interlude to let it go. As I gave her the bear, I caught her hand, made her look me in the eyes, said, "Sabina. Hey, Sabina? Look at me. I'm sorry. I won't disrespect you again."

"I don't need your fucking money, whiteman."

"I know that."

"Don't bring me to these fucking places."

"I won't again."

A black photographer came, said, "Photo for the handsome man and his wife?"

I pulled Sabina to me, and the camera flashed. I looked at the Polaroid in the cab on the way to the cheap hotel. She hadn't been smiling, and I was surprised to see just how black, how small against me she really looked. Why had she felt so much taller beside me than she was? She was a small African woman in the most obscene of Western dress. I brought the picture to my village with the intention of showing off my city girl to my friends there, but didn't. From time to time over the coming years, I'd pull it out of my papers on a strange urge, consider it in my hut in the night by my hurricane lamp's dim glow. It seemed to record an ancient time, people we had never been. How small Sabina looked, defiant and unhappy. Why had I made her do those things? Why had I believed that what I was doing was all right? The picture was lost with everything else when I fled the village at the outbreak of the real war. I wonder what they made of it, those people I knew who parceled out my things among themselves and found it.

That time during the security hold in Abidjan, word spread quickly, of course. Alan and Fred came back to the room in the night, turned on the lights, saw what was going on, and went out again. In the morning, they told everybody.

At that day's briefing at the embassy, the men acted as if they didn't know, couldn't care if they did, and the women wouldn't look at me. The stigma of what I'd done spread all over my shoulders as I held the Xeroxed security update in my hands. What was there to do but crawl into my heart and not care? Did these other people not need it? Were they not human the way I was? My only worry was that Ryan was embarrassed like this, too. I'd pressured him to do it in the end, hadn't I?

At the buffet lunch, a male voice said at my neck, "Gone completely native now, have you, Jack?" and later, as I ate a burger and chips in my folding chair with my plate on my knees, a girl I barely knew glided past and said, "Are they better than we are?"

I saw Ryan, drew him aside. I said, "I'm sorry I made you do that."

He shook off my arm and said, "You didn't make me do anything."

Chuck sat in the corner by himself. For the first time, I noticed how isolated he was.

The gray-haired CIA man took the podium in his polo shirt. He looked through his notes as if preparing for a lecture. "A-liss-san-ney Wat-tar-aye," he said, mangling the name nearly beyond recognition. "Anybody got the scoop on this individual?"

Alassane Ouattara and the RDR would rule the country when the war was over, I knew. In the afternoon, they released us back to our villages.

Every time I'd come to Abidjan, I'd find Sabina. I began to make excuses to come down: to research pump prices, to attend cholera information meetings. Always, there were weeks and months in the grueling Iron Age with nothing but the stars at night and the village's suffocating customs for company. Always at the end of them was a girl with long limbs who smelled like soap and sweat. My dreams away from her were haunted by her shape. She'd taken her place in the pantheon of women who were important to me. When I'd find her, we'd ride in a cab to Blockhaus, to the Ebrie Lagoon, watch the fruit bats cross its dark waters on their way to feed in the fields of the commercial plantations in their great evening migration, dance then to *makassi* music in the rough waterfront bars. The dirty hotel with the television in the cage was our rendezvous the first few times. Then, like any white-man in Africa, I made friends with another of my kind.

Martin was Belgian, handsome, alive, electrically intelligent. He wanted to know Africa the way I did, asked pointed questions about life in the village at the expat California Bar-B-Que bar while the CIA men sat in their shirts under the fan and glowered. He said, "You really live with them? As simply as they do?"

"I try to," I told him.

"And you genuinely like the Africans?"

"I do."

"Are you making a difference?"

"No."

"And still you believe in what you're doing?"

"Yes."

Martin paid the tab. I protested, but he patted my hand in the European way, said, "Let's not pretend." He worked for the World Bank, signed off on loans worth more money than either of us would ever know, got paid well to do it. His Mercedes was long and black, the interior upholstered with cream-colored leather that still smelled of the factory. He slid Ishmael Isaac into the CD player, and as the streetlights splashed down over the dashboard, I wondered if he was gay. But, too, I understood that we were in Africa, that he was lonely for a friend. The streetlights winked down on his hands in the night as we cruised Rue des Jardins. The girls stepped up to the curb, offered their rumps, their long legs, to the car's tinted windows for appraisal. Martin's hair was curly, neatly cut. His body seemed healthier than mine, though it may simply have been that he was able to stay cleaner, that his clothing was crisp and new. He said, "What do you think of these girls? It's sad, isn't it? War in Liberia, war in Sierra Leone. Poverty everywhere else. And now all these images from the West, all these products to desire."

I said, "It's very sad."

"Imagine? They offer their bodies to strangers for what it costs us to buy a drink at home?"

"I know."

"Some men do sick things to them."

"Some men are sick."

"It's a lonely life for us here, isn't it?"

"Martin, I sleep with these girls. If that's what you are trying to ask me, the answer is yes. It's something that I do. I won't deny it."

He wheeled the car around, accelerated. He said, "So much better than watching a stupid DVD. I have a special one, Jack. I would like to find her."

"I have a special one, too."

"Great. Let's get them. We'll have a party."

His girl's name was Fabienne. She sat up front in her long braids as if the car were her own. At the corner where I most often met Sabina, she stepped out of the shadows. She slid in back beside me, seemed glad to see me for a change. She ran her fingers along the supple leather, snapped her gum. "Good to see you, boyfriend," she said, kissed my cheek. She took my hand in hers, pressed it. "So long time I don't see you. I get worried."

Martin lived in a big furnished house with a pool in the expat district: a mansion. There were lights in the pool, and the four of us swam together in our underwear, drank Martin's wine, French burgundy he'd had imported. The maid, an old woman of the coastal Appolo tribe, brought out a platter of *alloco,* fried plantain chips; Martin gave her money from the pocket of his crumpled pants, told her to go home. We swam naked then, played a game where we each took turns holding our breath at the bottom of the pool. It was quiet down there, silent, like not being in the world at all. Sabina stayed down so long, I wanted to dive and bring her up.

"Good night, Jack. Good night, lovely Sabina," Martin said when it was time, showed us to our room. It was a four-poster bed with clean and cool sheets. The air conditioning was almost too cold to bear. As I turned down the covers, Sabina said to me, "Does this mean more money, boyfriend?"

"I wish it did, Sabina," I told her. She stuck her gum on the nightstand, stretched tall like a cat, rolled her neck, got into bed. Did she do that to become a different person, I wondered, the person who would let me enter her? Her hands were on me instantly; I caught them, stopped them, wanted to talk. About what, she asked, yawned. I didn't know. Something. Anything. I wanted to communicate.

So talk, she said.

I talked to her about America a long time. I explained what a garage door opener was, how everyone had a car. I talked about the lakefront, the jazz festival in Grant Park. Perhaps I was hinting at something, trying to impress her. If she caught on, she didn't say anything.

When the sex was over, Sabina said to me as I held her, "Hey, man. I'm used to you now. It's okay. You're pretty. So I let myself see it. You are different, good. I think about you. When you come, I like to see you."

I asked why her daughter had died, and she said, "Don't know. I loved her so much. Bought her every nice thing. It was like she did not want to live. She was fat, and then when she had two years, she got skinny. Every nice thing, I bought her it. She thinned and thinned, and then she died."

Starlight seeped in the window. There wasn't any sound but the faraway whir of the air conditioner. "I'm sorry," I said from the truest place in my heart. I wished that her presence next to me didn't have to be about money.

"Such a small girl. My girl. My best and only thing."

"I'm sorry for you, Sabina."

"Oh man, why is this the life? Why is it? Why is one rich and the other poor? Why is one black and the other white?" Sabina said, her face on my chest. For a long time, neither of us slept, the starlight making the top sheet covering our bodies seem as though plated with silver.

The maid fried us all eggs and toast in the morning, cut a cantaloupe. We sat at the table like normal people, two couples. Martin looked refreshed and healthy. He said, "We'll all take a trip to Man sometime. See the vine bridges. We'll all stay together at the beach in Sassandra. Eat lobster and escargot." The girls smiled and nodded, brushed their braids back from their eyes. Martin told his guard to let me in any time. Sabina kissed me good-bye at the door, told me to be safe in the bush; she wanted to swim again, to stay here now with her new sister, Fabienne. I took a transport up-country, longed for

Sabina in my heart, wished life could be the way Martin had said it forever.

In the village, I told Mamadou about what had been going on in the city, about Sabina, and he was relieved. As we ate rice with our hands from the calabash his mother had set out for us under the mango tree and stars, Mamadou laughed and said, "You were worried I'd think badly of it? Hey! It makes me happy. Adama, it's not normal to not have a woman, to be without a woman so long as you have. If you waited any longer, certainly you would fall sick. See how sick you fell for the Peul girl? Now it is fine again. As the ancestors say, 'Know the lion by his roar, the monkey by his cry.' What is the call of a man but for a woman?"

The news of my sexual normalcy won me the young men's trust enough that they were now willing to discuss AIDS with me, to listen to me talk about it in a way they hadn't before. And because I was having sex in Africa, I found myself talking about it realistically.

"A condom ruins the feeling, Adama," another one of them said as I sat in a group of them, smoking cigarettes in the late night outside the chief's hut.

"It's true. It makes it lose its flavor. But use a condom when you are in the city. Use a condom until you find your wife. Then you can be sure and enjoy forever."

"On the radio, they tell us to not have sex, Adama. But if a man does not have sex with women, then how can the world know that he is a real man?"

"Of course we won't stop having sex. That is nonsense. But we can be prudent about it when we do."

"If we get the test, and the test is positive, then we will lose all hope and our bodies will grow weak and die."

"We are men, are we not? We have the test because we want to protect the women we love. Of course it's scary. But we must be men and face this thing as we face anything else that frightens us."

Mamadou came to my hut in the night. He sat on the stool by my doorway and lit a cigarette. He said, "My *go* is pregnant."

"*Allah den balo.* God bless your children," I said to him.

"And your *go*?"

"She's a *maquis go.*"

"There is no shame in that, Adama. Many men marry *maquis gos* in the city."

"I'm not thinking about marriage," I said, and smoked.

"But do you love this one this time, Adama? The way that you whitemen must love your women? Or is this again as it was with Djamilla?"

"I don't love her, Mamadou."

"Not at all, Adama?"

"I worry about her when I am away."

"To worry about a woman is good. After all, the yam dreams of the sun as it sleeps. Perhaps this will become the love that takes time. The leopard is not born with all of his spots. Chickens are not eaten the day that they hatch. There will be time for all things, Adama. Time to live, time to work. Still, the ancestors say, 'The rice, even growing, knows that one day it must be cut.'"

With Sabina at Martin's house, Martin often away, I pretended in the pool that this was my real life, that this luxury was mine to give her. Sabina rose from the bed one night, stood at the window, and looked out at the moon. She said, "Tonight I feel sick. Tonight my heart is in my village in Liberia. But I have shamed myself and can't go back. So here I am. I want to tell you, man, that with you, it is okay. I want to do this with you as long as you like. I know that one day you will go back to your country. Still, it is okay for me."

"I like you, Sabina. I want to take you places if you'll go."

"Okay, man, let's go. Where do we go?"

Surprised, I said, "Really?"

I took her to the Abidjan zoo. Through American eyes, the zoo was a miserable place of stinking, fetid cells housing sick and bored animals. But the animals were actually marvelous. Arm in arm, we laughed at the baboons and their wide butts. We stood quietly before the sleeping lions. We reached up handfuls of banana leaves to the elephants' sucking mouths. People looked at us. Sabina did not seem to care.

At the mall, Sococé, Sabina came out from the dressing room of the couture shop in silk blouses, in skirts and matching heels. The Lebanese attendant seemed put out, refused to offer suggestions, busied herself with folding clothes as though what we were doing was distasteful. Sabina didn't seem to care about that, either. She was beautiful; the clothes lay on her body as though made for her, the pleats of the skirts fanned out about her knees as she twirled to show them off. Sabina walked out on my arm in the sharpest outfit in Abidjan: a cream blouse and skirt that brought out all the luster of her color.

We went to Legends on the lagoon and danced salsa together; Sabina's legs were as long as swords, her waist tiny in my hands. Every man in the city looked at her, all the respectable women. We went to Sassandra on the bus, ate steamed crab at the old hotel. Sex was different now; she'd become more to me than she'd been, and I didn't want to wear a condom any longer, didn't. Yes, I gave her money, but it was more than that. I signed us into the hotel as Monsieur and Madame Jacques Diaz. I wired home to my mother, told her to send me $500 from my savings account. I put Sabina up in a small apartment in working-class Anyamé, bought her a parrot, an African gray, which she named Levi, who knows why. She didn't call me "my boyfriend" or snap gum at me anymore. She'd brighten when I'd appear at the door, say, "Hey, man. Why so long time away?"

In my village, I thought a lot about AIDS. In the night outside my hut and smoking a cigarette to the stars, I wondered if I had it, ultimately didn't care. What was life but to let someone know you intimately, to be glad for what little joy you could scrape from the dark world? As I'd stub out my cigarette and duck under the thatching of my hut for bed, I'd say aloud to myself, *"Allahumdu lilah."* 'Thanks be to God.'

I avoided the few other Americans in Abidjan, had a different life. Still, when I'd check in at the office, others were always there: working on grant proposals, having a respite from their villages as I was. Now and again one of the men would corner me, say, "I know you sleep with those girls, Jack. How do you do it? Where do you take them? How much do you pay?"

I'd shrug, say, "Pay them what you can. They'll take care of the rest. That's their job."

Often, these men's faces would grow hard then. They'd say, "I'm trusting you. Understand me? Don't tell a living soul about this conversation."

History surrounded us in Africa, forward and back, white men, black women. But in the night with Sabina, neither of us seemed to have color.

The end of the story is this: I bought a school uniform, khaki, for Sabina's son, Max, who she'd brought from Monrovia to live with her. He was a small boy, timid; thin as a bird in his new clothes, his knees as round as apples. He'd never been so near a white person before, and was afraid of me, hiding behind his mother's legs until she slapped and scolded him to stop that.

At Sococé, I took him to the jungle gym, urged him with Sabina to attempt the long slide. The children there were both white and black, healthy and loud, attended by nannies who snoozed on the bench in uniforms as their charges played. Max took a long time to climb the steps. Steps were new things for him, hard to manage, as were the bright colors of the gym. He was terrified as he looked down at us from the height; the pleasure that it was supposed to be, lost on him. For a long time, he sat and looked at his mother as if pleading to be rescued. Then she barked at him, and he came down. I was waiting at the bottom. I caught him, swung him up onto my shoulders, and for the first time since I'd been there, he laughed. Sabina smiled and took my arm. I didn't know where it was heading, didn't care. "Give me 200,000 CFA, Jacques. I want to buy a sewing machine and make business, clothing.

I'm too bored when you are away. It will make work for me when I wait."

I gave Sabina the money, $300. I went up-country, came back again. It was raining all over Abidjan. I took a cab to Sabina's place. The apartment was empty. The floor was littered with bottles and cigarette butts. Even the parrot was gone. I asked after Sabina everywhere I knew. Nobody knew where she was.

I went up-country for four months, came back again, looked for Sabina. Everywhere, I saw her, girls like her: dancing too close with other whitemen, showing off their long legs from the shadows of the corners. A girl in an electric blue miniskirt came up to me from the shadows on Rue des Jardins and said, "Sabina, she gone back. Some months now. Visiting her daughter." I paid the girl cash to tell me this information. At the Hacienda, the bartender looked at me with hooded eyes until I brought out my money. He folded the bills into the pocket of his shirt, rubbed his face: numbed by things like this. He said, "Her daughter start school, man. She gone back to Monrovia."

I wandered through the city a few days, in the clubs and bars. Finally, I told the organization's doctor that I might have AIDS. She gave me the test in the sterile examining room, drew the blood from my arm. The doctor was middle-aged and gentle, from Ghana, a mother. Later, she held the results in her soft hands on her desk while I sat in the chair. Like pleading, like trying to manage emotions larger than she understood, she said, "What I don't understand is how you boys can sleep with women you don't know. Don't you want to find a special woman to love? Don't you want to hold her in your hands and protect her like an egg?"

She set the paper down on her desk. She said with a blank face, "You don't have AIDS, Jack."

There were years of service before me, a war. I wouldn't find Sabina that time. In time, I wouldn't care. Outside my hut the night I came back, I smoked cigarettes, gazed at the stars, wondered where Sabina was, who she had really been. Finally, I went to bed. In the morning, the village's mortars sounded with the women pounding rice for the hungry mouths of the new day.

SUSTAINABILITY

Midway into my second year, even as I was seeing Sabina, I rode my *mobylette*, a battered 49cc blue Peugeot, the sixty miles north from Tégéso to Ryan's village. I'd sent him a note to tell him I was coming. I'd visited him there once before, more than a year ago, when neither of us could yet ask for water properly in our village's languages. That time, we'd simply sat and stared at the people who'd gathered in his courtyard to stare back at us.

The *mobylette* was against the organization's rules, but as with a lot of things, I didn't care. We really had very little contact with the Potable Water International office in Abidjan once we'd been sent to our assignments in the bush. The secondhand machine had cost me $150 in Séguéla and changed my life. No longer did I have to wait hours in the dust on the hope that some transport or other would chug into my village and pick me up. With my *mobylette*, I could simply fire it up and go.

I loved the way the wind whipped my face, the way the forest and its shadows ran along as in a silent film as I rode my little banged-up horse. But to tell the truth, the bike was more trouble than it was worth. For every thirty miles of freedom it afforded me, it would break down for days. On the way up to Ryan's, I had to spend two nights on a borrowed mat on the roadside in Djirabana, while the local mechanic, a boy in oily rags, bent and scraped the copper of my bike's burnt electrical wires with his teeth. There were diamond mines nearby, and all during the time I spent there, shifty-eyed Peul in their blue robes tried to sell me stones that looked like rock salt, not believing that a whiteman could have no money.

When I finally arrived in Fadjiadougou, dusty and tired, Ryan stood up off his porch where he was drinking tea in a robe and said, "Hey, Jack. What took you so long?"

While I had spent my time hunting francolins and listening to fables about gazelles and bush pigs told to me by Mamadou, Ryan had started projects. He'd made a solar food dehydrator out of long scraps of tin sheeting; he'd instigated a vegetable-garden collective in the fenced area beside his mosque with the village women. And above and beyond all that, he'd begun breeding chickens for eggs. The coop was a fine constructed building of thatch and chicken wire across from his hut, and when we approached to feed the twenty chickens rice, they hurried forward in a group like pets. They clucked and cooed, and Ryan made kissing noises at them. None of these things had anything to do with clean drinking water, the focus of our mission, but it didn't matter. He was making the best of things. His village was so proud of him that every evening old men came to his hut from the fields to present him with fresh peanuts, papayas, and mangoes, and the women sang his name as they passed. He had so many peanuts, they filled great sacks inside his hut.

"What in the world are you going to do with all those peanuts?" I asked him.

"Don't know," he said, and sipped tea like a pasha. "Perhaps I'll sell them in Séguéla, buy pencils for the kids."

"Then they're really going to love you."

"Yeah," he said, and sighed as though he was tired of it, "I guess they probably will."

Back in my village, I ate dinner, cassava *toh* and okra sauce, with Mamadou. We talked about my trip, about what had gone on in the village while I was away. The blacksmith's daughter was having an affair with the potter's second son. Ama Fanta believed a genie was trying to crawl into her hut at night through the thatch. Bukari's cattle had eaten rice in Bébé's field and there had been an angry dispute about that. When we were done exchanging news, I said, "Guess what, Mamadou? We're going to start a project."

"A project, Adama? What sort of project?"

"We're going to teach the people about AIDS."

"Ah, you are going to talk to the young men again, as you do. That is good."

"Not me this time, Mamadou. *We* are going to talk about AIDS."

"Who we?" he said, and knit his brow.

"You and I, naturally."

"Adama!"

Of course the major problem of Ivory Coast was AIDS.

Because of my relationship with Sabina, I sometimes felt sure I had it, lived with it, whether I really did or not. As I'd gaze at the Southern Cross in the night from outside my hut, I'd ask myself, 'What are you going to tell your mother?'

"AIDS is our project, Mamadou. You and I are going to become the big AIDS chiefs of Tégéso."

"AIDS chiefs! Adama! What about my name?"

"This project will only enhance your name."

"AIDS? Are you crazy? It is fine for you to talk about such things. The people will let you talk about anything you want. But me? I won't do it. There is no possibility at all that I am going to stand before the people and talk about something like AIDS."

"Get some sleep, little brother," I said, getting up to leave. "We start tomorrow."

Not only was Mamadou my friend, but as the companion the village had assigned to me to help me learn their customs, he was also in some ways my slave. He was two years younger than me, beholden to me because of the rigors of the village age-hierarchy. But more than anything else, the chief had given him to me like a possession. I had the right to tell him what to do.

My standing among the Worodougou at this time was twofold. First and most important, I had learned the language, and second, I'd given away all my Western possessions soon after I'd arrived. The agency hadn't offered us any advice on this during training. What was most important to them was that we stayed. To this end, they wanted us to be as comfortable as possible in our villages. The last few days of training had included shopping trips to Abidjan so we could buy the things we'd need during our service in the field. For some, this meant haggling with Lebanese merchants in the clamoring Adjamé market for kerosene refrigerators, for butane stoves. Many went to their villages with portable stereo systems, frame beds, a cushioned chair or two. I'd never liked shopping, didn't do it there. Still, when I arrived in Tégéso with my small pack, no one could see past my transistor radio and tape deck, my fancy hiking sandals and array of Western clothes.

"Hey, Adama, you are rich!" a passing old man had said to me through Mamadou one of my first nights there. I'd been listening to Bob Marley on my tape player as I'd brushed my teeth before bed.

"Rich?" I'd said, thinking of the mat I'd sleep on, my few changes of clothes, my hut itself, black spiders casting webs all over the thatching inside no matter how often I swept them out. "How in the world can you say that I am rich?"

As the days passed and the scales of the West fell from my eyes, I saw myself as they did: my tall and healthy body, my unscarred skin, my thick and clean jeans, my wondrous electronics.

I turned off my tape player one evening soon after, carried it to the chief's hut, set it at his feet. My clothes, I parceled out to his sons. My shampoo and deodorant I gave to his wives. In this way, I let the West blow from me leaf by leaf. As though in exchange for what I'd given up, Mamadou's mother presented me with a wicker hat she'd woven herself to keep the sun from my face; Mamadou gave me an old machete so

I could work alongside him in the fields; I accepted tattered field clothes from the witch doctor. Just as soon as I had been naked among them, I was dressed again.

I began to teach Mamadou the specifics of AIDS under his mother's mango tree, made him record the information in a notebook I'd bought from a passing Peul merchant. I drew grossly detailed anatomical pictures in it to make things clear. He cringed at these, tried again and again to close the cover over the notebook as he held it on his knees.

Everything in training had been about "sustainability." It was the keyword of those who would aid the global south in the current era, learned through forty decades of big dreams and failed projects. Though I would reside in Tégéso for years, one day I would have to go home. For any project I would initiate to be successful, it would have to live on after I was gone. I'd decided that mine would live on through Mamadou.

I wrote to Abidjan about my plan and, for once, heard back from them. A small package came for me on a logging truck, and Mamadou and I closed the door of my hut to open it away from the prying eyes of the children who had gathered outside to see what was going on.

Mamadou slit the tape of the package with his thick thumbnail as I turned up the flame of my hurricane lamp in the dark of my hut. His hands drew open the flaps of the box, and inside, the round condoms glinted in their yellow wrappers like gold coins. There was a letter from the agency, from the under-director. It said, "Dear Jack. We're pleased with your perseverance up there despite the uncertainty of the times. Your new project is wholly in keeping with the mission. Take great care in how you impart this information. It's a conservative people you live among."

Mamadou sifted through the condoms like a kid searching breakfast cereal for the toy inside the box. He was as enraptured as anyone there would be by this package from the outside world. His hand found something, and he looked at me with excited eyes. He withdrew an oblong piece of wood that at first glance resembled a thick and short pestle.

"Adama? This strange wooden thing, what is this?" he said, waving it about like a sword, jabbing the air between us with it.

"What do you think it is?" I said.

He looked at it along its length, held it to his nose and sniffed it. He said, "It's some kind of whiteman tool."

"Every man possesses this tool, Mamadou. Every man of every color."

"What? Hey? A piece of wood like this?" He touched the carved knob at the end, looked at it again. Then he saw it for what it was, dropped it back in the box. He wiped his hands on his shirt, looked at me, and grimaced.

"It's a penis, Mamadou. A penis made of wood."

His eyes were wide. He said, "Oh, no, Adama. Oh, no, Adama, please. I want to stop. Don't make me do this."

Someone banged on the door. A young man's voice said, "Eh, Adama? Mamadou, Koné's son? What's going on in there? Something came from Abidjan, is it? What are all these children doing here sitting in the dust?" It was Bébé. The young men had come home from the fields.

"Adama, please," Mamadou said, like begging.

I nodded at him, smiled. I folded the letter into the short stack of correspondences I kept under my mat like a pillow. I took my wicker hat off the peg on the wall, put it on. I picked up the wooden penis, shook it at him. "You'll thank me for this one day, Mamadou," I promised. I filled my pockets with condoms. Then I pushed open the door onto the evening, onto the young men in their filthy field clothes who had gathered outside to find out what we were up to.

"Do you know what this is?" I said, holding up the penis like a revelation.

Their eyes widened, and they circled in. Even some of the nearby dogs crept closer.

"Sit down," I told them. "Mamadou will do his best to explain it to you."

For all of his initial reluctance and embarrassment, Mamadou quickly became an expert AIDS educator. I had a laminated ID card made for him in Séguéla, and he wore it everywhere: Méité Mamadou, Rural AIDS Instructor. He used money he'd saved over the years to have a professional *pagne* shirt made. We went together to Séguéla to report on our work to the Director of Rural Health. People in the village began to ask Mamadou all sorts of questions on medical issues. I think he got the idea that he was a doctor.

The dry season came, the harvests were in, the cotton stood in tall piles outside the chief's compound like snow. There were many people moving on the logging roads that ran between the villages now: Senoufo field workers heading home to Korhogo, Kulongho slaves heading to their distant homeland in the northeast to find out who had been born since they had been gone, who had died. There wasn't much work. The villages were full and lively.

In our wicker hats, Mamadou and I would set out with small bundles tied to our backs: a few cooked yams, stoppered calabashes of water. We'd bring our guns, shoot francolin and striped ground squirrel along the way. We traveled through forest and savanna in our flip-flops. We met many people and exchanged news with them. We came to swamps where the ibis nested in great flocks like white assemblies of the ancestors; we came out of the forest onto wide, open plains where the granite whalebacks stood up in the distance like old men's bald heads. We climbed one to see the great stretch of the land: the thick forest wall to the south with the lahou birds coasting above it like kites; the yellow savanna to the north with the acacias and baobabs standing like sentinels in the thick grass. We bartered cigarettes for milk from a band of Peul wandering with their cattle; Mamadou showed me pictographs on a stone outcropping: giraffes and leopards carved by an expert hand that we both understood belonged to a people much older than we were. We slept in the bush around fires of twigs with our wraps drawn about our shoulders like the stars. And here and there we would come to a village where the women and children would lead us to their old chief in a great entourage, everyone leaving their labor to witness these great goings-on.

"Old chief," Mamadou would say, his ID card affixed to the breast of his shirt, "we've come from Tégéso to salute you. We bring the greetings of our chief and people."

"Tégéso? Eh? How is old Méméfa? Is that sneaky pangolin still alive? He never was one to take up the machete. Happy to lie in his hammock until time came to visit one of his wives."

"He greets you, Father."

"Eh? You must greet him for me when you return."

"And who is this?" the chief would say, and look at me. Always what would ensue was a half hour or more of the chief asking me simple questions like, "What is your name again? How old are you?" just so everyone could laugh and marvel at my command of Worodougou: myself as a trick pony.

"Hey!" these chiefs would finally say, slapping their knees and looking at Mamadou. "Who could have imagined a whiteman speaking our language! And you are his guardian? Young son, you have honored yourself and your village. Now the world will know who we are."

In this way, Mamadou and I visited the fourteen villages of the Tégéso subregion, Tégéso *fo-ma,* the Worodougou district along the edge of the forest of which Tégéso was the ancient capital. We visited the great villages of Soba, Banandjé, Somina, Gbena, Wye, Kavena, Sualla, Kénégbé, Djamina; we visited the *campements* in the bush that were a handful of huts and would be villages of their own in generations to come. The teaching didn't begin immediately but required preliminary visits to introduce ourselves to the chiefs and state our intentions, and then the chiefs would announce a date when they would assemble their young people to hear our lesson. In this way, I learned the unity of the Worodougou in custom and language, understood how news spread by travelers kept these scattered outposts sealed in a cultural web.

The francolins rose out of the bush in the evenings, and Mamadou and I shot them. Then we'd pluck them, gut them, spit them over a small fire, talk about the world and our lives in it until Orion's Belt appeared square overhead and sleep came to us both. While he'd been ashamed of the wooden penis before, now he wouldn't let me carry it. He said, strangely, that it had begun to speak to him in his dreams. There were times now when he'd conduct the lectures almost by himself, and it was a visual thing, watching his estimation of himself grow.

One night, lying on the opposite side of a small fire in the bush while on our way to another village, Mamadou said to me as I looked up and considered the vast stars, "I never imagined I would travel as widely as this, Adama. I never could have dreamed that I would see the world. Imagine it! A poor farmer's son!

"I will miss you when you are gone, Adama. I miss you already when I think about it. In distant years, you must come back and we will share our children with each other."

But this is the story of Djigulachédougou, the village of 'Where the Men Fall Down,' and what happened to us there.

Djigulachédougou was a neat and traditional village a great length from Tégéso, miles in the forest. There were legends about it. Everyone there was rumored to be a sorcerer. Who knows why? Perhaps it was because the Worodougou were not a forest people. While many of their villages lay along the edge of it, the Djigulachés lived deep in the trees.

It was a day's walk in to it from Soba, which was already two full days from Tégéso by foot. There wasn't a road but a path, as there had been no roads to any of them before the French colonizers whipped long gangs to hack and burn tracks through the forest to facilitate the extraction of lumber, cotton, and, most of all, labor for the great southern cocoa plantations. Somehow, the village of Djigulachédougou had escaped that.

The chief of Soba, a teasing and happy old man with one empty eye socket and leprosy-eaten stubs for fingers, walked us to the path that led into the gloom of the forest the morning after our lecture there. This was the way to Djigulachédougou. He said a benediction for us at the trailhead, scattered some rice for the ancestors, and, in his laughing way, warned us again not to go.

"They are not people like we are," the old man laughed and said, pointed one stub at the sky as if warning of rain. "The *sous-préfet* came and offered to build them a road some years ago. They refused. Why approach the dog that snarls? Stay with us another night. Tell us more about these plastic bags that you say whitemen wear over their *mogos* to guard their health."

"We will come and speak about it again soon, Father," Mamadou told him. "But first we must do this."

"Tell me," the old chief said in a conspiratorial whisper, "can the plastic bags be washed and used again?"

"No, Father," Mamadou said in a slow voice, and shook his head. "Condoms must only be used once. Think of it like this: Once you have peeled the banana, you must throw away the skin."

"Then give me another, son. My wives eat many bananas."

The forest was thick around us on the narrow path to Djigulachédougou, dark and silent; it was like trekking through vast and cavernous catacombs. While excited to be going where few, if any, Westerners had been, I found myself nervously fingering the trigger of my gun. Mamadou must have felt it, too. When we took a break to smoke cigarettes and drink from our calabashes by a long-forgotten termite mound in the gloom, he said, "Who would want to live like this? No road? Always as though it's night? Why should we care about this one crazy village?"

"Why should we?" I nodded and said from my haunches, exhaling smoke.

"Ah, Adama, it's the penis. The wooden penis. Once, I feared it. Now, it calls to me in my dreams, tells me to carry it everywhere."

In the late afternoon, we heard the rhythmic thunking of pestles in mortars—the sound of the West African village—and soon enough saw light between the trees. We stepped out into the village, and as our eyes adjusted to the sun, we saw the round huts, their thatched roofs like pointed hats, and goats and chickens here and there. Some naked children were playing a skipping game, clapping their hands and laughing; they took one look at us, at me, and ran shrieking for the trees. An old woman cracking palm kernels for soap carefully set down her pounding stone, crawled on all fours into her hut, and shut the door. A line of women stopped where they were going, their mouths hanging open. What I noticed were the huge calabashes on their heads. They were the same size as the metal basins the women in Tégéso used to carry water from the swamp to their hearths: This village didn't even have the basic modern implements that women elsewhere took for granted. We walked into the village center, and adults came from everywhere to gather around us and stare. Not one person said anything.

"Sorcerers," I said to Mamadou under my breath.

The crowd shepherded us to a covered *paillote,* and under it on a carved stool was a great-bellied old man holding a gnarled staff: the chief. He wore a crown of rooster tail feathers around his thick scalp. We laid down our guns, sat in the dust before the chief with our legs crossed and our heads bowed. Mamadou took his laminated ID card from his pocket and clipped it to his shirt like an afterthought.

The whole village crowded in around us: I'd never seen people with so little in the way of Western clothes. Many of the women were bare breasted and the men wore the most modest of khaki shorts. The chief was the fattest I had ever seen, his skin like ink. He tossed a handful of monkey knuckles into the dirt, looked at them, grunted, gathered them again, and dropped them into an antelope-skin pouch. "The news!" he said in a booming voice.

Mamadou set a leaf package of kola nuts at the chief's feet. Then I saw that the chief's legs were swollen with edema. Mamadou said, "Great chief, we have come from Tégéso to salute you."

"Tégéso? Where is that?"

Mamadou glanced at me and I saw that his face was stricken. What were we to do in a place where they didn't even know what the neighboring villages were? He cleared his throat. He said, "The famous village of Tégéso? The village that Touré could not conquer? It is beyond Soba, Father. Beyond Wye. The most famous village of the great Séguéla *fo-ma*. Near the road to San Pedro."

The chief opened the leaf package, took out a pale nut, popped it into his mouth like a fat cashew. He waved away a fly that had landed on his nose. He said, "Of course I know where it is. I went to high school in Séguéla. I am only giving you a hard time."

Mamadou and I looked at each other again. Then Mamadou said, "Great chief, I have come with my white brother to bring news to your people. News about a great danger that threatens us all."

"What danger?" the chief said, and leaned in to look at us with a keen eye. The rooster feathers made him look regal.

"AIDS, Father. We've come to teach your people about AIDS."

"AIDS! The whiteman's great lie! There is no AIDS here. Small boy, go home. Who are you to bring a whiteman here and frighten all the women?" He clapped his hands, and a boy hurried forward to gather the kola nuts, to offer the old chief his shoulder and help him stand. "Don't come back," the chief said, clearly in pain from the swelling in his legs. "Do you understand me, child? Do not come back to my village." Then he went into his hut and closed the door.

Mamadou and I looked at each other, at the wall of people that encircled us. We were dumbfounded. Had anyone ever heard of anything so insulting? We spoke freely together in French, not worried that anyone would understand us here.

"Is that all he's going to hear from us?" I said.

"Apparently that is it."

"What are we supposed to do now?"

"Even I do not know."

We sat there awhile, and no one said anything. I could see their feet inching toward us as their circle tightened almost imperceptibly. It was clear that we wouldn't be offered a hut for the night, as was the custom for travelers. After all, they hadn't even offered us water.

"It is finished, can't you see?" An old woman clapped her hands and shouted as though we hadn't understood, and we stood from the dust and gathered together our packs and guns, which the crowd had picked up as though to hurry us on our way. It was already approaching evening, and if we really weren't to be given mats, it was long past time to go. Then the crowd pushed us along until we were at the trail-head that led back to Soba. If the forest had been dark before, now it was black. With a last look over our shoulders at those strange people, we started off on the trail. For a while, we walked along calmly, as though walking through unknown forest at night was something we did every day. All that could be seen were long snakes that were vines and glimmering genies that were last patches of light. Finally, something big went crashing through the nearby bracken. Mamadou shouldered me aside, and for two hours, I ran behind him, the terrors of this unknown stretch of forest close in on my heels.

The chief of Soba had rice and peanut sauce waiting for us in calabashes in the firelight. He laughed as we ate greedily; he wanted to know all that had happened. We told him of the long path through the forest, of the gloom, of the way the people had looked at us, of the fat and strange chief.

The chief of Soba smoked a cigarette that he held between the stumps of his fingers, grinned at the stars as he swung lazily in his hammock. He said, "That chief, he is strong. He is sick and should have died, but there he is. He went to school, you know. Very rich in his brains. The rest of them, they are like monkeys. They don't even believe in Allah. Did you see?"

Mamadou mumbled an assent as he ate.

"You boys, I knew you would come back. What you are trying to do is good. But that village, that is like the time before. That chief will not admit that the world has changed. He wants it to remain as it was when he was a boy. Too much magic there. Too much in the forest. Ah, but he is a great chief, very funny. Even the Senoufo who go there looking for field work come running back as though chased by dogs."

On our sleeping mats in our borrowed hut that night, Mamadou and I recounted what we'd seen. I said, "They didn't have metal. A few machetes, but that was it. They didn't have plastic."

"They didn't have clothes, Adama."

"Did you see those women?"

"How could I not? How can one not see mangoes in a mango orchard?"

"Well, little brother, now what? Do we go back and try again? Or do we go home?"

Mamadou thought for a long time in the dark. We hadn't been home in a week, were tired. Still, we'd talked about AIDS to hundreds of people, all of the villages but this last one. He said, "That chief, he said to me, 'Small boy, go home.' Did he not see my identification tag? My shirt? We'll sleep now, Adama, and I'll dream. The penis will come to me. It will tell me what to do."

In the morning, Mamadou said that the penis wanted him to go back. The chief of Soba saw us off. He touched Mamadou's face, then mine, with his stubs. He said, "How the gazelles prance when they are young! And in the evening, how they run! Don't go back there. Stay here and work in my rice fields for all the running that you will have to do."

We walked quickly, smoked once along the way. Then we came into the clearing that was Djigulachédougou. The village was shrouded in mist. The fat chief was wrapped in a shawl, drinking rice tea from an old calabash. He motioned to an attendant to sweep the ground before we sat. Then, as we looked at our toes, he said, "I think I've seen you before."

"Great chief," Mamadou said, "we came yesterday."

"Ah, yes. You are selling beads and *pagnes,* no? You are a Dioula merchant, and this fair one, he is a Peul, is he not?"

"Father, I am a Worodougou. And this one, he is a whiteman."

The chief coughed in a short fit. Though he seemed fat and healthy at first glance, he was really sick. "Ah, whiteman," the chief wiped his mouth and said to me. He wheezed as he talked. "You've come here to tell us a great thing and ruin our lives, is it not? Is it Jesus you've come to talk about this time? That is what you wanted the last time you came. I know all about Jesus. So great he was, wasn't he? You want to tell us about Jesus and that all our ways are foolish."

"We haven't come to talk about Jesus, Father," Mamadou told him. "We've come to talk about AIDS."

"Yes, you've come to talk about this AIDS today. You will talk to the children, and they will laugh. You will give them bonbons. Then tomorrow you will whisper to them, 'There are no ancestors. There is only Jesus.' I don't trust whitemen.

What good has a whiteman ever brought to us here? Go back to Soba, whiteman. You are not welcome. And, small boy, if you ever come back to my village, come back alone."

We went back to Soba. We smoked cigarettes with the chief, told him all that had transpired. "Don't cry for two eggs, Adama, when you have been given one," the Soba chief laughed and said from his hammock. "Be thankful. You never have to be insulted by that fat chief again."

Mamadou remained determined, slept with the penis under the mat beneath his head, and in the morning, he set out alone. I watched him recede into the gloom of the forest feeling something like longing, and he looked back a last time and smiled, as though he understood how I felt. Then the forest swallowed him up.

I passed the day harvesting rice with Soba's young men my age. At first, they teased me about my color, about if I knew how to do this work properly, and then we settled into the rhythms of the labor, the reaping songs. Under the heat of the midday sun, I forgot, as I often did, that I wasn't black.

Mamadou didn't return that night, and I sat on a stool beside the old chief in his hammock. Perhaps he could sense that I was hurt, because he didn't joke with me the way he had the days before. Beneath the laughter, he was a different man altogether. He said, "Is it easy for you to live here, Adama?"

"Not easy, Father."

"And why don't you go home?"

"Something inside me compels me to stay."

"It is good, Adama. You are an example for that boy."

The old chief told me a story. When he was a young man, the French came to the village: a French officer and his black soldiers. He imposed a levy. Soba had to give five young men to fight the war in Europe. Many ran away into the forest. Of those who remained, there were only cripples, half-blind albinos, dwarfs, and old men. But three fit young men had stayed in the village, and the French officer had his soldiers tie ropes around their necks to lead them away on the long road to the coast. "I was one of those three," the old chief told me. "As the son of the chief, I could not abandon the village. The other two were my cousins."

He was taken to Grand Bassam, put on a ship to France. The voyage was long, and many times he knew he would never see Africa again. It was very cold in France; the air burned his face, came out of his nose like cotton. There were black men from many strange tribes. No one shared a common language, and though they were all black, they could not talk to each other. The French put them into uniforms, then into ranks, made them march in the cold, taught them how to shoot. The French were very mean, but later, American soldiers they met in Stuttgart gave them chocolate.

One day during training, the French officer, perhaps the same one who had taken him from his village—who could tell, all whites looked the same—assembled the regiment in the yard. He had them build a fire in an oil drum. He said, "Tomorrow, you will go to war. If you brought medicine against bullets, throw it in the fire. War is a very serious thing. I don't want any of you to get reckless because you believe that bullets won't kill you."

Of course all of their mothers had given them medicine against bullets when they'd been taken from their villages. The officer came down among them, took the medicine bundles from where they'd hidden them in their boots, under their tongues.

"I swallowed mine, coughed it up into my hand later. I killed many whitemen. All the other black men died. I kept my medicine that my mother had given me. I did not die. I learned that whitemen are also men, that if you shoot them, they die. I saw many great cities, many great things we do not have here. I enjoyed seeing these things. I did not like the killing. I have no desire to go back there. It is finished," the old man said to end his story, and then he lifted himself out of his hammock under the stars, coughed and spit, blessed my coming sleep, and went into his hut to bed.

For three days, I stayed in Soba, working sometimes, often sitting with the chief, while Mamadou was in Djigulachédougou. The chief told me tales of his time in Europe, of the snow, of the stone cities of France and Germany where he fought. Part of me didn't want to believe him. How could this old man really have done all of that?

Mamadou came back on the evening of the fourth day, smiling, walking jauntily, and I understood that we would soon be going home. He lay on the dirt of the Soba chief's compound, lit a cigarette, and I pulled my stool in close as the old man roused himself in his hammock to listen. "That chief," Mamadou said, "he made me wait all of the first day in the sun! I watched him eat, I watched him drink. Then he called me to him. If he thought I would be frightened without you, Adama, I was not. I held up the penis and put a condom on it. I told him of the dangers; of Abidjan, of the men who come home from the city with the disease inside them.

For some time, that chief was quiet. I could see in his eyes that he was troubled."

The Djigulaché chief had called for the clown mask to dance that night, and the people gathered around the bonfire to laugh and sing at its tumbling antics until the moon was high. Then the chief had ordered them to sit and listen to Mamadou, and they had. Yes, the old man was a great chief, Mamadou said, very strong in his heart, though it was certain that his days were short. He had found the wooden penis funny, and Mamadou had left it with him. Mamadou's eyes gleamed. He said, "I will go back there soon and salute that great chief of our people."

We tied up our packs in the morning, bid farewell to the old Soba chief, started on the road home. Something was missing in me now that hadn't been before; Mamadou seemed taller to me than he had been as he walked along beside me. After some time, I put away what was troubling me, made myself happy for him. I said, "And what about your penis, Mamadou?"

"My penis? Ah, Adama, my penis now has a journey of its own. Besides, I can carve another one. After you have gone, I will carve many penises, take them to all the old chiefs. Now, if only I had a *mobylette.* If I had a *mobylette* to ride, I could move quickly on my own between all these villages. But as always, there is the problem of money. Do you have any idea how to remedy this?"

After a moment, I nodded at him. In fact, I did.

BAMBA

At the end of my second year, the regional supervisor, Cathy, came to my village to see how I was doing. In some ways, this was ridiculous as I'd already been there for twenty-four months. But that was how the organization worked.

Cathy's visit caused a huge commotion. Women set their pestles down beside their mortars to escort her to my hut like the arrival of royalty. They sang and clapped, danced as they came through the village, Cathy at their center with a smirk on her face as though she found the hubbub as embarrassing as I did. I was sitting in the dirt and sharpening my machete between my feet with a file after a long day of clearing brush with Mamadou in his father's fields. What could I do but accept that this was happening? "Adama Diomandé!" The woman came as they sang and clapped. "Rejoice! Rise up! Your white wife has finally come."

The women refused to understand that someone my age wasn't married, and even if they could have, they didn't want to. Their basic questions to me during my three years in

Tégéso were, "Adama, where is your wife? Adama, why won't you get married?"

"Your wife, Adama! Hey! Sing and rejoice! Adama, your wife has finally come!"

Cathy was tall and pretty in traditional wraps, into her fourth year in Ivory Coast. I smiled up at her. "Hi, sweetheart," I said.

"Hello, darling," she said sardonically.

"Looks like you've been welcomed to Tégéso."

"If that's what you want to call it," she said, and looked at the women who'd stopped singing now to listen to our strange English words. Ama Bintou, an old woman with strong limbs and steel gray hair, smiled and clapped her hands. She said to the others, "Don't you see what Adama is saying? He is saying to his wife who has come, 'How long you have been away from me, wife! How long I have missed you! Oh wife, my hunger has been great. Come now into my hut and feed me a great dinner!'" That made all the women double over with laughter, of course.

"What are they saying?" Cathy asked, and looked at me warily. The women stopped laughing again to listen.

"What do you think they're saying?"

"That we're about to do it?"

"Yep." I stood and brushed the filings off my field pants, picked up her bag from where the women had set it. "It's hot. Come on in and let's get away from them. It's nice to see someone from the outside. What's been going on in the world? Come in and tell me all the news."

Cathy ducked under the thatch of my doorway, and as I

followed her in, I paused to look back at the women who were ducking now to look inside, put my finger to my lips, and winked. Then I went in and shut the door. The women let up a cheer such as I'd never heard.

What was new in the world? What was ever new? Politics at home was depressing; we were at war again. Here in Ivory Coast, there had been massacres of Bozo fisherfolk along the Beoumi side of the lake, Peul murdered south of Korhogo. Berebi had burned out its Dioula for the third time. The government had built a plaza near Plateau in Abidjan to commemorate those killed in the uprisings the year before, which didn't do anything but cause more contempt that such serious problems could be salved as easily as that. Money was still frozen everywhere; it seemed reasonable now to think that there would never be any sort of funding. Despite everything, new relief workers had completed training, matriculated in. The retention rate was still running below 50 percent. Most of those I'd trained with had gone home. I knew as she told me the names of who'd left that I'd never cross paths with them again.

"And I went to Liberia," Cathy told me as she sat on the stool. Mamadou's mother had brought rice and mushroom sauce for us in calabashes; Mamadou himself had stopped by to greet Cathy and say hello. In fact, the day had seen most of the village ducking their heads into my doorway to call the afternoon salutation and take a look at my long-hoped-for wife. Even the chief had come to grin and exchange words. Cathy had been in Ivory Coast long enough to know all the basics of Dioula salutation, and that had pleased everyone, too, even though they were Worodougou. My old chief had put his hand to the side of his weathered face and said, "Adama, it is good. Your wife speaks our language, though she mumbles. Keep her with us for some time. Then she will speak Worodougou as you do. My heart is content, son. It is good that a man should have his wife close at hand. It makes the spirit happy and guards against insanity."

It had rained the day before, and as we talked into the settling evening, my neighbors placed hurricane lamps in their courtyards, wide basins of water around them. Soon enough, termites filled the air around the light of the lamps in fluttering clouds of gossamer wings, and the women and children knocked the fat insects into the basins with brooms, their hands. They plucked off the wings, fried the termites' white bodies in skillets of red palm oil. My neighbors brought us a steaming mound of them on a banana leaf, and we moved outside to eat them like popcorn under the stars.

"Liberia? What were you looking for over there?"

Cathy shook her head and smiled, gazed at the night as if deciding whether or not to tell me her story. She was from a small town in rural Oregon, had been homecoming queen of her high school: Though she didn't look it as she sat comfortably in her satin *boubous,* she was as far from home as anyone. "If I tell you, you have to keep it to yourself. I don't want word to get around. If the office knew about it, they'd send me home."

"Who am I going to tell? What do you think they'd do if they knew all the things I've been up to?"

"There's a girl in a Yacouba village on the border. Justine. She trained after you did. I'd never been out that way, so I went to check up on her. She's crazy, doing very well, really deep into it, everybody in her village loves her. She says to me, 'Want to go to Liberia?' Who wouldn't want to go to Liberia? The Yacouba are on both sides of the border; half her village goes across every day to trade in the markets and work the fields they have there. She'd been going across now and again with her neighbor. So we crossed the Cavally River in his dugout. We took food, water, *bangi,* like we were going on a picnic. We walked around in the forest, saw some monkeys, looked at her neighbor's fields: banana and cassava. It rained awhile and we ate our rice and sauce under his field hut. Everything was the same as here. When we went back to the boat, these guys with guns were there. Not little peashooters like yours. Real guns. AK-47s. They had on these uniforms, odds and ends. One guy had on a Mickey Mouse T-shirt. So right away I think to myself, 'Cathy, this is bad. You are not going to see Klamath Falls again.' I mean, how awful would that be? But I was scared. I said to Justine, 'You know these guys, right?' She didn't say anything. It was like she couldn't hear me.

"They were rebels of course. And they were pissed, Jack. They put their guns on us right away. They were shouting. Ever heard a Ghanaian speaking English? These Liberians were twenty times worse. They put their guns on Justine's neighbor. They were going to shoot him. They're shouting, 'Why not to shoot? Why not to shoot?' An old guy, right? He starts crying, sobbing. We just stood there. What did we think we were doing in Liberia, anyway?

"They marched us through the forest. We held our hands up. I'm stumbling around getting all wet, my hands in the air. Then we were in this nowhere village, and they locked us in a hut. The neighbor was outside, tied to a pole. We could hear them beating him up and him crying. Then it rained and they stopped. Then the raining stopped and you could hear the water dripping everywhere. We could hear them talking outside the door, all quiet, like talking about what to do to us. We could smell them smoking cigarettes, then ganja. Then there was music from a radio, and then it was nighttime. We didn't say one word to each other. It was like we thought that if we were quiet enough, they would forget that we were there. I fell asleep for a while, and then there was an argument outside the door. It was men. It was that time of night, you know? It got louder and louder. I thought, 'Man, we're done.' Then it got quiet again.

"In the morning, we heard a motorcycle pull up, the engine cut out, the guy kick out the stand. Then there was a commotion and they opened the door. We were blinking from the sun. It was an officer wearing mirrored sunglasses. He says, 'What are you doing in our country?' Justine says, 'We just wanted to go for a canoe ride on the river. We didn't even know we were in Liberia.' 'Are you spies?' he says. We both said, 'No.' He says, 'How can I know if that is true?' We just looked at each other. Justine looked like hell. Do you have any idea of what just one night of that can do to you?

"I got this bright idea. I said, 'We have money. We can give you the money we have with us.' He shakes his head. He says, 'This is not about money.' That's when I got really scared. Who's ever heard of things not being about money? I mean, I was scared before, but this was a kind of scared I didn't even know you could be. He asked a lot of questions. I remember those guns and my lips moving.

"They escorted us back to the canoe, kept their guns on us until we were across the river. Justine's neighbor was all beat up. He kept apologizing to us the whole time, his eyes swollen shut and his lips all bloody. The officer says to us just before we get into the canoe, 'You are very beautiful women. So sorry times are such as they are. Who knows what could have been in a better time? Perhaps even love, is it not?' When he let us get into the canoe, I thought that I loved him, too. It took us all day before we could even begin talking about it."

"Why did he let you out of it?"

"I have no idea."

"You don't remember what you said?"

"Justine did most of the talking."

"How can you not remember?"

"Come on, Jack."

Women brought mangoes for us to eat before we went to bed, grinning at us as if they knew what was about to happen. Cathy was ostensibly supposed to complete a progress report on what I'd been doing, but with the country the way it had been the past two years, she hadn't even brought the forms. We brushed our teeth in the starry night, turned in. In the dark of the night in my hut with the cricket's soft susurrus all around, I said to her on her mat a few arms' lengths from mine, "Are you sleeping, Cathy?"

"I'm not sleeping yet. The crickets. I don't get to hear them anymore since I've been in the city. It's too wonderful to sleep."

"Do you think about going home?"

"All the time. My parents have wanted me to come back for years. I imagine my friends would like to see me, too, if they even remember who I am. I've stretched it out as long as

I've been able. But I feel it waiting for me now. Sometimes it feels like something that's about to swallow me up."

"What are you going to do there?"

"Now? I have no idea. Drink too much, probably. I'll probably look for Africans wherever I can find them. I've liked who I am here. I don't know who I'll be back there anymore."

"Me neither."

"I can't even remember who I was."

"You can call me and we'll remind each other who we were when we were here."

"That sounds horrible."

"I know."

"I'm going to be lonely back there."

"I'm going to be scared."

We were quiet then, thinking, breathing. The thought of America hung before me like a cliff. I said, "What do you think about sleeping here next to me tonight?"

"No strings?" she said.

"None."

"It might be nice."

After a moment, she came over.

Cathy stayed in Tégéso two nights, and we had a good time. I showed her my old fields, everyone's fields, all the trails through the forest, and she remarked on all the work I must have done to clear such a farm. She squeezed my biceps as we stood with the fallen and dried stalks around us, said, "But it still hasn't made a difference." Everywhere we went, women set down their short-handled hoes to embrace her, to sing her welcome as my wife.

"Not my wife. My friend," I reminded them. It didn't matter.

I carried my shotgun with us, and though she wasn't interested in killing anything, she shot stones off a termite mound at forty paces. I showed her the green clearing in the forest where the girls were excised, the swamp and the yellow lotuses in it. We drank tea with the chief, with Mamadou, while his girlfriend Korotoum, her new baby tied to her back, smiled and plaited Cathy's hair. And in the night in my hut with the crickets singing around us, we made love.

"You know I've slept with girls down in Abidjan," I told her.

"I've had boyfriends here, too, Jack. So what? We'll use a condom. I'm used to that."

"Are you as worried about it as I am?"

"Every few minutes, every single day."

When Cathy left—the logging truck idling on the dusty roadside and the forest all around—we said good-bye with an embrace as though nothing had happened, as though we were simply the friends we'd been before. The chief's wives gave her a bolt of dyed red cotton as a gift, wailed as though grief stricken about her leaving, and she hung out the window and waved back to thank them for it. The village, my life in it, seemed diminished somehow: Still, I knew things would quickly resume their normal routine. Some of the women followed me as I walked back to my hut. Ama Bintou called, "See how he walks now? His head hangs like the donkey who has lost his mate. Oh, see that Adama's heart is as soft now as a rotten mango! Raise up your voices, oh, to sing a lament for Adama's lost wife."

Mamadou came to my hut in the evening, smoked with me under the stars. He said, "You looked healthy for a short while, Adama."

"Don't I always look healthy?"

"You always look normal. But for three days, you have looked like the forest after a rain."

"And what do I look like now?"

"Now? Like the rain has gone. Like leaves that brown and curl as the *harmattan* dries them. But don't worry, Adama. My eyes will adjust, and then this new look of yours will be normal again. Do you miss her?"

"Yes and no."

"Will you see her again?"

"Maybe."

It made sense in a lot of ways. We both enjoyed ourselves in Africa, enjoyed the Africans. We were both energetic and fearless there. Who hadn't heard legends about relief workers meeting in the bush, about romances in the sweltering nights, about couples going home together to start their American lives? While some did bring African spouses home, that often seemed impossible. They couldn't read, they couldn't write. They couldn't speak French, let alone English. What in the world would they do in America? Many of the young women in my village had never seen a lightbulb.

A few weeks went by and I borrowed the *mobylette* I'd given to Mamadou to help with his rural AIDS education project. I cleaned the carbon off the spark plug with a knife, greased the chain with palm oil, asked permission of the chief to visit my white wife, and then I rode down to Daloa to see Cathy.

The ride down was great: It didn't rain, the bike didn't give me trouble for a change, and the goats and sheep lying on the roadway wherever there was a village got up and made way like the parting of waters. The two times I took off my helmet to buy *gazole,* the boys selling the fuel from old pastis bottles asked me, "Hey, whiteman! Where are you going on a hot day like this?"

"To see my *go,*" I said, and winked. A *go* was any girl you were involved with romantically.

"White or black?"

"White this time."

"That is good," they said, and nodded, pulled crumpled bills from their dirty pockets to make change. "Crickets with crickets, ants with ants."

At thirty miles per hour, it took five hours to ride to Daloa. For the most part, the pavement had held up through the rainy season, and the forest around was tall and green. There was nothing better than humming through it at leisure.

In many respects, Daloa was like my hometown, Chicago. Certainly, there were no skyscrapers, no broad parkways, no low slate of the sky in winter, but even in its meager buildings, there was that same bustle of work. Daloa was the gateway to western Ivory Coast, the country's great intersection, and all manner of commodities passed through it on smoke-belching trucks to Abidjan: thousands of tons of cocoa, yes, but also cashews, peanuts, cotton, timber, beef. Cathy's house—the PWI regional office—was in the leafy residential section near the sugarcane fields. While the streets still weren't paved, there was real money in this neighborhood, and the homes reflected it. Cathy's was on a corner across from the gates to the university. Like every house of wealth, large or small, it had a serious security wall around it, and when I rang the buzzer, her houseboy, Bamba, turned the bolt to let me in. Inside was a wide and wraparound lawn, tall mango trees for shade, a vast porch with hammocks, open-air windows like eyes on a well-constructed French villa. I'd spent the night there a few times on my way to and from Abidjan but hadn't taken part in any of the parties it was famous for. When Cathy decided to throw one, she'd send word around on transport trucks, and the half dozen or so relief workers would come in from the area villages to get drunk, stoned, to listen to new music friends had mailed over on cassettes; to shit on a real toilet, take showers—though cold—and laze away the weekend speaking English in those hammocks.

Bamba helped me park my bike in the garage, took my helmet when I handed it to him.

"Where's Cathy at?" I asked, looking through the windows of the great house.

"Cathy? The *patronne*? Cathy has gone to Abidjan. But she is due tonight. I am preparing to cook *tcheb* for her. Now that you have come, I will cook for three."

"You know how to make *tcheb,* Bamba?"

"I lived for many years in Dakar, *patron*. I make it well. I do not overcook the vegetables or season the rice too strongly."

"Leave the cooking to me today," I told him. "I've got an idea to surprise her. I'll make us a big meal. We'll have a salad and rice, and I'll grill some meat. Why not?"

"Patron?"

"Don't worry, Bamba. I can cook, too."

I had heard about Bamba from Ryan, though this was the first time I'd met him. "You'll like him," Ryan had written in a letter some time back. "He's weird. I spent two nights there and all he did was tell me crazy stories."

Bamba wasn't young the way most houseboys were; in fact, he was a few years older than I was. He was a Peul, as his tall and lean stature suggested, as his blue robe defined. A Peul was a strange choice for a houseboy; as was Bukari, Djamilla's father, they were proud, devoutly Muslim men who'd come down from the deserts of Mali to make livings as they could in the forest, scorned by the Ivorian tribes, lonesome in their singularity. They had mystical roots and spoke fluent Arabic. But Cathy took her own path in many things, as she did in this. Maybe she thought it was funny to have a nomad as a houseboy.

Inside, I showered under the cold water, laid on the bed in the back room to enjoy the chill of the electric fan on my wet body. Then I wrapped a *pagne* around my waist and went into the kitchen, where Bamba was cutting carrots on the board for *tcheb* despite what I'd told him I wanted to do.

I said at his back, "I've heard about you from Ryan. Do you remember Ryan?"

"The blond one who enjoys to raise chickens? Oh yes. He is good. Not all are good. But he is very good. I have heard many things about you as well. You are the dark one who does not come down. Sometimes to Abidjan, but otherwise always in your village."

"Is that good, Bamba? To always be in the village?"

"That is good, *patron*. That is your job. You are living in the forest, shooting many francolin. You are with the Dioula, is it not?"

"The Worodougou."

"Is that a people?"

"It is."

"And why have you come this time, *patron*?"

"To see Cathy."

"Cathy?"

"Yes, Cathy. She came and visited me. Now I've come to salute her. Isn't that the way?"

"It is, *patron*. It is as you say. One visit must be honored with another. So that is very good."

"I want to make a meal for her. Will you help me? My clothes are dirty, too. Can I pay you to wash them? I'd like to have clean clothes before she gets here, a haircut, if there's time."

"You don't have to pay me to wash them, *patron*. I will do it just now. It is my job, and it is nothing."

"Is Cathy a good *patronne* to you?" I asked, thinking of her now as I had been on the ride.

"Cathy is an excellent *patronne*. Very honest. Very respectful of African ways."

"She's a good girl." I nodded and folded my arms.

"She is coming soon. Then you will be very pleased to see her," he said, and winked over his shoulder.

"What do you know about it?" I blushed and said.

"Oh, *patron,*" he said, and smiled. "I am only talking. Words are good to fill the air. How can I have any ideas about business that is not mine to know?"

Bamba lent me a T-shirt and jeans, filled a bucket to scrub my own, and I walked the few miles into the city. Daloa had a real downtown—three blocks of it, anyway—Lebanese *chwarma* shops with their curbside rotisseries intermingled among the electronics and *mobylette* dealerships. I bought a kilo of marinated *halal* beef in one, salad vegetables from another, made a few purchases in the sparsely stocked grocery; spreading money around, always a good idea when you stood out the way I did. There were even a few white people around on the bustling streets—three of them, in fact—two fat Lebanese men smoking cigars outside their hardware store and a woman hurrying by in her chador, a bag of onions hanging from her wrist. There were taxis there, too, green and rattling affairs held together by wire, and I took one back to the house with my purchases. The dirt and stones of the road showed through where the floorboards had rusted away, and twice it died and I had to get out and push so the driver could pop it into gear.

I planned on a meal of buttered rice, grilled steak, baked potatoes. A green salad with fresh tomatoes. Garlic bread. A bottle of French pinot noir from the Lebanese supermarket. Things I never got to eat or drink. I'd bought candles from a vendor in the *marché,* handkerchiefs we could use as napkins. And why not? It had been years since I'd sat at a table for a candlelit dinner with anyone, had any reason to.

Bamba watched me in his robe as I took over cutting vegetables in the kitchen, as I boiled water for rice and tore the lettuce. The afternoon sun streamed through the window, and I began to sweat like a real chef. Bamba said, "I have never seen cooking such as this, *patron*."

I stooped and lit the oven, waved out the match. "Think of it as learning, Bamba. You'll be able to cook this food for Cathy after I'm gone."

"This cooking is like exercise, like how the university students do on the field when they prepare for sport."

"This cooking is American. Like it or not, that's what I am, and this is how we cook."

"Then how can you say I will learn it, *patron*? I am a Peul."

"You can learn by watching."

"Then I will watch."

He watched me quietly a few minutes, and all the time I could feel him behind me, his arms folded, thinking. I knew that what he thought wasn't good. Finally, I said, "Bamba, aren't you glad you get to take the night off?"

"I don't want to take the night off, *patron*. This is my job. It is better if you let me cook. I can still manage to make a *tcheb,* despite what has happened to the vegetables. Please, *patron*. Perhaps take a nap? You are sweating very much. Perhaps you will make yourself sick if you go on."

"What will make me sick is if a tall Peul stands behind me all day picking at my back like a vulture."

"Like a vulture, *patron*? Oh, no. That is very bad. A very bad animal. Better that you think of me like an owl."

I shook my head, gave up. I scrubbed the potatoes in the sink. "Bamba, what were you doing before Cathy took you in?"

"*Patron,* is it that you refuse to let me cook?"

"Yes, Bamba. I refuse."

He sighed, closed his eyes, rubbed the bridge of his slender nose, seemed to resign himself. He leaned back against the wall, his long robe covering his feet. "I tended cattle in the bush, *patron.*"

"And how is settled life treating you?"

"Oh no, *patron.* That was many years before. Before when I was young. The next thing before was that I left my village and walked to Bamako. For some time I sewed *boubous* for my uncle, and then the next thing before I walked to Dakar and drove a taxi for my cousin. One day a whiteman engaged my taxi. His own vehicle was with the mechanic because his driver had taken it out in the night to impress his *go,* had gotten drunk and hit a donkey. Every place that whiteman told me to, I took him. Every question he asked me, I answered. He talked about his wife very much, about his daughters. He was a very fine man. At the end of the day, he brought me to his home. It was a very fine house. He was the assistant of the Belgium ambassador. I was his houseboy for two years. Then his wife and daughters wanted too much to go back to Belgium, and they left. He gave me a gold watch. Then I walked to Monrovia. My uncle was there. We made yogurt and were successful. Then there was the war. The soldiers took the watch from me. I walked to Freetown with my uncle. That was very good. We opened a spaghetti kiosk there. It was successful. Then war came again, and the kiosk was burned. I have a cousin here, so I came here. Some days I walked, other days I took transport. I had to go through Guinea and pay many bribes. My cousin had an omelet kiosk here, very successful. It was burned last year in the uprising. My cousin went back to Bamako. He left me one machete. I knocked on all the doors in the quarter to be a gardener. Cathy took me here. This is what I have done before."

"You walked all those places?" I said as I chopped the lettuce.

"Walking is what we Peul do."

"Such incredible distances?"

"I spent much money on shoes."

I nodded, smiled. "I once knew a Peul in my village."

"It is good to know Peul, *patron.*"

"I learned some Peul words, too. Sun, moon. Simple words. Pretty sounds."

"It is beautiful language."

"All the words I learned are gone now. Gone like the girl."

"It was a Peul girl that you knew, *patron*?"

"Very beautiful."

"And where did she go?"

"Home to her mother. I promised to marry her. But I got scared."

"*Patron,* that is bad."

"I know it is."

"*Patron,* I think that you are very much liked by women. Perhaps it is that you are liked very much by Cathy."

"Do you think so?"

"You don't know, *patron*?"

"I'd like to think I know. But Cathy is Cathy. She'll decide what she wants in the end."

"Is this the way with white women?"

"It is."

"And that is why you are cooking these things, though I am the houseboy?"

"That's right."

"Ah, then. Now I see and it is clear. *Patron,* this is very good. Very much it will surprise her and she will be happy."

"Are my clothes washed, Bamba?"

"They dry on the line."

"I'll give you some money."

"I won't accept it," he said, and held up his hand as if offering peace. Then he went out to take down my clothes for me, to heat coals for an iron and press them neat.

While the potatoes baked, we went out on the porch. I sat cross-legged on the tiles while Bamba kneeled and trimmed my hair with medical scissors from the kit inside. Something about him put me at ease. Perhaps it was the idea of all the things he'd seen in his life, that someone could undergo such hardships and continue on as he had. He drew my hair out in lengths, snipped it as cleanly as though he'd always been a barber.

"When Cathy leaves, whoever replaces her will have some village friend they'll want to hire."

"Ah, *patron,* this is true. When Cathy leaves, I will do business again. Already I am thinking of it. Always I attempt to make business." He paused the hair cutting to pack a short bone pipe from a beaded pouch with what I thought was tobacco, but as soon as he lit it, could smell that it wasn't. He inhaled a few times, released long plumes of smoke over my shoulders, traded the pipe for the scissors. Then his fingers again stroked my hair. "When I first came, I said to the *patronne,* to Cathy, 'All this grass here is good. Let me raise something, some animal.' That is what we Peul do. Cathy said to me that this was fine. So first I bought sheep. Three sheep. All my savings. Two ewes and one ram. They were small. Cathy said we must give them names. Very strange for sheep, but Cathy is the *patronne.* I name the ewes Aminata and Kadi. Very difficult to decide. So for the ram, I could not think of a name. I said to Cathy that I could not decide, and she said to me that the ram's name was Billy. So the ram was Billy.

"These three, they ate the grass, grew very well. I did not have to cut the grass any longer. So that was also good. But this Billy, his horns grew and curled, and then he became angry. Never had I seen a sheep such as this. Cathy had one cat. She called him Turtle. Then she had a duiker that her friend brought from her old village, when she was living before as you do now. The mother duiker they had found caught in a leg trap in the field. That one they ate. But the child duiker they brought here. The child was very good, very shy. I tempted him every day with mango leaves, and then he would sit in my lap as the cat would sit in Cathy's. So much like a gazelle. Imagine, *patron,* a duiker in one's lap!

"But this Billy. First he beat the ewes with his horns. All day it was running and beating, the house full of screams. Cathy did not like it. I tethered him to the wall. But Billy did not like to be tethered. He broke the rope. Then there was a screaming in the night, *patron,* such a screaming you could not imagine. Like a bat. Or a pig. We came running with flashlights. It was the cat. He was lying just here. His neck was broken. Still Billy was beating him. After I tied the crazy sheep, Cathy said to me, 'What must we do about this cat?' I said to her, 'We must kill the cat, *patronne.*' She was very much sad. How to kill it so that she would not be sad? I took an iron pole from the shed, but Cathy said no. She had been petting this cat very much, always in her lap. She said she must be the one who must kill it. She filled a bucket with water. She put the cat in a plastic bag, put it in the water. She held it down with her hands, crying very much. The cat was fighting so that I wanted to cover my ears. Then the cat was dead. But Cathy poked the bag with a stick, tore it, and the cat came out. It was not dead. It was wet like a rat, screaming, the neck broken like this. Horrible, *patron.* Then I killed it with the iron pole."

What could I do but listen, lethargic from the smoke, from Bamba's fingers in my hair.

"Soon this Billy broke that rope also. He killed the ewes, the child duiker. We woke in the morning and the bodies were on the grass. Billy was eating beside them. Imagine, *patron.* All my money.

"Cathy said to me, 'I don't care, Bamba. Billy must go.' But I said to her, 'Billy is very bad, but he is also like my cat.' Cathy said to me one last chance. I tied this Billy to the water pipe. The water pipe was very strong. In the morning, water was everywhere here, like a fountain. The pipe was broken. Billy was eating grass. This pipe cost much money to repair. Cathy said that Billy must go. But I could not kill him. So I sold him in the market and lost much money. Then I cried as Cathy had."

"That's a terrible story."

"*Patron,* that is not all. I took the money from Billy and purchased rabbits. You see how the grass is, good for sheep, but also good for rabbits. I purchased five rabbits. I did not know if they were male rabbits or female rabbits. In one month, there were twenty rabbits. In two months, there were thirty. Then there were rabbits in Cathy's shoes, in the kitchen cabinets, under the beds. They made so much mess, all day I was sweeping. Cathy said to me, 'Bamba, you must butcher some of these rabbits.' I fed them every day from my hands. But the *patronne* is the *patronne.* I took one by the ears, killed it with a hammer. Then I was crying. Allah, it was too difficult for me. I paid a Gouro boy to butcher the rabbits. Each time, I waited inside my room. I lost more money, paying this boy to do this silly thing that I could not. Cathy was very much upset. She said to me, 'Bamba, why did you decide to raise rabbits if you can't kill them?' I said to her, 'I am sorry. I did not know that I could not.' Cathy saw that I was losing much money, so she gave the boy 20,000 CFA of her own to come now and again and butcher the rabbits. Then we went to the market, and while we were away, he butchered them all. Cathy was very mad. But the boy said to her, 'Why have you paid me so much money if not to butcher all the rabbits?' She said to him, 'Now and again. Now and again.' Then he said, 'Ah.'

"What to do with so many rabbits, so much meat? We had to give them away to the neighbors. The neighbors were pleased, but we were not. Then the boy came again. He had gone into the latrine at his parents' compound. The cement had broken and he had fallen in. One hour he spent there. Then his brother let down a rope. He came out, but the money remained down. He used all his father's soap to take away the smell. He said to Cathy that she must give him money for soap. What could she do?

"Very strange things at this house, *patron.* Not good or bad, but very strange. Now my money is gone. Life is not to be understood."

I had moved to lie in a hammock in the telling of Bamba's stories, and he had swept together the clippings of my hair with his hands, burned them with a match so that no one could take them to work magic against me, as was the way. It was a calm evening, and as I'd listened, I'd grown drowsy, felt I could lie there forever. "Set the table, Bamba, won't you," I said, the darkness settling down. "If Cathy gets here soon, it would be a shame if we weren't ready."

"As you wish, *patron*. Cathy will be very pleased. Too often she is here with only me. Too much with the violence we are always inside. It is not good to be so much away from one's own people. It is the sort of thing known to make one strange."

The table looked romantic on the porch where Bamba had set it, the candles burning straight. As I lay in the hammock waiting for Cathy, he came and sat on a mat beside me. He was a tall man, lean and well boned, his blue robe handsome around him. I imagined him astride a camel, sitting like this under Mali's desert moon.

"And what about you, Bamba? Will you one day go home and buy a wife?"

"Buy a wife, *patron*? Oh, no. After so much time near white people, that is a thing I can no longer do." He touched a match to his pipe, drew on it, exhaled a slow plume. "To see the world is very good. But to see the world is also to change."

"And a family, Bamba?"

"A family, *patron*?"

There was a clamoring at the door and we both hurried out to it. It was Cathy, her arms heavy with packages. "Take the packages, Bamba," I told him. He carried them into the house in his sandals.

"Jack? Jack, what are you doing here?"

If I thought that we'd embrace at this meeting, we didn't. Perhaps it was the long trip up from Abidjan on the bus. But perhaps it was something else. Cathy looked very good in a blouse and jeans; she'd had her hair braided since I'd last seen her, her face was colored with sun.

"Did something happen in Abidjan?" I asked from across the table as we waited for Bamba to come from the kitchen with the food.

"Nothing happened in Abidjan, Jack."

"Then you must be tired."

"I'm not tired."

"It's good to see you, Cathy," I said, trying still.

"Jack, what are you doing? Why have you come here and done all this?"

I looked at my fingers holding the stem of my wineglass as Bamba came with the last steaming trays, and then, to do something, I lifted up the bottle that had spent the afternoon breathing. I reached across to pour for Cathy, but she covered her glass with her hand. The candlelight sparkled in her eyes, and she was beautiful.

"You don't want wine?"

"Bamba's a Muslim. He doesn't drink."

I held the bottle in my hand, wanted to say, 'What does Bamba matter?' Then I looked at him where he stood waiting to attend to us in his robe. For the first time, I understood how handsome he was.

"Jack," Cathy said, "there was no way to send word to

you, even if I'd thought I'd had to. I didn't plan it. Neither of us did. It just happened. Things happen like this."

"I will serve," Bamba said.

"Sit down, Bamba," I said, taking the spoon from him. As I filled their plates, I said softly, "You both know that I'm sorry."

For a long while, we were quiet, as though wondering what to do now. But the food was good, and as we ate, I let the embarrassment pass from me. Finally, I laughed aloud, shook my head, and looked up from my plate to see them blushing. What was left but to be happy, to share food, to sit together in friendship, to be glad that life was just the way it was, and that here now for a change, people were getting it right.

WU DIDI

Wu's story was simple: He'd come to West Africa from Shanghai in search of a better life. Chinese herbalists had established themselves in the major cities over the past decade; Wu's cousin was one of these, and he brought Wu over. Nearly every major and minor city of Ivory Coast had a Chinese herbalist but Séguéla. So Wu, with the help of his cousin, set up his practice there.

For the first few months, he didn't do anything but hire a local teacher to tutor him in the rudiments of West African French, and spend piles of his cousin's CFA entertaining the city's functionaries in the bars. Then he hung his shingle in the marketplace, and the patients began to come. Mostly they were soldiers and teachers who had contracted venereal diseases from the local prostitutes. They knew their names would get out if they went to the town's hospital, so instead they went to Wu and he cured them with acupuncture and erythromycin. Even the two Ivorian doctors came in now and again with embarrassing rashes. On weekends, Wu would ride his *mobylette* into the villages and treat the chiefs and their sons for these same maladies, at prorated village prices. His practice thrived, and, soon enough, he was able to send to China for his wife and son.

Wu became my friend out of the necessity of our foreignness, and in bits and pieces over the years, he revealed to me the totality of his misfortunes. I'd seen the wife around before I'd ever gotten to know Wu, was always surprised by the sight of that petite Chinese woman in a tight pink wrap mincing about the crowded Séguéla market on clogs that kept her elevated above the fish heads and mud, a pink parasol opened above her head like a flower to protect her from the sun. In her wraps, she was as decorous as a rose in brambles. Wherever she went, she was followed by a long train of market children singing, "Chinese woman! Chinese woman!" and by mangy and homeless dogs who were attracted, perhaps, by her strange scent. I was glad to see her because not only did her presence in that obscure market give me a pleasant shock but, also, she was even more alien there than I was. Whenever we'd cross paths, the children who'd been following me shouting, "Whiteman! Whiteman!" would abandon me to join her entourage. I understood that her life in Africa must have been hell.

"Peiching hated it here," Wu told me the night he revealed that part of the story. We were in his house drinking warm beer, playing poker for the shrimp tails that remained from our dinner. At that time, Wu was utterly alone, his house big and empty around him. "Everywhere she went, the children followed. In the market, the women always wanted to touch her skin. I hired a tutor to teach her French, but she never picked it up. Not one word. Her heart was in China. When

Wen died, she was ruined. A few months later, she went home."

Wu showed me pictures of his wedding. Outside, it was a rainy night, and, for a change, Séguéla was quiet. When they were married, they had both been poor students, and the best honeymoon Wu could afford to give her was a trip to Beijing, where they stayed with his relatives. The picture showed them in a garden outside the Imperial Palace, and if that garden had been full of the colors of the flowers of that long-ago time, they had faded, like the rest of the picture, to sepia. Wu looked thin and young, a cigarette in his fingers, and his wife looked shy. They were both wearing jeans, and if I hadn't known they were in China, they could just as easily have been a couple back home. Neither of them was smiling, but something in their rigid postures suggested an important event.

Everyone in China warned Wu not to bring his son to Africa; Africa was full of danger and disease; there were too many risks for a family's only child. But Wen and his father were close, always had been, and the boy decided to postpone university to follow his dad. Wu showed me pictures of his son, too, another time. Wen had been a tall boy, pale skinned and serious looking, his face neat and narrow like his mother's, handsome; someone the world would belong to one day. He was standing in front of a jade Chinese lion in a snowy square somewhere in Xian. He wore a heavy wool coat, military issue, and the snowflakes rested on his shoulders like petals. As he showed me the picture under the naked bulb of his room, Wu said in a quiet voice, "I took him here for his graduation. To sightsee. To celebrate. One child in China. One son. Can you imagine? In a world of rain, one single drop to belong to you."

For how difficult Africa had been for his mother, Wen took to it as though he'd been waiting his whole life for the release that it was. He was just eighteen when he came, and for whatever reason, the Africans took him in as though they'd been waiting for him as well. He played basketball with the soldiers' sons every evening at the stadium court, he borrowed his father's *mobylette* and disappeared into the bush for days with friends at the slightest rumor of a mask dance. He ate fried plantain chips from the street vendors, put away his leather shoes and wore foam flip-flops that he bought in the market. He went swimming in the distant Marahoué River, worked in the fields with people he barely knew for fun. In three months, he was speaking Worodougou as if he'd been born to it.

Every warning of his father about intestinal parasites, bilharzia, melanoma; about AIDS and the local girls, he laughed away. Six months after he'd stepped off the bus in Séguéla on a dusty Sunday with his mother nervous beside him, Wen had a local girlfriend, and two months after that, he told his father that the girl was pregnant. It had been the first hard rain of the season, and for the only time in his life, Wu struck his son. Who knows why? Perhaps it was the stress of worrying about the boy, perhaps the mounting difficulties of his own psychic isolation in a foreign land, perhaps his frustration with the corrupt Ivorian government, which always had a new document he had to buy, a new tax to pay. Perhaps it was all of these. Whatever the reason, Wu slapped his son again and again like beating him on that porch that opened onto the market, and even though it was raining, people watched this exchange between the Chinese men from every doorway, called to their friends, and laughed.

Wu said, "What sort of life will a half-black have in China?"

Wen shouted back at his father from the rain, "I live here now! I'm never going back to China!"

Wu ran out to grab Wen's arm, and Wen shook free, ran off into the night. For three months, there wasn't any word, and halfway through the fourth, a messenger came from the girl's village beyond Mankono, where the couple had fled. The messenger was a poor man in village rags. He never looked up into Wu's eyes as he broke the news he'd carried with him: Wen was dead.

As I looked at the photos of the tall and serious boy with snowflakes on his shoulders who was dead, I said to Wu, "What happened to him there?"

"It's Africa. Who knows what happened? Here, we sleep under nets. There, he was living in a hut. He wasn't on any medication. It could have been malaria. It could have been cholera, typhoid, plague, or fever. They could have poisoned him. He was dead, that was all we knew. It took me three days to tell my wife. Still, I know that she knew. She wouldn't talk to me, as though she was waiting. When I told her, she beat me. She blamed me for everything. A few weeks more and she went home. She said that she had made a mistake in choosing me for a husband. I can never go home now, do you understand? One child in China. The only possession of any value. They told me not to bring him here. Even if I went back, they would not forgive me."

My friendship with Wu developed cautiously. The weekends that I went in to Séguéla, I'd invariably meet Wu at the Club des Amis bar, beside the remnants of the Catholic church that had been burned in the uprising when I'd first arrived. For over a year, I knew Wu only as someone I drank with: the strange Chinese doctor who'd somehow ended up in this backwater, who chain-smoked cigarettes as though they were the secret to life, who wouldn't ever let me pay for drinks, as though trying to buy my camaraderie with them. None of the other relief workers of the region befriended him because his French was incredibly difficult to understand, and also, when they would come in to Séguéla from their villages, they were looking to get drunk in peace. I wanted this as well, but Wu sought me out. When I got used to his style of speaking French, I began to look forward to seeing him. He was educated and knew the world. We'd have long and drunken debates about Tiananmen, Kent State, the spy plane, 9/11, the bombing of the Chinese embassy in Belgrade, and the future relations of our countries. It was much better in the end than drinking alone. Often we'd go back to his three-room place on the edge of the market, drink some last beers that we'd brought with us, and begin to watch an old Jackie Chan movie on his portable DVD player. I'd wake in the morning on a wicker mat, under a sheet he'd covered me with, and for over a year, I had no idea that his wife had recently gone for good, or that his son had died. I also didn't understand that it was in his son's room that he'd put me to bed.

I'd always be embarrassed in the mornings to have gotten so drunk the night before. But Wu would put me at ease. I'd sit on a crate in the sparse kitchen and watch him cook noodles and shrimp in his underwear over his kerosene burner while he smoked a cigarette, tapped the ashes to the floor. We'd eat with the steel bowls balanced on our knees, chopsticks clicking and slurping loudly, which I understood was the Chinese way, and he'd tell me what teacher or other had recently contracted gonorrhea. One day, I would have to visit his sister in Queens and say hello to her for him, he'd tell me as we'd eat. She'd made it to America in a cargo container, now owned her own takeaway shop. He promised me that she'd treat me like a king.

"Let's go have a drink together at the Club, *petit,*" he'd lift his eyebrows and say, but it would still be early morning, and I'd beg off. I was here to live in my village; I had to get back to it. Then I'd hop on a logging truck to take me out to the bush, and for the next month or six weeks that I was out there, I wouldn't think of Wu at all.

I liked Wu because he was kind to me, and because we shared our isolation together. The children called him "Chinese man!" and they called me "Whiteman!" We were both literate in our languages and liked to read. We knew that there really was a world beyond the hot and violent here. I had lost my father when I'd been young. Wu, I was to learn, had lost his son.

His trust in me had been building for a year, and I don't know that it was any one thing that finally made him decide to take me into his confidence. Perhaps it was simply time, but perhaps, too, it was his need to unburden himself. We'd celebrated my twenty-sixth birthday together at Club des Amis, gotten drunk, and at his house that night, he showed me

Wen's picture, told me he'd died, and described what had happened next.

We sat on crates, lit cigarettes. The news was sobering and I didn't know what else to do but be quiet. Then Wu looked at the cracks running through the paint of his bedroom's walls and told me the story.

Together with his wife before she left, they'd ridden the thirty miles out to Mankono on his *mobylette,* his wife sitting sidesaddle behind him, which was her way. The road was cracked and broken, washed out in places from the rain, and often they had to stop so he could push while she walked. The forest was all around for a time, and then there was the long and lush savanna, baobabs standing up in it like sentinels. His wife had never been outside Séguéla; she was overwhelmed by how primitive the few villages they rode through were. People waved at them, but she pinched Wu to tell him not to stop. Again and again she said, "How could our son have lived like this?"

At the girl's village, the chief and everyone came out to meet them. For whatever reason, Wu wasn't angry, and under her parasol, his wife didn't say anything. The chief presented the girl to them, and she was clearly pregnant. What had his son seen in this small African girl? That she'd sold chilies in the market was all Wu knew of her. There were dozens of girls like that. His wife wanted to know every detail of what had gone on here, and Wu translated her questions to the chief, to the girl and her family. "Where did my son sleep?" his wife wanted to know. The chief led them in a great procession through the thatched huts of the village, showed them one at the back that looked like all the others. Wu and his wife peered into the gloom of the simple structure. On the dirt floor was a frayed raffia mat, nothing more. "This is where my husband slept," the girl told them. She showed them a ceramic cistern of water, a small calabash dipping cup. "This is the water I brought him to drink. This is the stool where he sat in the evening." The girl seemed frightened. If the chief's heavy presence hadn't hung over everything, Wu felt that the girl would have run off into the bush.

Apparently, Wen's few possessions had already been claimed by the living. These were brought forth from the crowd and set at Wu's feet. There was a well-worn machete that his son had held in his hand. There was a tattered green *boubous* that his son had worn in the evenings. The chief barked at a young man standing near him, and the young man removed his flip-flops. The chief set them before Wu and said, "These were his shoes."

The village was a nothing place in the middle of nowhere: a collection of huts and the meager people that lived in them. The gnarled witch doctor with his staff came in his rough Korhogo cloth robe, looked down at his feet, and told Wu, "The boy was sick for three days. The ancestors called loudly for him. He was strong, very strong in his heart. But the ancestors called to him with hunger. He died in my hut as I prayed over him. He was strong until the end." The old witch doctor pointed to another hut, where Wen had died. It looked the same as the rest.

The chief led them out into the tall grass of the savanna. They followed a path through it until they came to a clearing under a stand of yellow and red blooming acacia. There were old graves here, mounds of stony soil where the earth had been pried open, turned, and behind these was another mound, the soil fresh and red, soft looking, not so old. The chief said, "That is where he lies," and he scattered rice onto the ground from his hand for luck.

It was a heap of earth, pebbles all through it like rough gems, no marker of any sort, already settling down to anonymity from the rains. "Why didn't you bring him into the town when he was sick?" Wu asked the chief.

The girl spoke. She said, "My husband did not want to go into the town."

"Why didn't you bring us his body?"

The chief said, "He prayed with us. He died as a Muslim. We buried him here in the Muslim way."

Wu gave the girl money, told her to come to him in Séguéla. He promised to take care of her. He promised to help her with her every need. Wu's wife took the green *boubous* and the flip-flops. The girl's mother ran out with a blue *pagne* and wrapped these things carefully in it. Wu rode them back to Séguéla, his wife holding the blue package close to her chest. His wife had stopped talking to him days before; he knew his life as he had known it with her was over. Wu tried to see the village, the land, through his son's eyes as they left it. White clouds scudded through the blue sky, and for the first time—and only briefly—Wu allowed himself to admit that Africa was beautiful.

Wu's story was known in all the villages, was known in mine. The only reason no one had ever told it to me was because I hadn't known to ask. A year and a half into my service when I did know, I asked Mamadou, "Do you know the story of the Chinese doctor?"

"Oh, yes, Adama. Everyone knows it well. It has been happening since you have been here." Mamadou waved his hand before his face in the night where we sat smoking on stools outside my hut. It was as though he was trying to ward off trouble. He said, "A tragic story. Very sad. Who knows what sorts of genies have their hands in it? Now the doctor wants the small boy. The girl does not want to give up her son. For certain, genies have been conjured now. Trouble like this must be given a wide berth."

It took some time for the girl to take Wu up on his offer, but after the child was born, she came to live with her aunt in Séguéla, and brought the infant to Wu every day. I had only just become aware of the situation at this time, the beginning of my second year. Wu still had money then, and he lavished it on his grandson. He brought toys up from Abidjan, colorful balls, a plastic dump truck, and he bought the girl Dutch wax *pagnes* and closed-toe shoes so that she might dress nicely. The girl called the boy Moussa, a Muslim name, but Wu called him Didi. I was never exactly sure what this meant, but I had a sense that it meant 'little' or 'small.'

Wu stopped drinking almost as soon as he had told me his story, and for six months I didn't see him in any real way. Still, his story was on the lips of everyone, and I kept abreast of it that way. When I'd stop by his house to inquire how he was, I'd notice those toys in the entryway, understood that Wu was happy, that his grandson was suddenly in his life, that his life had diverged from mine in a good way.

Time passed. The rainy season became the dry, the harvest masks came out to dance their benedictions to the ancestors, the people had time on their hands. This was the beginning of my third dry season in Tégéso, and then Ramadan was upon us. Yet again, I rose at the imam's call to eat okra soup with my neighbors by firelight in the darkness, gave up food and drink during the day, observing the custom, though I didn't pray. There was a prolonged lull in the violence that had marked those years, and I and everyone began to wonder if Ivory Coast would now be good again. Perhaps it was the irritability that the fast put into its observers, but just when it seemed like the nation had righted itself, violence broke out everywhere.

I went into Séguéla once the government took control of the city again, to see what had happened. It was the typical scene I'd witnessed nearly half a dozen times already: the soldiers' and Christians' homes burned, the *préfet's* offices looted and in shambles. Club des Amis was still standing, and the proprietor and his sisters greeted me with troubled expressions, warm embraces. The owner's cousin was the subcommander of the region's military detachment, and the heavy machine gun he'd had set up to protect the bar was still on its sandbags like a testament to how dangerous things had been. Wu was drinking in the corner. I was excited to see him, but he didn't seem himself at all. As I approached, I saw that his ashtray was full of cigarette butts, that he'd set a long row of the beer bottles he'd drunk on the ground beside him. His face was dark with stubble. He coughed and looked sick.

"Did you ride out the trouble here, Wu?" I asked him.

He nodded. He said, "They looted my house. Everything is gone."

"And what about Wu Didi?"

"My grandson? The girl took him away weeks ago. She only wanted money. She told me I had to pay 50,000 CFA every time I wanted to see him. She refused to leave him with me because she was afraid I would take him to China. I told the police what she was doing. She heard of this, and ran away. It's her family who looted my house. I have not otherwise had trouble here."

We drank a few tall beers together, but the drinking didn't help his mood. He was maudlin, smoking. The evening settled over us and turned to night, and Wu, his head lolling, wanted to ride himself home. Instead, I made him sit on the back and, one eye closed for precision, rode us there myself. All the windows of his house had been broken out, the glass shards lay in the rooms like litter. They'd taken his television, his bed, his stove. On the floor in the debris were muddied aerograms covered in Chinese characters, and bent pictures of his son.

We sat on crates in his bedroom, lit cigarettes. Wu had composed himself during the ride over. "Jack"—he waved his hand at the mess—"this is the life I've made for myself, isn't it? I came here because of greed, and this is what I've earned." What was there to say? Wu picked up one of the pictures, smoothed it flat on his knee, then looked at it a long time like looking at a photo of someone he didn't know. He said, "You call me Wu. Everyone here calls me Wu. That is not my name. My name is Chang. Chang Gochiang."

"Chang Gochiang. What is Wu?"

"Wu is a sound. Someone else's name. 'Chang Gochiang' is too difficult for them to say. My cousin told me to tell them 'Wu.' It is the same name as he uses. Many Chinese here use it. It is easy for them to say. Every Chinese here is Wu. But my name is Chang Gochiang."

I helped him sweep up, bought a cheap plastic mat from a night vendor for him to sleep on. I worried that he might kill himself, but what could I do? When I left, he was sleeping on the mat in his underwear, the pictures of his life in a stack beside his head like a pillow.

Wu lingered on in Séguéla after that uprising, became something of a fool. To the locals, he was a strange man from China with troubling stories circulating about him: a dead son, a lost wife, a half-breed grandchild missing somewhere in the distant villages. And to the functionaries in the bars, he was a drunk, a wretch, a foreigner who'd come where he shouldn't have, who had lost everything because of it. Besides, he knew too many of their dirty secrets.

Wu bought another bed, another television set to watch the Ivorian news. He'd greet me perfunctorily at his door in his depression as though our friendship belonged to a time he didn't want to remember, and though he'd ask how I'd been, he wouldn't invite me in. When I'd come across him in the bar, he'd be buying beers for a table full of rowdy soldiers, sitting close to the magistrates and judges in their fine suits like a sycophant, offering them tumblers of neat Johnnie Walker. His French seemed to deteriorate to a buck-toothed caricature of the accent that it had once been. When the drunk soldiers would egg him on, he'd arm-wrestle shoe-shine boys, dirty *fous,* mugging when he'd lose with bright smiles to make everyone laugh. Now and again, I'd catch his eye from across the bar, witnessing his strange humiliation. Then his face would compose itself for an instant as though he wanted to say to me, 'You know this is not who I am.'

What Wu did or didn't do during that time, I'll never really know. I had no power to help him, and even had I, I don't know that I would have. When I'd bring up Wu to Mamadou, Mamadou would shrug and sigh. "It's terrible to lose a son. But the girl does not want to lose hers, either. Shouldn't a child belong to its mother? The Chinaman wants to have the boy to ease his loss. But doesn't the girl have a right to her son as well?"

Other times, Mamadou was more reticent. He'd say, "Why must that girl make so much trouble? The child is not a normal child here. Here, his life will be one of ridicule. That girl will have many children. Why does she want that boy if it isn't about money? Better to let this one go to the life the Chinaman will give it, and keep her new ones, which will be truly black."

It wasn't a secret that Wu was paying bribes right and left at this time. It was rumored that he'd given 500,000 CFA to the *préfet,* an equal sum to the district judge, and that each and every night he had drinks and cigarettes carried out to the soldiers who manned the checkpoints in and out of the city. A half-breed child was an impossible thing to hide. Soldiers in plainclothes went to the girl's village, searched it, searched all the villages of her family. Her father, then brothers, were brought into the Séguéla jail one by one. They were fined enormous sums they couldn't hope to pay on the premise that their identity papers weren't in order. But no one's identity papers were in order in the Muslim north. The girl's relatives were tortured and released. If they knew where she had gone, it wasn't squeezed out of them.

Rumors flew about. Some said she was living with a Senoufo cousin outside Korhogo. Others put her in a Bozo fishing village north of Beoumi. The more romantic versions said she'd drowned herself and her child in the Marahoué, while the most outlandish said that a French dignitary had fallen in love with her in Abidjan, whisked her and the child away to Paris.

The soldiers promised Wu that they were closing in. These reports made it even into the villages. Someone had seen a little boy with tea-colored skin and Chinese eyes wandering lost in a market in Boundiali, crying for his mother. Another had seen the girl with the child tied to her back trying to cross the Burkina border at Ferkéssédougou. Violence flared up here and there as it would: Dioula labor strikes in Abidjan, Mossi lockouts on the great palm oil plantations. That war was inevitable was like moisture gathering in the air. Soon the dry season would end in great thunderstorms, too.

Sometimes, I would try to imagine the girl. Who was she? What I knew was that she had sold chilies in the Séguéla market, that she'd grown up in a village as obscure and primitive as the one I lived in. Somehow she'd made it into town, where certainly the streetlights and few rusted taxis impressed her; where she'd fallen for Wu's son, made love with him, got pregnant.

The flirting stage of their romance played itself out in a thousand examples every day in the market for anyone to see: the bored girls teasing the unemployed boys about their rags, their muscles that meant nothing, the boys teasing back about the girls' servitude to their produce, their illiteracy and frayed *pagnes*. The girls were skinny as plucked chickens, the boys said, the girls would tell the boys back that they had donkeys' teeth. All day it went on. And in the night, after meals were eaten and dishes washed, the young people would stroll in tight groups under the orange Séguéla streetlights, half of them burned out, and once in a while some bold one or other would look both ways for aunts or cousins, cross the street, touch an arm, grasp a hand, pass some moments in a shadow beside the loved one, too shy at first to say anything at all.

Of course there would have been stars in the sky the night they met. Perhaps she had said to him, "Tell me about your country." Or perhaps he'd said to her, "Do you know about my country?" An unmarried girl like her would have always been under the eye of her aunt and her aunt's household. For his part, his mother always home, Wen couldn't possibly have brought her there. Maybe there was a grassy place in the bush that she knew of where they could sit and look at the town's lights. Maybe Wen had made a friend who could loan them a room. Somehow, somewhere, they had gotten to know each other, fallen in love. They made love together then, the cultures that bound them finally undressed to their simple bodies. The girl soon understood that she was pregnant; she called Wen "Husband" when she spoke to him, and he liked that. His father struck him when he revealed what had happened; the couple ran away together. Did she imagine they would live together in her village like that forever? Or had she hoped to one day travel with him to China? Had either of them stopped to consider the complications that would face their child? Or had everything seemed golden and bright in the throes of their love and youth?

What I finally wondered was this: Had her heart been broken? Did she feel the loss of Wen as much as Wu did?

Wu came to my village one Friday afternoon when the witch doctor was off hunting and everyone else was occupied at the mosque with prayers. I was sitting outside my hut eating the season's last guavas, and some small children led him to me, running before where he followed on his *mobylette.* The children were naked, potbellied, crusts dried under their noses; they stood quietly a short distance away from us as though stunned by malnutrition and fatigue. Wu parked his bike, looked at me in my field rags, peered inside the gloom of my hut, grunted. "It's a wonder," he said, "that you are not dead, too."

Wu looked neat. He was clean shaven, his hair had been cut. The wrecked and humiliated man I'd seen groveling in the bars the past months had somehow been returned to the doctor I had once known. "I need a favor, Jack. I've never asked you for anything. Now I need your help. They have the girl in the Mankono jail. My money's gone. I need to borrow 100,000 CFA, a document fee. But I also need a witness. Someone must sign that I am Didi's legal guardian. No one in Séguéla will do this for me. If you won't do it, then they will release her and I will never have my grandson."

Of course I did not want to have to make this decision. With everyone away, there was no one to lend me support, to make an excuse as to why I couldn't go. There was simply a thin, middle-aged man from China who had once been my friend, and some naked children staring at us numbly, not even blinking.

For a long moment, I didn't say anything. Wu looked away, and the children stared at me like a council of judges. The sky was blue, the day yellow. I set down the guava, went into my hut, took off my field clothes, and pulled on my green *boubous.* I slipped my identity papers in my pocket. When I went out, Wu kick-started his *mobylette,* and I got on behind him. "Tell the chief I've gone to Mankono. I will be back tomorrow, *inshallah.*"

The children nodded grimly. The oldest girl said in her delicate voice, "*Allah ee kissee,* Adama." 'God bless your route.'

Wu waited outside the bank with his *mobylette* running, and when I came out, I gave him the money. Then he rode us through the dusty streets to the courthouse, and the soldier at the gate told us the judge was in the bar. At the bar, the judge in his purple suit was drinking whiskey at a table of soldiers. The music was loud and they were all laughing. They laughed anew at me in my *boubous* when we approached: a whiteman dressed as a Muslim. In a minute, the judge wiped his mouth dry with a cloth napkin, grew serious, and said, "*Bon.* Do you have the money, Wu?"

Wu handed him the stack. The judge flipped through it quickly, tossed two soiled bills of it on the table, then folded the wad into his inner breast pocket. He put on his mirrored sunglasses, said something to the soldiers in Baoulé, and then we went out to where the driver waited in his black Mercedes.

The ride out to Mankono from Séguéla was long and silent. Even with the air on, it was hot in the car, and the judge in front in his suit smelled of his sweet cologne: lilac. The road was red and dusty, the savanna wide and dry around it, a flat yellow plain. There were no other vehicles on the road at all, and in the few villages we passed, people stood up from their labors to peer at the car's tinted windows.

"You'll witness for him?" the judge said to me as we sat in the car at the Marahoué ferry crossing, the old bargeman poling us across the dirty river on the oil-drum raft.

"I will," I told him.

"Never in my life could I have imagined this: both a whiteman and a Chinaman in my car at the same time. It was very good that you brought your son to Africa, Wu. So many unexpected things this decision has brought all of us."

In Mankono, a soldier opened the gates of the jail and we drove through in a cloud of dust. Chickens scratched in the dry yard, and the office was bare and hot, a metal desk beneath a metal fan. The judge dictated to the gendarme at the typewriter, who worked carefully and deliberately in his uniform. On the wall above him was a picture of the current general-president looking just as pleased in his suit and sash as he did on the nation's postage stamps. Beyond the door was the hallway of cells. Now and again, a yell sounded behind it.

A photographer came from the town on a bicycle and took Wu's picture against the bare wall. Wu didn't smile. The judge stamped and signed the documents, then he called Wu to sign, and then me. The documents seemed ornate enough, colorful with the blue ink of the round stamp, and I didn't bother reading what they said. The photographer, a Dioula in threadbare slacks, asked permission of the judge to leave, but the judge told him to take another picture. He had me stand on one side of him, and Wu on the other. "A white, a yellow, and a black," the judge said, and then the picture was taken.

"Now may I go, *patron*?" the photographer asked, inching toward the door. Wu gave him some coins from his pocket, said, "One of me and my friend." He held my hand as the photographer took our picture. Again, we didn't smile.

The gendarme barked for the soldier to come in from outside, gave him the thick ring of keys. The soldier went into the hallway of cells through the door, and I heard a tumbler turn, a metal door creak open. Then the soldier pushed a small Worodougou girl in by the shoulder. Her feet were bare, her wraps were dirty, and she didn't look at any of us. Something in her downcast eyes said that she'd had enough. In her arms she held a small boy, who blinked at the daylight streaming in from the window. His skin was the color of tea, his eyes were Chinese, and his hair was straight and black. He was a handsome boy, delicate and frightened, wearing khaki shorts and a collared shirt as though dressed for an occasion.

"No problems now, *muso,*" the judge pointed his thick finger and said to her, "and you'll be free to go. Understand?" She nodded. The gendarme lifted the child from her by the arm, and the boy clung to her wrap, began to cry. He set the child on the desk, pushed the girl out into the yard with the stock of his rifle. Through the window, I could see him push her all the way out through the gates and onto the street.

Wu called to his grandson in a tender voice, offered out his arms like coaxing a reluctant pet. I thought for an instant that Didi would cry, but he didn't. Perhaps he'd had enough as well. The gendarme passed Didi to Wu, and Wu held the child close to him, petted his hair, kissed the top of his head. He spoke softly to the boy in Chinese, and Didi set his arms around his grandfather's neck as though tired.

From the window of the car as we left, I saw the girl standing alone on the roadside, watching us go. She looked like any of the poor women there, but prettier, a small thing in the crowd. I assumed she would cry out, chase us. But she held her shawl closed at the neck, and then a line of women in colorful wraps came with basins of water on their heads, and the girl was lost among them, and in the swirling dust the car had left behind.

For a while, Didi complained and kicked, and then he was asleep. Wu closed his eyes and held him, oblivious now to the bumps in the road, to the film reel of Africa outside the window, which for him was becoming memory.

In a few weeks, the photographer came out all the way from Mankono to my village on a bicycle to present me with the picture of Wu and me at the Mankono jail. I asked if he had news of the girl, but he shook his head. Then he tucked the money I offered him into the pocket of his shirt, mounted his bicycle, and left. In the picture, Wu and I both looked more severe than we did in life, taller. That we'd been holding hands didn't make it into the frame.

There was a certified envelope for me from Abidjan at the Séguéla post office the next time I went in, and I waited until I was back in my hut to open it. Along with the money, Wu included a brief note, which someone had typed in French for him. The Chinese embassy had arranged a visa for Didi, they would soon be leaving for Shanghai. "Things are good now," he wrote. "What small thing I could have salvaged from this nightmare, I have." He thanked me for what I'd done for him, wished me the best. If I was ever to visit Queens, New York, I must visit his sister. If ever in Shanghai, I must see him.

Time passed, the war drew close. Everyone was thinking now, about what would happen to the country, about what would happen to the village and how they would survive it. I was thinking, too. Somewhere, in the bush beyond Mankono, a young girl gazed at these same stars and wondered after her son. Somewhere in a tenement in Shanghai, a boy grew taller each day, learned better in a new language how to articulate to his grandfather his needs now for rice, for candy, for juice, for toys, and soon enough, for his father, as well as his mother.

SOGBO'S WIFE

I remember a fight in the village. This was on a harvest night when the moon was full like a great silver coin, and the tall mask—the stilt-walker—had appeared in the witch doctor's compound, fortune-telling for rice and change, then dancing to the young men's drums, turning and leaping on those stilts like a great crane. Later, after the second harvest was stored in the granaries and the hot and dry *harmattan* wind had begun to blow, the leopard and crocodile masks would moan in the night, crawling on their bellies in the light of the great bonfire like beasts scenting the air for flesh, but this night, the moon was round, the land was moist, the first rice and cassava had been gathered, and the tall mask had made everyone happy. There would be a short lull in the field work now, and the sense of ease and festivity was general.

Perhaps for this reason, Gaussou, Bébé's arrogant older brother, thought to pay a visit to his third wife, the new one he'd taken as part of a debt settlement between his father and hers. Gaussou hadn't yet expressed much interest in the new girl. She was skinny like a chicken, her nose was thin, her eyes were narrow, and her teeth were set tightly in her mouth so her face resembled a beak. Gaussou often complained about this to anyone who would listen. But the air of the times was light, and perhaps he thought, Why not? She's terribly ugly, but she's my wife after all. Why not perform my duty and allow her the honors of a married woman?

Long after everyone else had gone to bed, Gaussou roused himself, went and pushed on the door of her hut, was surprised to find it latched. He put his ear to the planks to hear if she was sleeping. He heard moans instead. His wife was giving pleasure to herself! With a carrot or slender sweet potato, women in need were rumored to do this. But what a waste of life energy, what an insult to the ancestors! If only he had known, he would have come to her hut more regularly. Yes, the girl was ugly. But what did that matter in the face of duty?

Gaussou listened more intently, grew aroused at the sounds his new wife was making. He imagined her writhing on her mat, the carrot between her legs. Her plastic bridal beads were white as cowries around her hips, and it was only in this way that Gaussou finally understood the great beauty of his third wife's long thighs, supple belly. He parted his evening wrap, took his erection in his hand. Yes, this was a great sin, too, but listening to the girl moan, he could not help it. Suddenly, he was on the verge of eruption. He shouldered in the door, stripped off his wrap and said, "Remove the carrot, wife! I am going to possess you."

In the darkness of her hut, he fell on her to mount her, thrust his penis vigorously between her legs. A male voice yelped: Gaussou was prodding the buttocks of the boy who was fucking his wife. All three tumbled apart, found their feet, ran out of the hut. For their part, the lovers, anxious in their hearts already, assumed they were under attack by a genie. Gaussou, for his part, understood instantly that his name had been ruined beyond repair: Not only had he been cuckolded, but his *mogo* had touched another man's anus. Naked, he began to beat the boy, and after taking a few blows, the boy began to fight back. He was the blacksmith's fourth son, and his arms were muscled from endless hours turning the bellows' crank. The wife, Shwalimar, began to scream at the top of her lungs, because, at times like these, everyone must do something.

We all ran out into the silver moonlight at the commotion. Newly roused from my dreams, I had the impression that the village was covered in snow. People were in all states of disarray and dress: Women were bare breasted, men wore only sleeping shorts. Even I was nearly nude; my chest bare, my long legs bare. No one stopped to take in the sight of me.

I have rarely seen anything so vicious. We were humbled, quieted, by the fury with which the men fought. How strange, how awesome to see the primal rage of two furious men who weren't wearing any clothes. Gaussou's brothers jumped in, hitting the boy repeatedly in the face until it leaked like a cracked melon, a swollen mass of liver. Then the blacksmith's sons arrived, and the fight was a general rumble of elbows and grunts, of locked forearms and teeth. In the moonlight, it was like looking at a living field of marble statues, hoplites, in battle. The night was punctuated with the root consonants of human language: chokes and shouts. The women of the two families scratched each other's faces, pulled hair; soon men punched women, women leaped on and bit men. Even the dogs snarled and cursed.

The chief's sons came running with braided cattle whips, cracking them in the night, applying lashes liberally, and the melee began to be subdued. But then even the chief's sons fell into a lust for it. Soon they were running about, whipping people who hadn't been involved. It was pandemonium, people running in circles at three in the morning, the whips cracking like the end of the world. Then the chief himself arrived with his staff, his withered limbs. With a voice much louder than that body had a right to produce, he shouted, *"A bana! A man-yee! Dougoutigi a nah! A bana! An Allah a nua laka?"* 'It's finished! Evil people, your chief is before you. Would you open God's eyes onto us?'

Of course there was a history to it, not between the boy and Gaussou per se, but between this man and that, this old woman and her neighbor, between old lovers, or the parents who had sold your true love to someone else for two chickens and a wicker hat. There were always lingering debts, festering for generations. It was life in the village.

In the end, the boy was driven into the forest then and there, naked as he was, banished to whatever village would take him for two years on pain of death. The girl was carried into the forest by her husband's women, her vagina stuffed with chili peppers. And Gaussou received kola nuts and a red hen from the blacksmith in compensation for his shame, though this would never be enough. When we'd see him walking to his hut in the evening, alone as all men are, Mamadou would swallow a mouthful of rice and whisper, "Remove the carrot, wife."

This was my last year in Tégéso, and soon a war would ruin that place and separate me from it forever, but then, that time was my favorite. I spoke the language, I practiced the customs as well as I ever would, and I lived in the village as a member of it. I was a man and a hunter. I'd grown my own fields, proven myself to the Worodougou in every way I thought I could. The reason I had come to the village—to find clean drinking water—felt like an old and confusing dream. I had gone here and there with Mamadou and taught people about AIDS, but really, I was simply there, my heart beating, my lungs taking in air, growing older as the sun rose and fell. I wondered if I had AIDS. The stars looked so wonderful to me at night. One day, maybe soon, I would take my place among them.

One afternoon, the witch doctor and I went hunting for mongoose, which we both liked to eat. We crawled into a dense thicket in the forest where the leaf litter was a damp and warm humus, full of worms and grubs: what mongooses liked to eat. We sat with our backs to an old termite mound, held our shotguns, waited. The hours turned toward evening, and nothing came. The sun set, and still we stayed where we were. Then in the dark of night, I heard the flick of his lighter, smelled the cigarette smoke. I lit one, too.

"Adama?"

"Yes, Father?"

"You've learned patience."

"Thank you, Father."

"Before, I could feel your heart beating like a drum. Now you are like the air.

"Adama, I am old now. Things have changed badly in the world. The world has become more than we can understand. These days, I like to come to the forest and simply look at it. The people come to me with their ailments, fears, and I gather those things from them and bring them here. I give them to the forest, and then I go home to the village. I like to look at the small children eating dirt. Sometimes I take a pinch of dirt and eat it, too. You should go home, Adama. Be with your people; you should sit in your village and look at your children. Eat dirt. Gather your children's fears, take them to your forest, sit, remark at the beauty."

"I will soon, Father," I told him, and we crawled out of the thicket, followed the path home.

The first time I noticed Mariam was in her hut. Her husband was visiting the village from Abidjan, and like all visitors, what he wanted to do before anything else was meet the whiteman. His name was Sogbo, and he was nice enough. He worked in a plastics factory in the city's Adjamé quarter, punching out durable cups and bowls from a press. I didn't ask him about his life in the city because I knew what it was like and didn't want to make him lie: He lived in a squalid shantytown like all village men there did. Here now, he'd brought soap and a new *pagne* for his wife, held his small son on his knee as he watched me eat the plantain *foutou* and peanut sauce that he'd had his wife prepare to honor me. In the corner, his wife undid her top wrap in the lamplight, smoothed shea butter over her chest and breasts with her hands from a jar.

"You really eat this food, Adama?" Sogbo said, and smiled under his thin mustache.

"See," I said, whisking a glob of that great treat through the peanut sauce, popping it in my mouth, "I'm eating it."

"But won't you get sick and die if you eat black men's food? The whitemen in Abidjan, they eat this thing, *'chwarma.'* They eat this thing, 'cheeseburger.' Don't you need to eat those things not to die?"

"Two and a half years now," I said, and tapped my chest. "Still alive."

"And you sleep in a hut? On a mat?"

"Sometimes I sleep in my fields. When I'm hunting *agouti,* I don't sleep at all."

"Hey!" he said, shaking his head. "You hunt the *agouti*?"

His wife snorted from the corner. Though she was deep in the shadows, the lamplight shone on her moistened skin. She rubbed her arms with the butter, said, "Don't pester him with questions, Sogbo. It's you who are the stranger here. They call him *u-a-o fa* because he kills so many francolins. Don't ask him what he eats, where he sleeps. He plays in the forest with the witch doctor." She looked into my eyes in a hard way as she said this. Why had I never noticed her before? "Look at how he speaks our language. Look at how he eats our food. How can he be white? He takes off his skin and hangs it up at night. He's black underneath. He's a sorcerer."

"Hey?" Sogbo said, looked at his wife, at me, seemed confused.

I said, "The zipper's on my back."

He looked at me a moment as though not sure what to think. Then he bounced his son on his knee, smiled. "You even joke like we do."

I ate, sucked the thick sauce from my fingers as I did. I looked at the wife, and she at me. Her presence was all over me. Her skin was black and supple with the shea butter. Her breasts were pendulous with milk. We'd both worked hard in the fields that day and were tired in a way that her husband wasn't. I said to her, "Sogbo's wife, you've pounded the *foutou* as smooth as cream."

"I thank you, friend of my husband's. I thought of you as I pounded it."

"The sauce is as rich as honey."

"It was with thoughts of you that I mixed it."

"Sogbo's wife, I have eaten it all."

"I will rise now and prepare more, friend of my husband's."

"Tomorrow I will eat it, my friend's wife."

"As you say, Adama whiteman. Tomorrow. Tomorrow I shall think of you again."

Sogbo looked at his wife, at me, like trying to decipher this exchange, which I was, too. The wife looked down at her hands, rubbed the shea butter into her shins. Sogbo said to me, "You are satisfied, Adama?"

"For now."

"You are welcome," he said, and smiled.

I spent the next days close to him because I wanted to be close to his wife. Just the bowed presence of her as she served us food brought the blood up under my skin. Sogbo had left the village years before, visited now only irregularly. I could see that the conditions depressed him, that the labor of the fields wasn't something he wanted to do. But I honored him with my presence, and in that way, helped make his short visit a pleasant one. The men who came from the city went into deep debt to return to the village, to distribute gifts in it. The villagers had no concept of the poverty of city life, and so nothing brought back to them was ever enough. All that they could see was Sogbo's Manchester United jersey, his knockoff

Reeboks, fine modern things to them. I understood that these were probably the only clothes he owned.

"Good-bye, my friend," Sogbo said to me as I saw him off onto the logging truck that would carry him away. He had tears in his eye. "We are great friends now, and when you come to the city, you will come to my home and allow me to honor you."

As the logging truck coughed to life and raised thick veils of dust behind it, I waved good-bye at it, understanding simply that I would never see Sogbo again.

Time passed as it does in the village. In the evenings, after a long day setting up an AIDS lecture in a neighboring *campement* or uprooting yams in the fields with the men of my age group, I'd wash from a bucket behind my hut in the last light, pull on my *boubous* like a nightgown, and walk to dinner at Mamadou's.

Since Sogbo had left, I'd found myself taking a roundabout route. There on the east end of the village, I made a pretense of saluting the blacksmith, of asking after the well-being of his banished son. He'd recently repaired the lever of my shotgun for me, and as I'd sit and smoke a cigarette with him under his mango tree, I'd look across his courtyard to the next: Sogbo's. There, Mariam turned cassava *toh* in the pot with the long paddle, while Sogbo's decrepit mother sat nearby on a mat, watching. Sogbo's mother was an ancient woman; she often sat with her head bowed and eyes closed as though in pain, or asleep. I understood then that Mariam took care of her and the son both. Mariam's arms were long and strong, the skin on them without flaw. She never looked up.

At dinner, Mamadou would note the direction I'd arrived from. He'd often have his baby daughter on his lap, but when I'd arrive, he'd send her away and brush off a stool for me. "What's there, Adama, this new direction you've been arriving from?" he said to me one night as his mother set calabashes of *toh* and okra sauce on the ground between us.

"The blacksmith's," I said, and washed my hands in the water bowl.

"Even the constant dog is led away by a new scent."

"What's that you say, Mamadou? I'm not in the mood for proverbs."

He lowered his eyes to eat. Just as he was about to put the first ball of *toh* in his mouth, he said, "Women don't really satisfy themselves with carrots, Adama."

"I know that."

"And men don't use empty calabashes. Nobody needs to visit the cross-eyed blacksmith more than once a month. You know your way around. I won't say any more. Many things have happened since you've come. Now we'll see what you've learned from them."

I put Mariam out of my mind. Except one night, overcome by the image of her smoothing shea butter into the skin of her chest by lamplight, I lifted the corner of my mat and scratched her name—Mariam Dosso—into the dirt of my floor. Then I took an ebony leaf from the bundle the witch doctor had long ago given me to protect my hut, and laid it over the letters of her name. What good would it do? Could the ancestors read? Could she?

My dreams were troubled that night. I dreamed of Sabina,

dancing salsa with me at Legends in Abidjan before she'd disappeared, of Mazatou pounding rice and opening her wraps when no one was looking to tease me before she'd been sent away. I woke up in a sweat, pressed my belly to feel my liver in the dark. But my liver was not swollen; it wasn't malaria, for a change. I lay in the dark a long time, the thoughts I always had at times like these whirling through my mind: Who did I think I was? What in the world was I doing here?

The next evening, I shot two francolins in the rice of the chief's fields, tied them by their spurs to my belt. The nightjars were calling the coming of evening, and as a last thing, I hunted the swamp in the forest near the edge of the village. There was a large lizard that lived there: I'd long been eager to shoot him. The people called it *varan-o* and I don't know the Western name. But it was like a small crocodile without teeth, and if you happened upon it and startled it, it would whip your legs with its tail before diving under the water.

Here now, I crouched in the rushes at the swamp's edge, breathed, let the scene come to me. The evening light between the trees was blue all over the black water. There were gray stumps in the water like broken concrete pilings, and on one, its eyes closed, lay the *varan.* I aimed, exhaled, watched the air sacs under the creature's throat fill and deflate as it breathed. The meat and skin were prized. If I brought it back to the village, the children would holler and sing my hunting prowess to everyone.

Perhaps I had been there too long. I looked at the sleeping animal a long time, wondered why in the world I should want to kill it. I lowered my gun, simply looked at it. Why did this great lizard live in the same world that I did?

Nearby, someone was chopping wood. I circled through the forest and crept in close to the sound. I could stalk people even more easily than I could animals. It was a woman with a child tied to her back, collecting some last wood before returning to the village for the night. I crept closer and saw that it was Mariam. She thwacked the long ax into a dried stump, worked the blade free again with her foot. Her son was asleep on her back, and each time she raised the ax high above her head and swung it down into the wood, she exhaled like coughing. She seemed as oblivious to everything as her sleeping son. From behind the tree where I watched, she was Africa embodied, struggling with her work beyond the eyes of the noisy world. I stepped into the clearing. Mariam turned and looked at me.

"I felt you behind me, Adama. How long have you been watching?"

"Why didn't you turn if you felt me there?"

"Who turns and looks at danger?"

"Am I a danger to you, Mariam?"

She looked at me. She didn't seem frightened. She said, "I don't know what you are."

"I've wanted to see you."

"I've seen you, at the blacksmith's. Every night you come and look at me."

"Should I not?"

She didn't say anything. I slung my gun over my shoulder. I went to her and touched her bare arms. She looked up at me. She said, "Not here, Adama. Not in the forest."

"When I breathe, I think of you. When I sleep, I think of you."

"When the moon is new, come to me. The old woman sleeps early. It will be dark all over the village. Come to me then. Even after you go back to your people, I must stay here. When the moon is new, Adama. Then come."

I pressed her arms with my rough hands, was surprised at how soft her skin really was. She gathered the shards she'd cut from the stump, arranged them into a neat stack on her head. She said, "I know that you are a man, Adama. I know that the skin you wear is your own. Every night, I am glad to see you looking at me. Every night I've wondered how we would meet." She squeezed my hand, left on the trail to the village, and I lit a cigarette and waited in the swamp for the full cover of the falling darkness.

Mamadou said that night, "The old gazelle knows his way past sleeping lions."

In a few more nights, the moon was new, and after dinner, I went to my hut, made all my typical signs of retiring—brushed my teeth and spit, pissed a last time in the grass—then closed the door, and lay on my mat, waiting. I could hear the witch doctor's sons laughing around their hearth fire. A long time went by as I willed everyone to go to bed, and finally there were last coughs, and then there was quiet. I went out through the dark village in my bare feet, the dust of the paths soft like powder between my toes. Some dogs barked at me, and I hurried on. Even the stars were covered by clouds. Under her mango tree, I whispered, "Mariam, Mariam," to the night.

I heard someone trying to hide her footsteps. Then her

hands were on my arms. "To your hut," she whispered. "The old woman is sleeping."

I led her by the hand through the dark. Inside, I closed the door, lit my hurricane lamp. Mariam's son was asleep on her back, and she untied him now, spread the wrap on the floor, laid him on it. Then we stood and looked at each other in the lamplight. We weren't teenagers. We weren't in the throes of some adolescent lust. Still, we were afire. I offered her my hands, and she took them, stepped close to my body. She unhitched her wraps, let them fall; the lamplight shone warmly all over her clean body. I pulled off my shirt, undid my belt, and let my pants fall. I stepped out of them. I pulled down my shorts, stepped out of them, too. Her marriage beads were like pearls around her waist. Milk hung in drops on her nipples. What was there to say? We didn't say anything. For the first time, I held her to me, nothing between us but flesh.

"Hurry, Adama. There isn't time."

She looked at me, put her fingers in the hair of my chest, touched my stomach, wrapped her hand around me. Everything was a marvel: my body, hers, the colors of our skin, our desire. She lay on my mat, and I lay on her. I kissed her, held her face, drank her milk. I had a condom, began to put it on. She took it off me with her hand.

"You should be afraid of me, Mariam. I've been to the city."

"How can I fear? My husband lives there."

It didn't last long.

In a few minutes, she dressed, tied her son on her back, and I led her to her hut.

We made love everywhere. It was difficult, it was dangerous. But every breath that I took, I thought now of Mariam.

I asked the witch doctor for the leaf wash that would make me invisible to genies in the forest, shared the leaves with Mariam, and we made love in the rushes of the swamp, in the forest's dark glades, her son asleep on a bolt of cloth beside us. We contrived stories to travel in to Séguéla: she to sell onions from her garden, me to mail letters home, and when her onions were sold, she'd come to the small house I shared with the aid workers of the region. Melissa or Shanna, or whoever was there, would entertain the boy in the front room while Mariam and I made love on a real bed for a change, showered together afterward. The others had their own affairs. They were happy to help me in mine.

After a few months of this, Mariam received word that her mother had broken her leg back in their home village, Djamina. She told me as I passed by her hut, "Meet me tomorrow in Gbena." Gbena was the village where the bonesetter lived. I told Mamadou I'd be hunting gazelles in the forest beyond Soba-Banadjé, and he took it at that. I wound my way through the forest, found Mariam in Gbena with her mother. The mother's shin was swollen with the break, and she had to stay at the bonesetter's for a week. Villages kept secrets like this from each other, and after presenting the chief of Gbena with a bundle of kola nuts and a pair of francolins I'd shot on the way, Mariam and I were able to live there a week, discreetly, as man and wife.

Her mother was kind to me, and this was the finest week of my life in Africa. I hunted francolins in the Gbena chief's rice fields during the day, and in the evening, returned to the hut he'd given us, and a meal of *toh* that Mariam had prepared.

I'd hold Mariam's sleeping body in the night, imagine I was holding the whole of that hot continent.

When I returned from Gbena, I ate dinner with Mamadou. "No gazelles?" he asked.

"No luck," I said, and brushed off my pants.

He wouldn't look at me. I washed my fingers in the water bowl, and we ate his mother's *toh*. I pretended for a while that his silence didn't bother me. Finally I said, "What is it?"

"Don't you know what it is?"

"That's why I'm asking."

"Sogbo's my kinsman. We were circumcised together."

"What if I say I don't know what you're talking about?"

"Adama, you are my brother. You were like an infant when you came, and you have grown before me until you have become more important to me than my children. Don't you respect my name? Don't you respect our ways? Her mother-in-law has made accusations to the chief. Were you going to their hut after the village slept during the last new moon? Don't you know that old people don't sleep well? Old people are the bridge to the ancestors, are almost ancestors themselves. She says they've been speaking to her in her dreams. She's made claims against you."

"What did the chief say?"

"He sent her away. If it was anyone else, Adama," he said, and shook his head. "But it is you. Our whiteman. The old woman's gone to Wye. The only reason anyone goes to Wye is to see the witch doctor there. He is blind and has a white beard. Everyone fears his magic. You should be careful now. If shame comes upon me because of you, I don't care. But the old are old because they have learned to protect their lives. She needs Mariam to care for her. Be careful, Adama. You think you know a lot here, but you don't. Get medicine from Chauffeur. Do whatever he says. She's set genies on you. Everyone is expecting you to die."

I met Mariam in the hut of my old fields. The work had been too difficult alone, and after the first year, I'd let mine fall fallow to help Mamadou enlarge his instead. All around us, my old farm was a tangle of weeds and young trees. Even the old paths through it were lost in the surging reclamation of the forest. Mariam set her son down on the cloth to sleep. She lay beside me. She wasn't well.

"What's the matter, Mariam?"

"I haven't eaten in three days. I'm afraid of the old woman. I think she's going to try to poison me."

"She's an old witch."

"She's not a witch, Adama. She's Sogbo's mother. If I were in her place, I don't know if I would do any differently. Adama, I have to leave the village. If I go to my mother's, they will find me. I have to go to Abidjan. I've wanted to anyway. I learned how to weave as a child. I can go to Abidjan and weave market baskets. Everyone will buy them. All women need a basket to go to market with."

"And I'll be alone here?"

She petted my face. She said, "You will go back to your people. Give me money, Adama. Let me run away. I will write you, and then you can join me. I'll find a house in Abidjan, and when you come to me, it will be like when you came to me the first time when the moon was new."

For a few days, we kept a low profile. I went into Séguéla and withdrew 150,000 CFA from the bank. People in Abidjan were lucky to make 15,000 CFA a month, people in the village 15,000 the whole year. It was nearly all the money I had. I gave the bundle of money to Mariam in my field hut, and she tied it into her wrap. We made love one last time.

In the morning, Mariam was gone. On discovering this, the old woman let up a lament that brought even the old chief to her hut. No one—not even Mamadou—spoke to me for days.

For many weeks, the old woman and I battled with magic. I was constantly sick with malaria, and killed first one cobra, and then another, that had somehow gotten into my hut. After that, I visited the witch doctor of Kavena because I knew that Chauffeur wouldn't help me with what I wanted to do, and I sacrificed the black-and-white speckled chicken the one-eyed Kavena witch doctor told me to at the black granite boulder outside that village.

"It needs to be strong magic," I told him when I came back from the cleansing sacrifice. "I need to protect myself from her. I'm guilty of what she claims."

"It will be as strong as what you feel in your heart, white-man," the old man said. He tossed bones—antelope joints—on his mat, read them, then assembled a packet of herbs and fur drawn from the many bundles of them he had tied in the rafters of his hut like an alchemist's workshop. He wanted

5,000 CFA—about $8—three kola nuts, and six eggs to get the old woman's genies off my back, gave me the burlap concoction to bury behind my hut.

For some days, the old woman and I exchanged hard stares when we'd pass each other in the village, as hard as what we felt against each other. The whole village seemed to await the outcome of this battle, and everyone, even Mamadou, kept their distance from us lest the genies circling about our huts would think they were caught up in it, too. Soon enough, the old woman cut her foot while chopping wood for her hearth fire. She was carried to her home village, Kenegbé, on the back of a young nephew, and there, despite the Kenegbé healer's best efforts, the wound grew gangrenous, and she died.

After he returned from her funeral, Mamadou said to me, "So it's over, Adama. Good. But know that the bush pig who uproots a baobab tree eats well for one day. After that, he starves."

I'd be leaving soon because of a war, though I didn't know that yet. In many respects, the death of the old woman was my end in Tégéso anyway. It wasn't about the way people treated me. It was how I felt about myself.

Nothing I'd done there was what I had been sent there to do. Now I'd killed an old woman. What was the meaning of this? How had any of this love or witchcraft made my life or theirs any better?

A letter came on a logging truck addressed to me, Diomandé Adama, Whiteman, Tégéso village. On the seal, it read: *"Devine."* 'Guess.'

Inside, there was an address in Abidjan. The words on the paper said simply, "I wait for you as on the new moon."

I took a transport to Séguéla the next day, was in Abidjan within three. The address was in a squalid and dangerous neighborhood of Adjamé, and as I made my way through the fetid alleyways of tin-roofed shacks in the darkening evening, youths and menacing toughs followed in my wake. At her shack, I rapped on the door. Sogbo opened it. His smile was broad and open under his thin mustache. He said, "Adama! I told you that you would visit my house. Come in, Mariam will prepare a special meal, a feast! I hear my mother has died. I'm very sorry for that. But first I thank you for the help you gave Mariam so that she and my son could join me here."

In the corner, in the lamplight, she was spreading shea butter on her chest; unconquerable, unknowable, as beautiful and resolute as always. She did not look up at me.

COLORS

The times were ugly: massacres on the coast, massacres along the lake, whole quarters of Abidjan burned down. For two weeks, the principal towns of the north revolted against the Christian government, and the flagpoles that hadn't been broken in half by the people now flew the colors of Burkina Faso in declaration of a Republic of the North that hadn't yet had time to design a banner of its own. Businesspeople abandoned the country in droves for Europe and America. For the first time in my nearly three years there, real news of Ivory Coast made the front pages of the world's dailies.

Of course, the Republic of the North was short-lived. With no infrastructure, army, or export commodities to speak of, the north had no real access to foreign currency or negotiating power. We were all called down to Abidjan and put up in those same fancy hotels where the bellboys had long since learned our names. Behind us in our villages, the government sieged and starved the north into submission while the television station played music videos and the national anthem on a loop as though bedlam wasn't really happening. Half of the PWI workers went home. I said good-bye to Ryan. He was the last one of my old friends from training still there. Still I stayed. What was any different now from my first days there?

The voyage back to my village after the embassy sounded the all clear was what my flight south during the beginning days of this uprising had been: endless checkpoints beside piles of burning tires, search after search of my small daypack and documents by jumpy young soldiers who held beer bottles in their hands and cocked their weapons at the slightest hint of complaint. Where fires had raged on my way down—in markets, roadside huts, government outpost buildings—now lay piles of ash. The back roads teemed with refugees carrying their households in bundles on their heads. Everyone was wary and tired. The northern Muslims had been humiliated and beaten again. Though the land was fecund and green, the mood was gray.

Half my village came to meet me when I arrived on a crowded transport truck. Many of these covered pickups were rolling now: People who'd gone to try their luck in the city were coming home for safety, as empty-handed as when they'd left. Everyone I cared about came to greet me from the maze of huts of the village: The chief embraced me a long time, the witch doctor's sons quarreled over who would carry my bag, and Mamadou pushed through the women who'd come to touch my hands and welcome me home, to lead me to my hut with his arm around my waist. No matter how many times I'd failed these people over the years, they'd forgiven me. Again and again, Mamadou said, "Adama, you cannot know how these past weeks have been. Every day I waited for you. Every night I felt certain I would never see you again."

This time, I had seen dead bodies, body parts. I saw an arm lying on the side of the road in Séguéla, across from the great mosque. Bullet casings lay around it like gold. The arm had looked like the severed talon of a great bird, as much a piece of trash now as any dung pile or torn bag that always gilded the streets of that city. As for my own safety, this time I'd been concerned.

Outside my hut after unpacking and drinking water from my cistern to collect myself, I sat on my stool and considered the children who gathered in my courtyard to look back at me. Always, there seemed to be more of them. I lit a cigarette, passed one to Mamadou. We smoked together and let the past weeks settle over us, and the hungry children pressed in as though expecting a story. Who had the energy now to chase them away? Why had I ever done that in the first place? "Were things bad here?" I asked my friend.

"Not so bad, Adama. Not bad like other places. Everyone stayed in the village. When troops came by, we hid inside. What else could we do? There was gunfire at the Kavena checkpoint. We could hear it here. Some people took food and slept in their fields. Others stayed at home. Where was there to go? The teachers left again. They haven't come back. What does it matter now? What did it matter before? Many of the Senoufo have headed north. The cotton will soon be ready for harvest. Who will harvest it? We stayed quiet and prayed. What else was there to do?"

"It was the same in Abidjan. We sat in hotels and listened to the fighting."

"Was it frightening?"

"Yes."

"But you did not go home?"

"Here I am."

"Adama, dark days are ahead of us. Ahead of the whole country. All that was good before is now silly. All that was bad has risen up to take the place of the good. Now is not a time of sense. Now is not a time of men like we are."

My mother, in her letters, wanted to know why I wouldn't come home. Her words were urgent—almost frantic—and I could hear her voice as I read them in my hut by lamplight. What good did I think I was doing in such a dangerous place? How did I think I could help the world if I was dead? It had even made it onto CNN, she wrote, so I shouldn't try to lie to her about how fine things were. What in the world was I still doing there?

What I wrote back to her was this: I don't know what good I'm doing, and: I'm not dead yet.

Though the radio spent hours recounting a fashion show at the Hotel Ivoire, the high test scores of children in the southern schools, we knew it wasn't true. This was a tense, new way of living, and soon enough, as people always manage to do, we got used to it. The villagers worked harder in their fields, trying to put up more food than usual. Men regretted aloud now in the evenings that they hadn't taken this growing season more seriously. The mosque was full every evening, parents huddled at night with their children around their hearth fires, and the witch doctor's compound was a long line of people seeking magic.

I went on the unregulated back roads to Séguéla more frequently than I ever had. Many people were moving on them now. Whole families were walking; the smallest of children were walking in their bare feet. There seemed to be no sense to the direction they were taking: For each one heading north, another went south, east, west, all the directions. It was as though everyone knew safety lay at the end of none of them. At the PWI flophouse in the city, I called my mother every other week when the phone was working, assured her that I was okay. Sometimes I was scared, other times excited to be witnessing something I'd only otherwise read about in books. There was a glamour to it, a sense of pride. At times I let it quicken my pulse, though I know I shouldn't have.

There were eight of us left in the region, an unusually robust number that I attribute to the welcome our villages had shown us over the years. We bought newspapers, tried to follow the daily developments through the government's Pollyanna rah-rah. If a peaceful strike in a cocoa plantation was reported, we tried to puzzle out how violent it had actually been. If a temporary curfew for "security, peace, and wellness" was announced, we wondered what street fighting had happened to cause it. We drank heavily, told raw jokes in the Club des Amis bar, smoked stacks of cigarettes and grew sentimental about our villages and our African friends. In the fog of our morning hangovers, we mapped out evacuation plans. Would it be better to sit tight in our villages when the fighting started, or should we head south? Sean was adamant that we should forget crossing into Christian lands to get to Abidjan, and instead head west through the forest to Guinea. Shanna, with a wink, said Mali was a better choice because they had finely tooled leather purses to buy in their markets.

We knew we'd be targets wherever we went. Our only real decision was that we would stick together, once the war started.

One day when I went into Séguéla, I saw that the Lebanese hardware store was having a going-out-of-business sale. I hadn't had many dealings with Hassan, the proprietor, over the years because I knew that he hated Americans. After the missionaries had been driven out two years before, he was the only other non-PWI whiteman left in town, and the Africans assumed we would become friends because of that. Even Mamadou had asked me in the early days when I'd come home from market, "Did you eat with Hassan? Do you have any news of your brother?"

"Hassan is Lebanese. I'm American. We're not brothers just because our skin is white. Is a Baoulé soldier a brother to you? It is the same way with me and this man."

Hassan and I had one conversation early on. I'd gone into his store to buy batteries for my flashlight, and also because I was drawn to him as though we might in fact share something. As I'd passed him money through the slot of the wire cage he sat behind, I'd said to him, "I've just arrived in the area. With Potable Water International. I'm in a village not far to the south. I'm American."

"Of course you are American," he'd said, and waved his hand, like waving away the sentiment. "What other country can throw away money sending its people to live with savages? Let us not waste time. You want batteries, you are welcome. Come and buy them anytime. I thank you for your business." He was a thick man, balding, black hair on his hands and wrists; he was short and sturdy like a wrestler, the sort of build that explained how he'd made a living in this outpost. He dragged on his cigarette, punched numbers on his till; the drawer slid open, and he made change for me. As he passed it to me through the slot, he had something more to say. "We are in Africa together. So what quarrel do we have here? But don't think I feel sympathy for your Trade Center. Every day is a Trade Center in my country, for my Palestinian brothers. It is because of your country that I must live here. So we find ourselves together in Africa. A bad fate on both sides. Come into my shop anytime. Buy what you need. But don't think that we are other than we are."

West Africa, they'd told us during training, had taken in southern Lebanese entrepreneurs who'd fled their country after the Israeli invasion. Ivory Coast had the highest percentage of Hezbollah of any country other than Lebanon itself. Katyusha rockets launched into northern Israel were bought with money earned in shops like Hassan's. His lecture served to remind me that the world would be what it was no matter what I wanted.

But a sale was a sale, and I wandered about the aisles of the dim shop, looking at all the nails and cement and tin sheeting he'd marked down. The place was a warehouse, not clean, not modern in any way other than a whiteman owned it. It was empty inside because Hassan had a policy of allowing only two Africans in at a time. Still, he'd been successful over the years. No one else in Séguéla had the capital to offer the inventory of dry goods that he could. His guards with submachine guns were off-duty government soldiers, and he lived upstairs with his wife, who was never seen in public. Looters had been shot on the steps by those guards during the uprising. They'd locked themselves inside and shot through the slats of the metal security shutters.

Hassan called to me from his cage that last day as I wandered the aisles of his shop. He said in French, "What are you still doing here?"

"What are you, Hassan?" I said back.

"I live here, isn't it? Where else have I to go?"

"Don't I live here, too?"

"You don't live here, Jacques. You are on a long vacation. When the war starts, your Marines with their night-vision glasses will come and retrieve you. But I will have to stay. Twenty-two years I've lived here. When the war starts, they will loot my shop and eat me, these animals."

"You are nice and fat, Hassan," I said as I looked at the price of a sack of couscous. "Sometimes when I look at you, I get hungry myself."

"Ah, Jacques, perhaps we could have been friends in another life. You are right. Every meat tastes good when sprinkled with salt."

"I'd sprinkle Lebanese meat with paprika."

"Then American meat should be grilled with barbecue sauce, is it not?"

"Why are you closing your shop?"

"Why? Because I'm not crazy. This eating business is not a joke. They eat baboon and monkey. So why not man as well?"

"Haven't you earned enough goodwill here not to worry?"

Hassan grunted, laughed. He said, "We should have been friends."

In the end, I bought paint. It was almost free, how cheap it was. Red and blue and yellow and green; the colors of the lids called to me in the dark of the shop, and I bought them all.

Hassan rang me up at the till, took my money through the slot in his cage. He said as he pushed the buttons, "You can paint each child one color. Any color would be better than black."

"Good luck to you, Hassan," I told him as I folded my change into my pocket, checked the receipt. "Let's hope they can see the color of our hearts when it's time to look."

"Hope, Jacques? I'm not going to be around to hope. I learned that lesson once from your people. These people are even worse. I'll be in Abidjan with my dear ones when it happens. The Lebanese quarter is a big one. Let them come for us. This time we are ready. We'll be happy to teach these Africans what it means to suffer. We learned this lesson from you, don't forget. Good-bye, Jacques. Go with God in all you do, *inshallah*."

The twenty paint cans stood stacked under the eaves of my hut like containers of foreign-aid food. With the lids the bright colors of the paint inside, they looked like they held ice cream. Eager boys came and tapped the cans with their fingers, to hear that they were full. "Adama," they said, "there is enough paint here to color the whole village!"

"Maybe that's what it's for," I said as I wove shredded palm fronds into a sling for hunting on my stool outside my hut.

"Hey, Adama! You mean that you don't know?"

"Perhaps I do know," I said, and winked. "But can the monkey know the plan of the guava he wishes to eat? Do I matter in this? Only the paint can know what it intends to color."

The boys looked at me strangely, lingered a bit as though trying to figure out the proverb I'd made up to confuse them, and then they shuffled away.

I asked the witch doctor to fashion a brush for me in the morning, and he wrapped an *agouti* tail onto a thick stick with gazelle sinew. Then I painted the planks of the door of my hut blue. Not the blue of the sky, but the blue of water, clean water, the reason I'd been sent to Tégéso, the thing I'd never been able to accomplish. A crowd of children gathered to watch me work, then Mamadou arrived, many of the young men. As I stroked the bright color onto the wood of my door, the smallest children let up a cheer.

Older women pushed through to the front, chewing their lemon-root sticks like cigars. They stood so close at my shoulders as I worked that I could feel the heat of their bodies, their breath on my neck. "Oh, Adama," they said like moaning, "it is so beautiful. Paint our doors for us, too. Let us enjoy this color that you have brought."

In the evening, I closed the lid on the paint, wiped the makeshift brush on my mango tree's trunk until the bark was streaked in long lines with blue and the brush was clean. Then I sat and smoked with Mamadou, as was our longtime ritual. My blue door stood out in the evening as though lit.

Mamadou said, "Your door is very beautiful now, Adama. It shows how much magic you have. The chief has told me that he would also like it if his door was painted such as yours is. So would I. Color makes everyone happy. It is wonderful that you have brought all this color to the village."

"I should have thought of it sooner."

"That you have thought of it today is as well as if you had thought of it last year. Better. Now it is new and good. If you had thought of it then, we would have already tired of enjoying it. Adama," Mamadou said in a voice like whispering a secret, "it is not long now that you will leave forever."

I nodded, smoked, didn't say anything. We wore the stars on our shoulders like a spangled cape.

"I miss you, Adama. Even though you are still here, I miss you. All of these years together, you are not a whiteman to me any longer. You are Adama Diomandé, Jacques Diaz. You are my friend. This is the way that I think of you. To say goodbye to you is a thing I can't imagine."

"Mamadou, let's never say it. Life can be long, why not? Every dawn will bring a new day when we can hope to be together."

"I will hope that."

"I will, too."

"We will smoke together and hunt the francolin in the fields."

"We will sit in the night under a mango tree and talk about women."

"We will clear brush together and sing the working songs."

"We will watch our children play in the dust."

"Am I your friend, Jacques, though I am African, a black?"

"Adama. Call me Adama. Soon I will go to where no one knows that this is my name. Mamadou, you are not my friend. You are not even my brother. You are something to me beyond words. When I think of you, I think of myself."

"I'm scared, Adama."

"I am, too."

"Nothing will be as it was."

"We're going to have to change. We're going to have to become better men than we are."

The women lined up outside my hut in the morning to beg me for color, and one by one, I painted their doors. I worked as quickly as I could. I began with my close friends, worked my way down. With the four colors that I had, I was able to make each door unique. The chief's was a yellow star painted on a background of green, the color of Islam. Mamadou's was blue like mine. The witch doctor's was red with yellow dots representing the stars of his vast knowledge. On the blacksmith's I painted the yellow flame of the forge on the blue of the water he cooled metal in. On each of the witch doctor's four wives' doors, I painted various plants at the fruit stage of their growth: corn, yam, cassava, rice. On the doors of the chief's four young sons I painted the symbols of a deck of cards, representing their affection for the game they played together every evening, Huit Américain. For the tailor, I painted stripes, representing bolts of cloth. Weeks went by and the village was awash in color. Every night I listened with Mamadou to the news, to vague reports of trouble in Abidjan.

Working for PWI had become the major event of my life, though I'd done volunteer service before. Why this value had gotten instilled into me had to do with how hard my father had worked at selling life insurance, our comfortable life in Chicago, the idea that my Catholic parents had that life was about giving back. My mother, a schoolteacher, had spent the late '70s helping resettle Vietnamese boat people; my father always donated money to the Red Cross.

One of the first volunteer jobs I'd ever had was spending evenings with seniors at an old folks' home in Rogers Park, where we lived. It was a part of a work service through our parish, and I remember the antiseptic stink of the place that barely covered the shit smell of the incontinents. Every Saturday afternoon I went there on the bus and helped the old people play bingo. They wanted to touch me as I moved about making sure they recorded the numbers on their cards with beans, they wanted to grasp my arms with their cold hands, to make me listen to their stories. In many ways, being among those old people had been much worse than the worst times I'd ever had in Africa. But one old man I had liked. He hadn't yelled for me to come to him, hadn't beleaguered me with laments about his kids who wouldn't visit. He waited, months, saying hello now and again from his wheelchair, letting me attend to the others who seemed to need me more. Then one night, exhausted from listening to another old woman tell me a long story about how important she'd once been, how beautiful, I went and sat in the foyer under the statue of the Virgin, where there were poinsettias lined on the sills for the coming holidays. The old man was in his wheelchair with his oxygen tank beside him. I realize now he'd stalked me all that time.

"What do you think about all of this, Jack? All these old people whining how they're about to die? What do you really think about all of us pathetic wretches?"

"I don't know, Mr. Pociask."

"How old are you? Twelve? You're a kid. You shouldn't have to think about all that yet. Am I bothering you? Let me know. The last thing I want in my life is to think I'm bothering somebody. I know you work hard. I've seen what you do for all these whiners. I was in a war, Jack. World War II. The Asian theater. I fought the Japs. I killed some. I killed three men. Now I'm here. What do you think about that?"

"I don't know."

"That's good. That's better than a lot of people. It isn't good to kill. Not even for your country. Do you believe me? We fall for the bullshit when we're young. Then we do things we shouldn't have. Then we have to live with it, and then we end up here. Do you understand what I'm trying to tell you?"

"Maybe."

"Don't ever kill anyone, Jack. It isn't worth it. It's better to die. Do you believe me?"

"I don't know." It was snowing outside. I looked at the falling flakes.

"Do you believe in magic? You should. I'll tell you a story. I was marooned on an island. For three weeks I was stuck there. Then the fleet got me. I was lucky. Everybody was drowned when our ship was sunk. Good friends of mine. But I lived. While I was there, I lived in this village. Couldn't even communicate with the people. There was this pretty girl. I wanted like hell to talk to her, but I couldn't. I saw magic there. People flying around. Devils. But I was sick, swallowed a lot of seawater. Maybe that was it. There isn't any god, Jack. Do you understand me? Not any god in the way that people can say it. Not that statue or anything like it. But God is everywhere. Not all this hocus-pocus and knowing what God wants us to do and funny robes and prayers they tell you God wants you to say. Nothing as simple as that. You ever look at a candle when you were a little kid?"

"Yes," I said.

"That's good. That's what you are supposed to do. That's why kids stare at fire. It's magic. You have a piece of wood and it burns. Who says it's supposed to burn? But it does. That's magic. God. Water is magic. Look at it sometime, put your hand in it. Then your hand gets wet. That's magic. And that's God."

He'd gone on awhile like that, and I'd stared at the snow, the way it covered the walkway, the way it dressed the two shrubs outside until it looked like they were wearing coats. Then my mother had come in our car and honked the horn, and when I looked back at the lighted foyer from the window as she pulled us away through the snow, I saw the old man sitting there, looking at nothing.

But the other thing he had told me was this: The only proof of God in the world was color. Everything would have worked the same without it. So why would the world have been made so full of color if there wasn't a God?

It became my goal to paint every door of the village, so long as the paint lasted. It went on for weeks, and though I kept expecting people to get bored with it, they never did. The rowdy young men who never seemed to have enough to do wanted to help me, and though I didn't want to give up this task I'd made for myself, I handed over the brush and let them. Then I became a supervisor. The hag's door was painted, the griot's. Even the dwarf's door was painted red, as though in warning against the magic of his strangeness. In this way, I was able to spend time at each and every hearth in a way I never had.

People stayed home from the fields to sit with me as the rowdy boys took turns with the brush, painting their doors. They were old people and young: some were missing fingers from leprosy, one old man was missing both front teeth and his left eye. They wanted to know about America, and I told them what I could. Many of the oldest women wanted to hold my hand to thank me as their doors came to life in vibrant hues.

In the night under his mother's mango tree, Mamadou and I would smoke and contemplate the stars. It pleased me to see his daughter, Bijoux, born since I'd been there, attempting to walk now. It made me nervous how quickly she'd run to her father; when she'd fall, I was the first to leap to her rescue. I liked to hold her warm body. I felt proud of her for my friend. Often, she'd fall asleep in my arms, and then Mamadou would call his girlfriend from the fire she sat at with his mother to take the child in to bed. I'd say to Mamadou, "I haven't accomplished one thing I was sent here to do."

He'd say back, "The ant cannot see the road that waits for him over the next grain of sand."

I, like everyone, expected the war at any moment. I knew now that I'd be going home. Every man who had a radio walked about with it pressed to his ear, every rider who came into the village was greeted with ears hungry for news. I talked to Mamadou about how I planned on sending him a little money each month once I went home and found a job. "A letter now and again will be enough," he told me. "I am content to know in my heart that you are my friend."

After a month of it, the paint ran out. The cans stood in lopsided stacks under the eaves of my hut like the detritus of a party. It cast a sadness onto the children; it cast a sadness onto me. The witch doctor received a crate of guns from a Burkinabé rider late one night. He put them in the back of his hut, but we all still knew they were there. Who of the village would fight in this war? Mamadou had no interest in it, and, though I sympathized with the north, neither did I any longer. The rowdy young men came to the witch doctor's hut night after night, asking to see the guns. The witch doctor smoked his cigarette at his fire and said that it wasn't yet time.

It was at this time that the chief died. He'd been ancient from the day I'd first set foot in Tégéso, but something about the way he cared for me promised that he would live through the whole time I was there. He didn't.

It wasn't until he was dead that I understood I loved him. He was funny in his old age; he had always had a smile for me. When I'd visit him to honor him as was his due in the evenings before dinner, without fail he'd tell me some story or other, about the spotted cat, about the mole. He'd been another of the old men who'd been conscripted away to fight in Europe in World War II, though he'd never talked about what had happened to him there.

The village entered a period of mourning. The women shaved their heads and smeared their faces with ashes; the men gave up meat and cigarettes. An important imam came from Séguéla and sang an all-night vigil over the chief's corpse as his wives washed and anointed it, wrapped it in fine gauze. I shaved my head, beat myself with knotted palm straps as we walked in procession behind the corpse on a mule cart to the graveyard in the bush.

I was crying. I missed the man, yes, but I was also crying for Ivory Coast. The old generation that had known the terrors of war was leaving us. The new generation was taking its place, and all that the loudest among them wanted was that same thing.

The graveyard was nothing really, a cleared patch in the forest where holes were dug, bodies lowered into them. There were many mounds there, most tamped and weathered by time, weeds on them; others new like scars against the earth, the record of what AIDS was reaping. The chief's sons—boys, really—stood sobbing as those of us unrelated to the family by blood took turns jumping into the hole to dig. I wanted my turn, but had to wait a long while. Every man of the village wanted to show that he'd honored the chief on his last day. When it was my turn, I jumped into the hole in my ceremonial *boubous,* and Mamadou tossed the spade that the blacksmith had spent the night hammering into shape down to me. The hole circled my shoulders; the soil was rocky, red, thick with stones and roots. I worked until the sweat began to trickle down my neck. I tossed bladeful after bladeful in a high arc out of the hole, and even when they called my name to tell me that I'd done enough, I dug as if trying to reach another world. Then hands pulled at my shoulders, the spade was taken from me, and they caught me about my arms to lift me out. Soil spilled to the bottom from where my feet sought purchase. My *boubous* was filthy.

The old chief was laid in the bottom of the hole wrapped

like a mummy. Then the imam said a last prayer and the women let up a trilling wail. The imam tossed in a handful of red dirt and it soiled the white muslin. Then everyone tossed in handfuls of dirt to say good-bye, and the blacksmith's sons began to fill in the hole with their short-handled hoes.

"Now we have no chief," Mamadou said to me as we left the graveside. I walked back to the village, through it, out through the forest, and into my old field. That there had ever been a farm there was now impossible to believe. I pushed through weeds taller than I was and found my old field hut, sat under it, reclined, closed my eyes, let the faces of the past years whirl through my mind as I mourned my chief in my own way.

The news spread through the region, reached Séguéla, and the *préfet,* who had been driven out the month before by mobs, came in his long Mercedes to pay his condolences. Why was the village willing to receive this man who so many of them wanted to kill? But a thatch sunshade was constructed of palm branches, and the virgins painted their faces white and danced in a procession to meet his car. The *préfet* in his French suit and mirrored sunglasses was flanked by commandos with automatic rifles. He sat on the chair under the sunshade, and we each went to him in turn, bowed our heads, and thanked him for honoring our chief. When it was my turn, he said to me, "You are the white Worodougou I've heard so much about, is it not?"

"I live here with these people."

"And do you think you are doing them any good?"

"I don't know."

"Come, boy, help me with my jacket. It's very hot here in the bush. Hold it up so that it won't be wrinkled."

I held his suit coat as he shucked his great body out of it. For thirty minutes I stood holding his coat, and after being honored by every last man, he stood for me to dress him again, and the soldiers led him to his car.

"Why did we receive him?" I asked Mamadou in the night.

"To honor our chief," he told me.

"Was the visit of a man like that an honor to our father?"

"What is a greater honor, Adama, than for those who hate us to acknowledge what we've lost?"

"It was humiliating."

"Now is our time to be humiliated."

For one week, the village was allowed to drift without a chief, without any real discussion about a new one. Then a council of elders was called. They met in the chief's courtyard in their finest *boubous.* Word had been sent to the chief's eldest two sons who were away working in France, but neither of them wanted to come back to take charge of a nondescript village in the West African bush. The chief's other sons were still too young. A list of candidates was determined by the old men as we listened to their lengthy deliberations. Gaussou, Bobi, Chimokro, Shwalar; great care had to be taken to choose our new father.

The old men retreated to their huts to weigh the options. The new chief should not be so old that he may also die soon; he must not be so young that no one would respect him. The times were difficult, the list of choices short. People began to campaign and loud arguments could be heard in the night.

Gaussou was too vain in his heart, everyone knew, too

shamed in the people's eyes by his public cuckolding. But he was the eldest son of an important family and had to be considered. It wasn't beyond him to demand a tithe of yams from each compound in exchange for filling the position, to use its power for punishing everyone who had laughed at him. Shwalar was kind and old but knew nothing but growing rice. Chimokro owed money to many men in surrounding villages. Bobi, though strongly built and of the perfect age, had a violent temper: In his youth, he'd shot dead a Peul who'd let cattle into his father's rice fields. Bobi had served two brutal years in the Séguéla jail for this, before the old chief had finally raised enough money from the village to pay the Peul's family's blood money and buy him out.

Who would it be? Mamadou and I hunted francolin together in the afternoons, spitted them now and again over a small bush fire as we had on our travels the year before: It was as though we were trying to relive old times. We smoked cigarettes, lay back against termite mounds to gaze at the clouds scudding across the sky. Among the rowdy young men, sentiment ran toward Bobi; the fact that he'd killed a man had changed in these new days from a stigma to a boon. Many of the older people felt Shwalar was best in his measured and deliberate ways. Though he knew nothing of the world but the cultivation and growth of rice, weren't people also like rice in that they also had to be developed? Old Shwalar was closer to the ancestors in his respect for the earth, but Bobi seemed more prepared to deal with the times as they were. The young men wanted Bobi: Only a man like Bobi could see the village through the coming days of war. As we smoked, both Mamadou and I wanted Shwalar. What we really wanted was our old chief, but Shwalar was enough like the old man had been to keep the village on its peaceful course. Even as we debated it, we knew that the decision had been made.

The young men painted white stripes on their faces, danced in a thick group in the evenings through the village holding up their machetes like swords. Bobi was a warrior, they sang; the men of the old day should listen to the men who owned tomorrow. Old women walked about in the mornings, visiting hearths. Shwalar knew the difficulty of the growth of rice, they pleaded; he could guide the village to harvest. Neither man campaigned in any way. They spent their days at their hearths, awaiting the outcome.

The old men picked Bobi.

The rowdy young men had shadowed the deliberations with much murmuring, with menacing poses, and when the decision was announced outside the old chief's hut, they let up a cry to celebrate, raised their machetes. Some came and circled Mamadou and me where we stood. They said to us with their painted faces, "Tomorrow has arrived, older brothers! Regret that this day is not of your time. No more shall we cower. No more shall we bow before those who listen to the weak talk of women." A bull was slaughtered, Shwalar making the killing cut as though to accept the decision, and the old men who had voted on it wandered back to their huts as though what had been determined wasn't a thing worth celebrating. For three days, the village feasted, and girls of the last excision sought me out as a bachelor to dance with them in the ancient and rigid *pass.* They were like younger sisters to me now. Though I danced across the bonfire from them, I knew that none would ever become my wife.

During the days, Bobi sat on a chair beside his hut in a fine filigreed *boubous* the tailor had sewn for him, receiving the honors of the village men. I stayed at my hut and occupied myself with trivialities: scraping gourds clean for bowls, knotting wires into loops for *agouti* spring traps. On the third day, Bobi called for me as I knew he would.

I kneeled before Bobi where he sat outside his hut. He was a big man, bigger in his flowing robe. I knew him from exchanges we'd had over the years. He'd found it funny that I liked to hunt, often stopped me in the forest to praise the quietness with which I walked, to tell me jokes about *agouti* and francolin, to say that he respected my resolve in succeeding in the village. Why didn't I take a wife? he often asked. What was I really doing here?

"Rise up, Adama," Bobi said after I'd recited the benedictions, "you've saluted your chief well." He took my hands in his. He said, "Know that you are welcome here, Adama Diomandé. Know that nothing has changed. You were like a son to the old chief. Now you are like a son to me."

"I thank you, Father."

"Adama, times have changed, have they not? You see how we have lived under the Christians. Now another time has begun. The old chief loved you. Therefore, I will love you. You are welcome here so long as you wish to stay. Do you understand me, Adama whiteman?"

"I do."

Soon after, the young men came to the witch doctor's hut. They demanded to see the guns, and the witch doctor brought them out, stood on his stoop, and looked up at the stars. There were three guns, AK-47s. The young men pawed them like women's bodies, pointed them at the sky, shot them, though they were empty. Mamadou and I sat smoking outside my hut, watching this. Mamadou said, "When is it that we shall say our final good-bye? What will the world look like? Will there be a wind? Will it rain? Will we have eaten? Will we have thirst? How will you look in that final moment when you turn your face from me forever?"

Long into the night, the young men handled the weapons, laughing, passing them around, the firelight coloring their eager faces. All around them in the night, the doors of the village were painted in many and beautiful hues. They didn't notice this anymore, though they had been the ones who'd painted them.

PETITE AFRIQUE

For a time in Africa, I had a dog. My dog was small, amber haired, chestnut eyed, she had a white tip at her tail: She looked like a deer, a doe. I called her Jane.

Though Jane looked like the other dogs, she wasn't. She'd been raised by my friend Samantha, a gift to her from someone in her village. When it was Samantha's time to return to America, I rode on my *mobylette* the day's journey north to see her for the last time. I didn't really know her, had only talked to her now and again on weekends in Séguéla, but we were kin in that we'd gone through Africa together. I was dusty from my ride, and she hugged me at the door of her hut. Her compound was full of her villagers in their finest robes; the men on stools, the women on mats in the dirt. Her boyfriend, the chief's son, sat in a chair in the Western clothes she'd bought for him in Abidjan, and Samantha passed parcels to him to distribute to the people: her radio; batteries, razors, candles, soap. She gave away all of her clothes. She gave her toothbrush to a small girl who had been special to her.

Later, in a supermarket in Cleveland on the other side of the world, she would watch the store's employees tossing barely wilted heads of cabbage into a garbage bin one after the other. She would try to stop them; she would take the cabbage from their hands and try to put them back. Then she would notice her mother, with whom she'd gone shopping, her mother's frightened eyes, the customers staring, the store's workers, and she would stop that. At home that evening, she would unwind the long braids her village mother had tressed for her on her last day, which she'd worn for months in America after her return until the plaits were frizzy and unkempt, even beyond what she knew her village mother would have tolerated.

In her bathroom at her parents' house, she'd drop the *boubous* she'd been wearing from her shoulders, untie the hip beads her boyfriend had given her, look at her white body in the mirror a long time, fold all of these things in the silk of her *boubous,* place them in the bottom drawer of her dresser. She would take a long, hot shower. Even as she soaped herself, she could feel that her muscles were softening. Then she would write me a letter.

"They don't get it here, Jack," her words said to me by lamplight in my hut as children drummed and sang outside in the night. "If you want it to mean something, don't ever come back."

But the day she left, she had a gift for me: her dog. She called the dog "Denny," 'Child,' a joke against all the teasing she'd endured as a grown and childless woman. "Where are your children?" the village women would stop and ask her. She'd whistle to her dog, say, "*Voilà,* here is my Denny."

"She won't know how to survive without me," Samantha had said, and handed me the rope leash. "I should have gotten papers to bring her home. But there was so much else to do. I think she'll be happier here anyway. She's yours now, Jack. I hope you'll care for her as I have." The dog sat on my lap on the ride south. She whimpered, cast long glances behind us on the yellow road as if looking for Samantha, and I petted her ears to hush her. In Tégéso, I called her Jane, after a girl I'd had a crush on in high school, and she slept that first night beside me on my mat. I wondered how Samantha's boyfriend felt that night alone on his mat; how she herself did on the plane later and watching as the forests of Ivory Coast dwindled into a long and even green, covered then by clouds.

I liked Jane, enjoyed her company. It took a few weeks of hand-feeding her rice to make her belong to me, and when she did, she'd dash out like a yellow ribbon from the village as I'd come home from the fields, would tumble in the dust as her speed carried her past me, her tongue hanging out over her teeth as if she were smiling. Her body was lithe and young, and she'd nip my heels as though she couldn't contain her love.

Samantha had treated her like an American dog: She'd fed her boiled eggs and bits of meat, bathed her now and again, petted her constantly, and let her sleep in her hut. I wanted Jane to be able to hold her own in the village once I'd left. She ate the cold handfuls of cassava *toh* I'd place on the ground for her after Mamadou and I had eaten all we could; at night, she slept outside. The other dogs tormented her at first: She toughened, learned to snarl back; soon enough I saw her running among them now and again, hunting bush rats in an excited pack, being social apart from me. I didn't pet her because

Africans would not touch anything so filthy as a dog. Sometimes I'd even hit her to remind her to be wary of people. But my violence impressed her about as much as it had the children at the school when I'd taught there. Jane would whimper outside my door for hours to be let in. As I lay listening in the dark, I told myself that I loved her, that I was doing this to prepare her for when I would have to leave.

I could have made plans to bring her home with me. But I believed that Africa belonged to the Africans, worried often that my presence among the Worodougou eroded their traditions, and in my heart I knew that Jane should never have to learn a leash, a cage, neutering, vaccinations, sedation, a transatlantic flight; the cold of Chicago, the confined spaces she would live in there. It was better to leave her to run in the forest with the young boys, to the rain and stars and hearth fires and drumming for the whole of her life as I imagined I wished I could with mine.

Still, she was an American dog. Samantha had caressed her so she'd lost her fear of people; she'd taken her for walks through the village on a rope leash and tugged her away from the road when logging trucks would rumble past.

I went away from the village for three days. Maybe I was teaching AIDS somewhere with Mamadou. Maybe I was hunting bush pig with the witch doctor. When I came back to the village, some of the small boys were waiting for me, smiling. They were naked, dirt-streaked from wrestling in the dust. They took my hands and led me home. They said, "Adama, where is your dog? You know she is very bad. She never listens. A very bad dog."

"She's terrible, isn't she? The worst dog in the world."

"You know that she likes to lie in the road, Adama. We threw stones at her, but she chased us away."

They smiled widely, looked up at me. "She was in the road, Adama. Everyone yelled at her, but she wouldn't listen. A truck hit her. She is dead. The chief had her body thrown in the grass so that you wouldn't see. We went to look at her for you, Adama. Her body swelled. Then the birds and marching ants came and ate her. Do you want to see her bones?"

I shook my hands free of them. In my hut, I lay on my mat. The boys were shadows in the doorway.

"Are you sad, Adama?"

"Yes."

"Are you going to cry?"

"No."

"Do you miss Jane?"

"Yes."

"Come and see her bones."

After a while, the boys grew bored of watching me, drifted away. Between mouthfuls of *toh* in the evening as we crouched in the dark over the serving bowl, Mamadou finally said, "I'm sorry about your dog."

I nodded, balled *toh* with my fingers for another bite. Jane was finished like that.

The war began like this: The radio station went out in the early morning, and because this made everyone nervous, Bobi the new chief had the old chief's television fired up from the car battery they kept charged for that. Yes, the television station was out, too. This had happened regularly over the past three years. Still, nobody went to the fields. Every hour or so through the day, Bobi turned on the TV to check, and finally in the evening an image came through: five young men in combat fatigues and holding AK-47s flanking another who was seated at the news studio desk and reading a statement. The government had fallen. They were the new government. Everyone should remain calm. Then that image went out, too. The stars had come out over all of us in the meantime, and we blinked up at them. Who were those men? What would they tell us to do? A rumor had spread in the past week that a troop of forty commandos had marched on the highway toward Séguéla. That meant something, too. People began to argue, voices grew heated, fists were waved at the night, and then the witch doctor came and shouted at us to go to bed.

The television was out all the next day, and we occupied ourselves with simple tasks: the women cracking palm kernels for soap, the men weaving mats, sharpening hoes and machetes. Everyone stayed close to the village. In the evening, Laurent Gbagbo, the latest president, was on the TV, in a stiff suit and reading a prepared statement from his desk. He stuttered, seemed aged and nervous; he didn't bother looking up at the camera. General Guei had staged another coup. But this time he had been defeated. The country was secure. Guei was dead. His whole family: His wife, his kids, all of his bodyguards and servants were now dead. Even the cook. The government had won the battle and Ivory Coast would now be safe and prosperous. The president thanked God, said good night, the anthem played, and the studio faded into an image of the waving Ivorian tricolor. Then that went dead, too.

In the morning, men on bicycles came out from the path through the forest from Séguéla: messengers. They were harried and winded. Bobi and the old men gathered to hear them. They straddled their bicycles as they poured out their news. Korhogo had fallen. Tengréla had fallen. The Muslim quarters of Abidjan had fallen. Great and Christian Man had fallen! Berebi had fallen. San Pedro. Kong. Even Bouaké was now split in two. A great Muslim army had risen up to throw off the Christian shackles. The young men let up a cheer. The old men were somber. "And Séguéla?" the old men asked. "What of our capital?"

"Séguéla has not fallen yet. All around here there is fighting. There have been massacres. People are moving on the roads. If you have Christians here, kill them, or send them home. This land is the frontier. The rebels will come for Mankono, and then they will assault Séguéla. The military is all over the roads, in the woods around Séguéla. They are going to fight. But the rebels are coming. They will fight and win, and then we will be free!" The young men cheered. The old men held their chins in their hands and murmured to each other.

And for me? My instincts told me to stay put, that I would be safest among these people I knew. But I also had orders. The organization had drilled contingency plans into us for this: Don't move until commanded, and once commanded, I had better do so if I wanted anyone to try to help me.

I went into my hut and tuned my shortwave to the BBC. Mamadou sat beside me on the floor at the radio, his legs crossed like a boy. After recapping the Japanese and European markets at the top of the hour, the female announcer said, "Fighting has broken out in the major cities and surrounding countrysides of Ivory Coast. Massacres have been rumored. It is too early to report on casualties. Two hundred Western children are caught in the crossfire at a missionary school in the country's second most populous city, Bouaké. Paris and Washington have convened emergency discussions. The BBC will update coverage of Ivory Coast as the situation becomes more clear. Also, the relief agency Potable Water International has convened a training mission immediately in Abidjan."

That was my cue: the secret message ordering me to evacuate the village to my regional capital. My regional capital was Séguéla. I looked at Mamadou and he knew.

"You'll be safe here, Adama," he said, and squeezed my hand. "You know that we'll protect you."

"The others need me with them now."

I made a small and inconspicuous bag: a change of clothes, my passport, my talismans—feathers and bones that the witch doctor had given me in a gazelle-skin pouch to guard my health—and nothing else. In my heart, I readied myself. I embraced Mamadou, went outside with him with my arm around his waist. I embraced Bobi as I would have the old chief. I embraced everyone. They walked me to the path that led to Séguéla; the secret way. The witch doctor came to me with my gun from my hut, but I shook my head at it. Around us, it was a hot and sunny day.

"We'll guard your things for your return, Adama," the witch doctor told me.

"I know, Father."

"Allah ee kissee," Bobi said for all of them. 'Go with God.'

I looked at their faces for a last time. It was like looking at the gathered faces of my beloved family. Then I hurried into the forest, and when I let myself glance back, it had closed around them.

I reached Somina in the late afternoon, the last village before Séguéla. Somina's courtyards were crowded, old women were sitting on the ground wailing. I had passed many people on the path in the forest. I had been jumpy, they had been jumpy; some of them bolted off into the trees at the sight of me. Here now, an old woman gripped my hand from where she sat and said in Worodougou, "Everything is lost now! Adama, everything is lost, Allah!"

The chief of Somina did not offer me food. Already, they were hoarding it. I passed out my cigarettes to men who asked for them until they were gone. The *dossos* of Somina met in groups outside their huts, were dressed in their magic Korhogo cloth shirts and pointed caps, shotguns and black-powder guns on their shoulders. Men sped through on bicycles. Families packed up rice and mats and headed out to hide in the forest.

"Why didn't you stay with your village, Adama?" the old Somina chief asked me as I sat in the circle of men at his compound, everyone debating what to do. "All night we heard guns. All morning."

"I have to go into the city, Father. My brothers and sisters are waiting for me there."

"Can't you see all these people? Can't you see that Séguéla is no place to go?"

"My white chief has ordered me. I have no choice."

"I won't let you go. We'll bind you and carry you back to Tégéso by force."

"Father, each man must walk his own path, isn't this true? I wish it was otherwise, but the path to Séguéla is mine."

A man on a bicycle came with news. He said, "The soldiers are hiding in the trees. I was the last to get out. Now they circle the city like a python. Nothing can pass."

I slept on the ground that night, didn't really sleep. People were lying on the ground everywhere, some moaning, many whispering, old people coughing, men arguing. Babies cried long and uncomfortably as their mothers tried to succor them in this strange place. Small children lay together in piles for warmth. Séguéla was not far away, and now and again we could hear gunfire. Everyone quieted to listen. Then the night would fall silent again and the arguing would start anew. What could I do but look at the stars?

For hours the next morning, I hid in the elephant grass at the edge of the western road to Séguéla. Two men were with me: a rural teacher—a Christian—and an old Peul who'd been selling glass beads in the villages. Both men were trying to reach their families in the city. Flies found and worried us as soon as the sun hit the grass, and the Christian alternated prayers in his language with crying out every one of his worries. He kept gripping my arm and asking, "What should we do? You are Christian as I am. How can we tell the soldiers not to shoot us?"

I shook his hands off me, wouldn't look at him. His nervousness made things so much worse. The old Peul was as calm as wood. I said to him, "Father, what do you think we should do?"

He stroked his long beard awhile. Then he said, "We have to make a choice. Either we step out onto the road, or we do not. If we step onto the road, either we may be shot, or we may not. If we stay here, we wait to make this same decision later. I think it better to go now in the light than to be found in darkness. Also, you are white. Perhaps they are afraid to shoot whites."

"Let's go together, Father."

The old Peul said a prayer in Fulani. I twisted dirt in my fingers as I waited for him to finish. The sky was blue as usual; I was frightened. We stepped out from the grass and onto the asphalt as though it was any other day. The teacher waited in the grass to see if we would be shot. We weren't. Then he scrambled out after us. "Don't leave me," he said, and held my arm. I didn't shake him off. There was gunfire far away, across the city. Here, it was quiet, the sun on us, the roadway hot under our flip-flops, and we walked a long time, approaching the city from the west. The road usually bustled with traffic and people. Today, there weren't even dogs.

We came to Séguéla's outskirts where the first huts were. Some were burned, cinders smoldering in cone-shaped piles where they'd been, ashes drifting down through the air like a black snow. There didn't seem to be anyone left. We heard a truck rumbling ahead somewhere. I grasped the old man's arm. He was walking with a tall staff, and I hadn't noticed that until now. The buildings were shuttered everywhere. There were brass bullet casings on the ground in piles like rice spilled from sacks. The walk took over an hour. We saw no one, though as we entered the city proper, I began to feel people everywhere, behind every shuttered window. The old man came to his cross street, turned to say good-bye. I embraced him, felt how old his frail body was under his robe. He stank of perspiration, and I knew then that I did, too. He smiled for me and I saw that he didn't have any teeth. He said, "*Allah ee kissee,* good man. Go with God."

I walked faster now, came to my street. The teacher was holding my arm. "Take me to my house," he begged me. I shook him off. "Please. Please," he said, "it's not far." I jerked my arm from him, didn't look back. I heard his flip-flops slapping up against his soles as he ran away. Then I began to run, too. Everything was shuttered. Fires had scorched the walls. A dog was dead with black flies on its face like a mask, flies crawling in and out of the nostrils, sucking at the black holes on its side that were the cause of its death. I didn't stop running until I was at the security door of our flophouse. I pounded on the door. "Open up! Open up! Please! It's Jack!"

Melissa opened the door, the crowbar in her hand. She looked worn and pale in such a way that I wondered how I looked. We locked the door and embraced a long time.

"Do you have any idea how shitty it's been? I've been alone in here since Gbagbo was on the television. What took you so long? Why isn't anybody coming in?"

"You're the only one here?"

"I've been the only one here for two nights."

"And there hasn't been any word from any of them?"

She shook her head.

Inside, the water was cut, the electricity. I picked up the phone receiver to listen to the nothing I knew I'd hear. There was no food in the house. I sat on the couch and ran my fingers through my hair. Melissa sat beside me, slipped her arm around my waist. We were quiet together a minute in the silent room. Then Melissa said, "Do you have any cigarettes, Jack?"

"No," I said, and shook my head.

"Then you'd better go back out again."

A dog came from the bedroom doorway, stood in the short hall, and blinked at us as though it had just woken from a nap. It sniffed the air as if tasting it, yawned and stretched, then came over with its nails clicking on the cement floor and licked my dirty toes as though we were old friends. It was a typical amber-haired African dog with paws like white slippers and a white tip on its tail. "Who's this?" I said, and scratched the dog's face roughly.

"This is Petite Afrique."

"Who'd give a dog a name like that?"

"Nancy would," Melissa said, and petted the dog with me. "She went to Abidjan to meet her boyfriend. They were going to go to Mali together. A big vacation. She asked me to watch her dog for her. I said sure."

"Little Africa, huh?"

"Yeah."

I scratched Little Africa's ears, and she set her forepaws on my lap to stretch up and lick my face. "So you want to be friends?" I said to the dog as I clamped her mouth shut to nuzzle her. "I think we can manage that."

Over the next days, the other six came in. Marcus and Sean rode in from the east on bicycles, had been held up by a squad of soldiers who stepped out of the trees near the approach to the city, had to sit with their hands behind their backs for hours until the soldiers received word on their radio to let them through. Nikki and Shanna negotiated a ride on the last logging truck piled with teachers and their families fleeing the northern areas. Rachel came in on back roads, holding tight to a Malian contrabander on his motorcycle. And for three days, Courtney had walked through the forest with her boyfriend, had paid bribes to get through checkpoints while her boyfriend picked his way around them through the trees. Finally, at the city's edge, they'd said a hurried farewell, and he'd stayed behind in the grass.

There was nothing to eat, and we didn't. We had a few bottles of water among us, and we rationed sips from them. We couldn't bathe, we couldn't flush the toilet. It filled with shit, and then we didn't shit anymore. We listened to the BBC all day, gleaned nothing new from it, lit candles at night and played hearts. Once in a while, there were sudden bursts of gunfire, mostly not. There was nothing to do but wait. Four days went by like this.

Perhaps it was hunger that finally made us brave. But perhaps, too, it was the long confinement, our desire to know what was happening. None of us had any cash but Rachel, who had 370,000 CFA, which she'd gotten from her church at home to build a well in her village. It was a huge sum. We took turns volunteering to go out into the city in pairs, to pound on doors, to pay extortionate rates for rice and sardines; for water, cigarettes, cookies, candles, beer. No one was ever on the streets, and when we'd hear a military jeep rumbling near on rounds, we'd plead through shuttered windows until the frightened families would let us in. In this way, we got news: The rebels were on the edge of Mankono; the rebels had taken Mankono. The rebels were on the edge of

Touba; the rebels had taken Touba. The rebels were consolidating; they were on their way to Séguéla. Séguéla was now the last Muslim city to be freed. We played cards, drank warm beer, smoked cigarettes, waited for the rebels.

The new ones were excited to be going home. The older ones regretted the unfinished projects they were leaving behind. We all talked about our village friends, times we'd had, crazy things that we could never have imagined before getting here: waking up with a sheep standing over us, a neighbor giving birth to her eleventh child in the morning, chopping wood at night. Melissa, who'd been caught in the city, wished she could see the women of her compound one last time to say good-bye. Courtney lamented her boyfriend. The girls slept on the mattresses in the bedroom, Sean and Marcus and I on the floor in front. Someone was always out on the porch, smoking in the dark. Sean said to me from where he lay one night, "You should have gone home when you had the chance, hey, Jack?"

I shrugged, didn't know that. I kissed the neck of the dog asleep beside me.

When the phone rang in the morning, I jumped up to answer it. The others in their bleary eyes gathered to listen. It was the Abidjan office, our security coordinator, Judith. She said, "Everyone okay, Jack? Everyone accounted for?"

"We're all here."

"What's your situation?"

"We're fine. We're calm. We have food. We have no idea what's going on here. We've heard the rebels are on their way. Everything's a rumor."

"First thing in the morning, we want you to get out. Do

you understand? Do not tell anybody. Not any neighbors, not any friends. You guys are too far north for us to get you. Pack your things today, make a plan. Pack light. First thing in the morning, go down to the transport stand. Arrange whatever you can. Any price. But don't mess around. If it's not safe, then stay where you are. The rebels have been helpful so far. But we still want you to move."

"Is everyone else okay?"

"Everyone's fine, Jack. Worry about yourselves now."

"Tell our families we're all right. Tell them we're together."

"We will."

"Everyone's been good here. Everyone's been brave."

"We're proud of you."

"We'll make it out."

"No foolish chances, okay? No heroics."

"Okay," I said. Then we lost the line.

We made our packs, stripped the house of anything valuable. For ten years, PWI workers had shared this flophouse, good times in it; had left behind photos of their happy selves tacked to the wall, colorful batik tapestries from trips to Guinea and Mali depicting the village scenes: women pounding rice in mortars, men weeding corn rows with machetes. Once stripped of these things, the house looked just like the three-room cinder-block structure that it was. The dog came to me where I sat in an armchair looking at the blank walls, yawned widely, wagged her tail. Her eyes seemed to sympathize. I scratched her ears. "Feel like traveling?" I asked her. She wagged her tail as though to say yes, set her face on my knee to be scratched more.

One of the strangest incidents of my years there happened that last afternoon, toward evening. Someone pounded on our security door. We'd been reading, playing cards, and we looked at each other. The pounding only got louder. With the others' eyes on me, I finally picked up the crowbar and went outside. *"C'est qui?"* I said in a menacing voice.

"Eh, *blofwé,* we know you are in there. Open the door! We won't hurt you."

They'd said *"blofwé,"* the Christian word for 'whiteman.' The only Christians around were the soldiers controlling the city. I looked at the others back on the porch, and they looked grim. I said, "Say who you are and I'll open the door."

"Le militaire."

For a last time, I looked at the others. How strange they all seemed. How filthy and haggard and scared and tired. But they were stone-faced, too. I turned the lock.

There were half a dozen soldiers in mirrored sunglasses and fatigues. They held automatic weapons, index fingers extended over the trigger guards as if pointing. They were young and smoking cigarettes. One also had a basketball under his arm. The leader said, "Come on out, *blofwé,* and play basketball with us."

"Basketball?" I said.

"Oui," he told me, "basketball. Our commander has sent us off duty for now. We want to play basketball with *vrais Américains.*"

Marcus, Sean, Shanna, and I went out and climbed onto their covered troop carrier. What choice did we have? Then the soldiers got on, too. The two in the rear hung their legs out the back, trained their guns on the receding road as if ready to shoot. We hurried through the deserted city. The sky that I could see was wide and blue, cleared of the smoke of the week's fires. This was Marcus's fault. He'd taken to playing pickup basketball at the stadium the weekends he'd come in.

The young soldier beside me said from behind his glasses, "You've been here many years, no?"

"Three."

"You speak Worodougou, isn't it? You must really love these Muslims to have learned such a tongue. Or is it only that you are good with languages?"

"I love them. I'm also good with languages."

"That is good. Do you speak German?"

"Ja. Ich spreche ein bischen Deutsch."

"Wie geht es?" he asked me, looking down his nose.

"Es geht mir gut."

"Ja. Gut. Deutsch ist gut, nicht wahr?"

"Ja, Deutsch ist gut."

"I taught myself with tapes," he said in French.

"Sehr gut," I said.

We went past the mayor's office. The windows were all broken, the great doors hanging off the hinges as though a tornado had run through. There were scorch marks above the windows so it was clear that the inside had been burned. The flagpole in the yard was broken in half.

"*Ich heisse* Girard."

"*Ich heisse* Jacques."

"Sehr gut, mein kleiner Kerl," he said, and slapped my knee.

At the stadium of Séguéla, we played half-court basketball, four on four. The grass had grown out on the soccer pitch, and sheep grazed there, between the two cement grandstands in their few and meager tiers. The facility was just outside of town, and because the basketball court sat on the hill above it, being on it was like playing on a dais: the lush savanna open and yellow and green to the north, an endless tableau; the black wall of the forest to the south. The sky was pink and yellow in the evening, as beautiful toward the horizon as the feelings I had for the place.

The soldiers could sink jumpers, but didn't like to pass. We worked the ball in to Marcus, who'd post up, or swing it out to Shanna, who sank them from the top of the key. We played to twenty. They won, then we did. Then they did, then we did. They played in their boots. We played in our flip-flops. The thoughts that went through my head as we played were: I'll never see this land again, and, these young men will all die tomorrow.

At dusk, they took us home. Girard took my hand. He pointed his finger at me and said, *"Du musst morgen gehen. Verstehst du das?* Tomorrow morning. Not any later."

"Ich weiss," I told him, and nodded.

And Little Africa? She'd eaten more in the past seven days than the rest of us combined. Every scrap we could find was hers, whole tins of sardines. Why not? She was calm as she spent the days watching us from her perch on the couch, and her calmness soothed us. It was like taking care of a child. Still, Courtney had been saying for days, "How can we take a dog with us and leave my boyfriend behind?"

Melissa and I met in the bathroom the night before we left. I sat on the toilet lid, and she sat against the wall. The bathroom was a tight and humid space, thick with the smell of the shit piled in the toilet. With the power out, we sat in the dark. I said, "We call the shots tomorrow. You and me. We can't have anybody making any other plans. Courtney can complain about her boyfriend as much as she wants tonight, but tomorrow morning it ends. If she stays, she stays. But she's not going to stay. We'll hide money on each of us. If it gets bad, we come back. No last-minute plans about Mali or Guinea."

"They're going to listen to us, Jack."

"I know they will."

"I'll back you up."

"We'll back each other up."

We lit cigarettes. The stars shone in the small and high window.

Melissa said, "We're not coming back this time, are we?"

"No, we're not."

"I've loved it here. I've felt alive and important for the first time in my life."

"Me, too."

"Jack, what about the dog?"

"I'll manage the dog."

"And if something bad happens on the way?"

"I'll worry about it then."

We finished our cigarettes, sat quietly together an instant as the thought of tomorrow settled in. Then we went out to where the others were waiting.

At first light, we shouldered our small packs, and I tied a rope around Africa's neck for a leash. Rachel was trying to take too many bags with her, and after watching her wrestle with them a minute, Melissa told her, "One." We left the security door swinging open behind us. The house would be looted today, regardless.

We were eight Americans and a dog. The mosques were silent as they had been, a mist hung over the city's streets in diaphanous folds. As we walked through it, doorways opened, people crowded in them to see us go. If they'd had any illusions about what was in store for them, this ended it: the departure of the whites. All along the way, people called out our African names. *"Allah ee kissee!"* they said. 'Go with God.'

It began raining immediately. We banged on the shuttered window of the transport shack, bribed the *gbaka* driver hiding in it ten times the rate to take us out of the city. As soon as he started the engine, teachers and functionaries hiding in the Christian *bangi* bar across from the terminus ran out in the rain with their handbags to try to board the minivan. They were fish-eyed and frightened, and we let them on until the seats were full, the driver shouting huge fares at them. Others tried to push in, to lay across our laps. The dog between my legs squirmed to get free. I tried to slide the door shut, but men kept thrusting in their arms. "We'll die!" they pleaded with me. "We'll never see our families again."

"Drive, goddamn it! Drive!" the others shouted at the *gbaka* driver, banged the roof with their hands to urge him on. The Christians who had seats yelled this at him, too. I pushed the men's arms away with my hands. I shut the door hard on their arms and fingers, shut it again when it was clear. They ran after us in the rain, hung from the *gbaka*'s sides. I shoved them off through the windows. We all did.

The driver went fast. Suddenly the forest was tall on either side, the rain falling hard. We came upon a checkpoint. The driver swerved around the nail-studded board, the minivan tearing through the tall grass at the roadside, and we could hear the soldiers' shouts. When I looked back, the checkpoint was already receding into the rain, figures running both ways across the road. The dog squirmed where it was pinned between my feet, tried to clamber out onto my lap. I hit her hard on her head and she yelped, settled. Then she thrust her face up between my knees, nuzzled me to apologize, and I scratched her snout to apologize back. We crested a rise, and before us on a short bridge was a logging truck toppled over on its side. It looked like a dead dinosaur; it spanned the bridge from side to side and there was no way around it. The driver pulled right up to the truck's belly, to the great driveshaft as thick as my chest, and the river below was a muddy torrent from the rain. The forest around us was mighty and primal. Then we heard an engine, and a military jeep with its lights out crested the rise behind us. There were so many soldiers on it, their legs hung off the sides like bristles.

The *gbaka* driver jumped out and ran into the trees as the soldiers hopped down off the jeep, ran toward us on the road. Then there were guns in all the windows, banging them open, soldiers passing before the windshield in the rain, all around us. *"S'il vous plaît! S'il vous plaît!"* the old functionary beside me was yelling. *"Déscendez! Déscendez!"* a soldier outside yelled. He slid open the door, pointed his rifle at me. I put up my hands.

"Who said you could leave the city!"

"No one!"

"Who said you could leave!"

"No one! No one!"

Another soldier came up, pushed down the barrel of the first gently with his hand. Despite everything, he grinned. He said, "Jacques! *Wie geht es? Wo gehen Sie alles?*"

I looked at him. I tried to understand who he was and what he was saying. The soldier laughed, slapped my knee. He shook his head and said, "You spoke good German yesterday, didn't you? But not today."

He shut the door on us; the soldiers gathered to talk. They went to the roadside, called the driver out of the trees, and when he came out with his hands in the air, one of them booted him in his seat back toward the *gbaka.* The German-speaking soldier leaned in the driver's window, smiled, and said an amount, and we rummaged in our pockets and met it. Then he said a second amount. We met that, too. Then they hooked a cable to the rear axle of the logging truck, winched it back just enough for the minivan to get through. The driver hit the gas. No one said anything to him about running away. After we drove through the gap, the soldiers pushed the truck back across the bridge, closing Séguéla behind us. They didn't know, as we also didn't, that Séguéla was falling at that moment.

We negotiated a half dozen more checkpoints over the next hours, all less severe, and four miles north of Vavoua, the first Christian city south, the driver ordered us out onto the roadside and drove his vehicle onto a narrow track through the forest to someplace safe that was known to him. We waited a while as though he'd come back, and then we began to walk. Refugees came out of the forest to walk with us, their households in ponderous bundles on their heads. One man was carrying a sewing machine, another man a crate of chickens. No matter how much I blinked, I couldn't clear my eyes of the rain. The dog stayed close to my leg, often looking behind her the way Jane had when I'd first brought her to Tégéso.

At midday, we crested a hill and came to the edge of Vavoua. There was another bridge here, another river. There was an immense pile of wood blocking the bridge. It looked as though every household of the city had carried chairs, tables, bedframes, firewood, wall planks, boards, pallets, fencing, and piled them there. At the pile's core were enormous felled trees, twice as wide as I was tall. No vehicle could have passed through that; a tank could not have passed through that. People looked like ants beside it. It was the annunciation of the south's fear of the north.

To get around it, we had to hold on to the railing and step along the half inch of bridge that hung over the rushing water below. The water was frothing and brown, and I held the dog under my arm. For the football-field length that I danced us over that plunge, she didn't squirm once. When I climbed back over the railing and set her down, she shook out her coat, wagged her tail, and sneezed.

After a seven-hour journey, we had crossed the war zone. There were many men with guns here, many, many refugees sitting on the highway in the rain. The men with guns wore street clothes. They were soldiers who'd chucked their uniforms in case the rebels breached their defense. They barred the highway with tires and studded boards, were searching one by one the long lines of people waiting to get through. We waited our turn. When we got to the head of our line, they dumped out our bags, asked us if we were spies. They kept their submachine guns pointed at our bellies, were nervous, yelling. One by one, we paid them bribes and got through.

Then it was my turn with the dog.

"Vaccination papers? Title of ownership?" the man asked me. He had a paunch, wouldn't look me in the eye. His white T-shirt clung to him for the rain. I shook my head, looked down. "Dog doesn't come through," he said.

Another man came over, tall, thick with muscles. He said, "We can issue those papers here."

"I don't have any more money."

"There is always more money, whiteman," the second man shouted at me. He stepped closer to me, like trying to crowd me in. "White people are the richest in the world. Therefore, when there is a whiteman, there is always more money."

"No more money," I said and shook my head.

He jerked the leash from me, pulled the dog to him. "No money, no dog. Hey," he said to the one with the paunch. "Shoot this dog."

The other man raised his machine gun, aimed at the dog's face. She was looking at me, straining at the rope that bound her. She was soaked from the rain, looked even smaller than she was. The others were far ahead now, moving away among the refugees for Vavoua. Only Melissa waited. I pulled the leash back, picked up the dog. "Shoot me," I said.

The big one took out his sidearm, pointed it at my face. I could see that he was angry. I didn't care. I held the dog, felt the rain on my face. He pointed the gun at me a long moment. Then he grabbed my shoulder and pushed me through. I dropped the dog and we ran up to Melissa and the others.

In Vavoua, there was no gasoline to get south. We were across the lines, but there was simply no gas. We still had money: Of course we still had money. After long negotiations, a car was arranged and we rode in it an hour. There were checkpoints everywhere, tires burning, black smoke pouring off them into the raining afternoon. They stopped us, searched us; mile by mile we moved along. At Daloa, the great market had been burned. Blocks and blocks simply gone. A gang of young toughs followed us to the bus station. We kept a tight group, and they kept another close behind us. The guards at the station let us through, shut the great gates on the growing mob. Again there was no gas. Again we made up the necessary sum, along with the wealthy Ivorians on the bus eager to get out. Finally, the bus shuddered to life. We left Daloa with hordes of young men running alongside, beating the bus with their fists. There were checkpoints after checkpoints. We piled our bags on the dog to keep her hidden. The soldiers made us all get off again and again. The dog lay still and they didn't find her.

In the early evening, we came to Yamoussoukro. We could see the American helicopters circling the tall dome of the basilica. The driver announced over the PA, "We are safe now." Nobody cheered.

At the bus station, I called Abidjan from a phone kiosk. "We're here," I told Judith. "We're all here at the bus station in Yama."

"Don't move."

A bus rolled up fifteen minutes later, flanked by U.S. jeeps. The bus was crowded with white people, the first we'd seen. Marines encircled us, shoved away the shoe-shine boys who had gathered to gawk so that some of them fell down. A Marine grabbed my arm, pulled me close. "We got you now. You're safe," he said in English.

"Don't touch me," I said, and yanked myself free.

I was the last to board the bus. A Marine grabbed the dog's leash. "No dogs," he said.

I picked up the dog, got on the bus. They shook their heads and shut the door. Then we set off in the night in a convoy for Abidjan.

There were chocolates on our pillows that night, psychologists to talk to if we needed it, handshakes from the Washington people, food and drink coupons. We were put up in the Hotel Ivoire, the finest hotel in West Africa. From my ninth-story room, I had a view across the Ebrie Lagoon, and the rain had cleared, and the lagoon glittered with stars. They'd take us in convoys to Ghana in the morning, and mobs protesting the American and French military presence in their country would rush us, pelt our vehicles with stones and bottles. After three more weeks in the Hotel La Palm in Accra, we'd be given our walking papers, and while most everyone went home, I wandered another half year around the far reaches of the continent. I tried, and mostly succeeded, to enter every war-torn nation there was: Burundi, Angola, Congo, Zimbabwe. Whatever I was looking for, I didn't find it, and I finally came home.

The desk clerks at the Hotel Ivoire that last night hadn't wanted to let the dog in, and she pissed in the elevator on the way up to our room, as though to let them know what she thought of it all. I petted her a long time as I stared at the stars on the Ebrie, missing Africa already, wondering what was happening to my village, my friends. Then I took her up to Nancy, whom she was very excited to see.

The dog lives in San Diego now. She likes to sit on the couch, and Nancy lets her. Nancy called me where I was staying at my mother's in Florida soon after I returned. "Jack?" she said. "Someone's been waiting to talk to you."

"Who is it?" I said into the phone.

"It's your friend. It's Africa."

ACKNOWLEDGMENTS

First thanks to Barry Spacks, whose artistic advice released this book from my despair.

Thanks to Joel Dunsany.

Thanks and love to Merle Rubine.

Deepest gratitude to my agent, Liz Darhansoff; to Kristin Lang, Michele Mortimer, and everyone at Darhansoff, Verrill, Feldman; to my editor, Tina Pohlman; to Becky Saletan, Stacia Decker, Jennifer Gilmore, Jodie Hockensmith, Lynn Pierce, and everyone at Harcourt.

In memory of my chief; in concern for my friends.

Thanks to Cathy Martin, Jack Rolls, Brian Spillane.

Thanks to Bill, Tim, Penn, Sandra, Helen, Mary Ann.

Thanks, Sokung.

Thanks, Suzanne.

Love to Mom, Alyson, and Irene. Thanks to my teachers.

Finally, to Armin: for loyalty beyond reason.

Dunsmuir, California, July–November 2004.